GALAX

EDGE

KILL TEAM

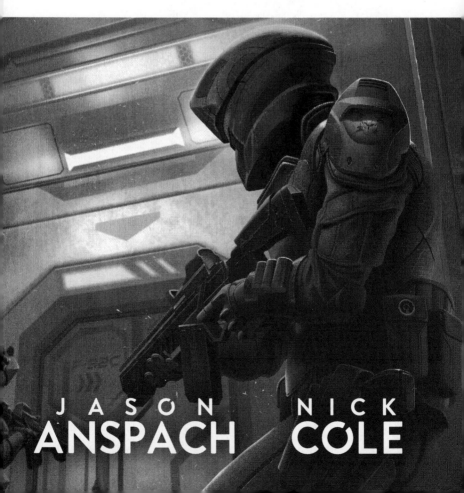

JASON
ANSPACH

NICK
COLE

Edited by David Gatewood
Published by Galaxy's Edge Press

Cover Art: Fabian Saravia
Cover Design: Beaulistic Book Services
Formatting: Kevin G. Summers

For more information:

Website: GalacticOutlaws.com
Facebook: facebook.com/atgalaxysedge
Newsletter: InTheLegion.com

OTHER GALAXY'S EDGE BOOKS

A LONG, LONG TIME FROM NOW
AT THE EDGE OF THE GALAXY...

GALAXYS
EDGE
galacticoutlaws.com

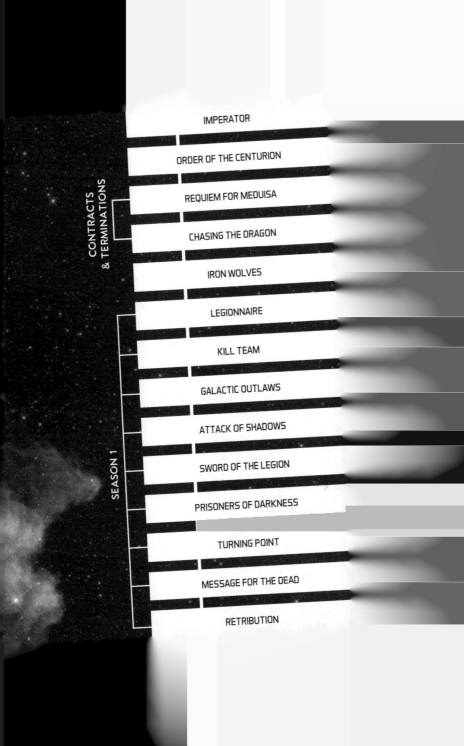

PROLOGUE
Kublar Orbit
Contested Space Following the Battle of Kublar

"It's hot out here. I've never seen so many—Oba!" A shudder reverberated through the hull of the drop shuttle. "Hang on back there!"

Captain Ford—Wraith to his fellow legionnaires—grabbed an overhead safety bar. His legs went out from beneath him, and he hung from the bar as Republic marines tumbled across the deck. The hullbusters rolled over a few wounded legionnaires and Repub-Army basics—the lucky few who were extracted from Kublar before orbital bombardment. One Navy corpsman shielded a severely wounded legionnaire with his own body, doing his best to prevent a vicious-looking gut wound from becoming further injured or contaminated.

Boom!

The lights on the shuttle flickered as blaster fire strafed across the shuttle's shield array.

"Damn it!" the pilot shouted from the cockpit, the words accentuated by the sharp sounds of incoming blaster fire. "Tibeel, get that tail turret firing! They're chewing us up!"

The pilot sounded like he was on the verge of panic, a far cry from the usually calm and matter-of-fact tone

Wraith was used to. He'd heard pilots talk through crashes as if they were reading a technical manual, right up to the point of impact. Whatever was going on outside must be really bad.

Wraith looked down the corridor to the rear gun emplacement. The Navy gunner was sprawled, unmoving, on the deck.

The shuttle stabilized, and Wraith eased himself down from the bar and onto the deck. He ran past marines helping one another up and crawling for jump seats. "This is Captain Ford." Wraith's voice was dispassionate. "Your gunner's no longer combat effective. I'm moving to take his position. Call out priority targets."

"Pick one!" the pilot shouted back.

"Copy."

Wraith guided the twin control arms to raise the weapon from its resting position. He looked through a superimposed targeting reticule on the emplacement's viewport and swept for targets.

He had never seen so many starfighters. The MCR must have bought up every Preyhunter starfighter in this sector of the edge and loaded them into the Ohio-class cruiser they'd salvaged from who-knew-where. They were everywhere. Spinning and looping in furious dogfights with Republic tri-fighters launched from the super-destroyer *Mercutio*. Others buzzed the Republic drop shuttles returning from the planet's surface. A trio of rebel starfighters focused their blaster cannon fire on a shuttle, sending it into a brilliant gaseous explosion that quickly extinguished itself in the darkness of space.

Wraith clenched his jaw at the bad luck of the legionnaires and basics inside that shuttle. Plucked last minute from certain death on the planet below, only to get atomized in the rescue craft.

The Preyhunters zoomed past the debris, the lead starfighter waggling its wingtips as it closed the distance to Wraith's shuttle. The targeting reticule flashed and beeped, and Wraith pushed his thumbs down on the firing buttons.

Green blaster cannon bolts streaked toward the lead spacecraft. The pilot attempted to nose down away from the fire, but wasn't quick enough. Four consecutive bolts ripped along the top of the starfighter. The first blew apart the cockpit canopy, killing the pilot, and the next three scorched holes in the craft's fuselage, causing a breach and explosion.

The other two Preyhunters banked away, one left and one right. Wraith went left, leading the craft with well-placed shots that blasted away a wingtip cannon and disabled a main thruster. A Republic tri-wing starfighter swooped in and finished off the Preyhunter before roaring past Wraith's shuttle, close enough for Wraith to make out a mole on the pilot's cheek.

"Nice shooting!" said the pilot over the comm. "We're sixty seconds to entry at the *Mercutio*'s docking bay. Keep those insurgents off our tail just a little longer and—"

A crack sounded across the comm, and the ship shuddered violently. Wraith felt as though the temperature had increased a good fifteen degrees. An onboard alarm gave a looping, ominous warning. *Eht-eht-eht-eht-eht-eht...*

"What's going on?" he asked.

The co-pilot answered. "Oba—we came within ten meters of flying right in the path of one of the heavy emplacement blasts from that Ohio cruiser. Overloaded Mero's control panel. He's dead. No stabilizers online. Sensory array cooked. Request tractor guidance."

Wraith realized the co-pilot wasn't talking only to him. The traffic controller for the *Mercutio*'s docking bay answered. "Too many targets to obtain an early lock. We can pull and drop from your angle once you are in range. Will deploy deck netting on entry through hangar bay shield."

"Acknowledged," answered the co-pilot. "Be advised, life support is disabled, and we have an onboard fire."

The MCR fighters were keeping their distance from the Republic super-destroyer. Wraith couldn't see a target in range.

The co-pilot noticed as well. "Captain, you'd better get strapped in. We're approaching high, and once we enter the hangar, we're going to drop like a bot in water. It's gonna be bumpy."

The port hangar openings on a ship this size were large enough to pull in the big bulk freighters. Dropping from the top of the shielding would leave a few marks. Normally a tractor beam brought the ship in close to the deck, where repulsor plates could float it to a stable landing once the beam lost contact. This... was doing it the hard way.

"Copy." Wraith left his emplacement and made his way back to the jump seats.

Most of the marines and leejes were strapped in, save for the corpsman who was struggling to secure his wounded patient to a built-in stretcher beneath the shuttle's re-charge station. Wraith knelt to assist, then patted the le-gionnaire's shoulder armor as he rose to strap himself in. "Hang on, buddy."

The drop shuttle boomed and shook as the *Mercutio*'s tractor beam locked on and began to pull them in. Apart from the landing itself, this was when they were most vulnerable, moving in a straight line with only the capital ship's bristling laser batteries and fighter escorts protect-ing them from enemy Preyhunters. Just like the sleds in the ambush back on Kublar.

"Hang on back there!" the co-pilot called over the all-ship comm. "Once we enter the docking bay, we're going to drop like a nib-stone."

"We're all gonna die, aren't we?" a grimacing ma-rine asked.

"Probably," Wraith replied.

The ship's interior lights darkened for the landing. The co-pilot announced that the shuttle's nose had entered the hangar, and seconds later, the tractor beam lost its lock and the drop shuttle went into free fall.

Wraith's stomach lurched up into his throat. He gripped the restraints crossing his chest and braced himself for the landing. A twisting, screeching shriek re-verberated throughout the craft as the shuttle plunged into the impervisteel cable netting installed beneath the retractable hangar deck plates for just such an occasion. As if they were on some core-world amusement ride, the craft bounced up, and the accompanying twangs and snaps of broken netting gave a good indication of just how hard they'd fallen. When the drop shuttle stabilized into a steady up-and-down rhythm, Wraith released his harnesses and headed for the shuttle's disembark door.

"Where you going, man?" asked the same marine who had spoken before. "Ship's not gonna blow up, is it?"

Wraith pulled the manual override and waited for the shuttle's door to slide open like a curtain revealing the stage. "War's still on, Marine."

He hopped over the small gap of netting and landed on polished black deck plate. The hangar was buzzing. A squad of Repub marines sprinted past and loaded themselves into a Spiker assault-boarding shuttle. Signal landing bots guided in new shuttles and damaged tri-wing starfighters—a lot more starfighters than shuttles—while tow-sleds pulled the craft into the side storage hangars, clearing as much space for incoming landing craft as possible.

Wraith looked around the hangar for survivors from the battle below. He saw a few basics and legionnaires being whisked away to the medical bays. Only a few. How many had still been down there when the orbital bombardment started? How many had already died before the shuttles even arrived?

Wraith watched the fierce dogfight happening just outside the hangar bay. He winced every time a drop shuttle took enemy fire. The legionnaires inside those shuttles—if there were any—deserved better than to be dusted inside a tin cup, unable to fight back.

"Captain Ford!"

Wraith turned—and saw a corpsman and leej medic sprinting off with Captain Devers, who looked dead.

Wraith replied to the legionnaire who'd called his name. "Lieutenant Chhun, I'm glad you made it out."

"Thank you, sir," Chhun said, stepping forward, his N-4 still in his arms. Behind him was Exo, who was probably due for a world of hurt if Devers survived.

"Same goes for you, Exo," Wraith said.

"Thanks."

"Sir?" Chhun said, his face stained with blood and dirt and sweat. "What now, sir?"

"Always make 'em pay."

The *Indelible VI*
Present Day

The cockpit door of the *Indelible VI* swooshed open, and Leenah, the ship's resident princess-mechanic, stepped inside. She wiped her grimy pink hands off on her coveralls and dropped herself into the navigator's chair, next to Captain Aeson Keel.

Ravi's chair.

Leenah felt a pang of regret. She missed the holographic navigator who'd disappeared while defending the life of a scared little child. Everyone did. And though he didn't show it, she imagined Captain Keel missed Ravi most of all.

She watched for Keel's reaction, wondering if he would show some subtle displeasure at her being so familiar with his lost navigator's place. That was, after all—or so Leenah presumed—the real reason Keel had banned the woban-ki, Skrizz, from the cockpit, and all the hair and dander the catman left behind. But Keel had been reading when Leenah entered the cockpit, and he now seemed more preoccupied with quickly powering down and stowing his datapad than with any perceived breach of crew protocol.

"What were you reading?" Leenah asked, careful not to leave smudges on the arms of Ravi's chair.

Keel shook his head. "Nothing. Just…" He hesitated, as though unsure how much he was willing to reveal. "Just remembering. Dredging up the past so I won't forget. How's Garret progressing?"

Pushing aside an intense desire to follow up on what, exactly, Keel was trying not to forget, Leenah thought of how to answer him. Garret, the beanpole code slicer, had spent days pleading with or circumventing the *Six*'s limited AI in an attempt to "find" Ravi and reconstitute the noble hologram. Without much luck.

Leenah felt a need to be delicate. She looked at her feet, the pink tendrils hanging from her scalp dancing across her forehead like delicate locks of hair. "Still looking. The ship's holocores are very segmented, and making your way through it is nearly impossible. And that's a verbatim report from a slicer who makes the impossible look routine. Ravi seems to have done some remarkable work. Garret's not sure how long it will take him. He says a lot depends on whether Ravi left a way for his OS to be found."

Keel gave a lopsided grin and bounced his knuckles gently off of the ship's dash. "Well, he didn't exactly come with the ship, but have the kid keep looking."

Leenah nodded. The two sat in silence beneath the swirling blue waves of hyperspace.

"I was thinking about Prisma," Leenah said, lowering her voice to a whisper, as if she expected the girl to overhear. "She needs a stable life. She can't just travel around the galaxy with a crew of... whatever we are."

Keel frowned. "Let's just focus on one problem at a time."

The comm chimed.

Leenah furrowed her brow. "How are you receiving while in hyperspace?"

A look of concern flashed across Keel's face, but only for a moment. Like a spotlight sweeping across a dark night sky. He leaned forward and tapped the comm to display. A black screen superimposed itself over the ship's front canopy, with a simple message written in green text.

Wraith. Return to shell. LS-33.
P-1.

"What does that mean?" Leenah asked. LS-33 was a legionnaire's identification number. Keel—Wraith—had the leej armor, yes, but that sort of thing could be come by with enough credits.

But Keel only leaned back in his seat and chewed the tip of his thumb, staring into the unfolding layers of hyperspace.

**Years earlier. The *Mercutio*,
fifteen minutes after exfil from Kubļar.**

01

I don't hang around to thank the pilot. No one claps when our drop shuttle lands on the *Mercutio*'s deck. Instead the shuttle's doors burst open and Captain Devers is rushed straight to the med bay on a repulsor sled. He's pale, most of his blood covering his armor. If you ask me, he's dusted.

But I'm not going to go on record with any predictions. If he pulls though, it won't be the first time Devers lived when he should have died.

I hop onto the deck as bots and sailors rush to get the ship out of the way. The crew, marines, and wounded are following the orders of a deck officer, moving to their appointed stations. I ignore their commands. Ignore the green arrows that light up the deck plate like a roadside cantina's sign: *this way*. I hear boots hit the deck plate behind me, in spite of the ringing in my ears and the frenzied hum of repulsors.

"Lieutenant Chhun! Wait up!"

I turn around and see Exo, his N-4 in one hand and bucket in the other, moving to catch up. There's a part of me that wants him with me, a sympathetic soul to stand with me as I wait in the wings of the hangar and see who else made it. Another part of me wants to tell him to get some chow and take a shower so I can be alone. But I don't express either of these things. Instead, I stand there like a mouth-breather staring at our drop shuttle.

It's shot all to hell. Black scorch marks from blaster fire and exposed circuitry decorate the hull like some sort of tribal tattoo. I'm amazed the pilots were able to bring this bird in for a landing. Maybe I *should* have clapped when we touched down.

"Yo, Lieutenant..." Exo realizes I'm looking past him, and he slowly turns to take in the view of our riddled craft. His arms drop to his sides, the barrel of his rifle just inches above the deck. "How am I not dead?"

I don't have a good answer, so I just shrug. "Let's see who else made it back. Maybe we can lobby the leej commander to get us back down to the planet's surface."

"Sir..." Exo's face falls. He looks tired. "They're dead, sir. There's no point going back down there, unless it's to wipe out koobs."

"Then let's see about doing that."

We move across the hangar, disregarding the "helpful" instructions of the signal bots and not giving a damn about the glares we're getting from the naval spacemen. We aren't far before I see a drop shuttle that took a greater beating than even ours did. It's tangled up in the crash netting beneath the deck. These guys came in hard. Exo and I change directions and head toward it. There might be legionnaires on board.

Survivors.

Brothers.

Sure enough, I see a legionnaire, his armor showing black scorches from near misses and caked brown from the Kublar dust. He has a Specter squad insignia painted on his shoulder. I could find out who he is if I were to move close enough to read his name and serial number, but I don't need to. His walk—full of purpose and hard as durasteel—tells me all I need to know.

"Captain Ford!"

Captain Ford—Wraith—turns his helmet to follow the medics carrying Devers off, then he faces me. "Lieutenant Chhun. I'm glad you made it out."

"Thank you, sir." I step forward, cradling my N-4.

Wraith looks around me at Exo. "Same goes for you, Exo."

Exo sniffs like he has a runny nose. "Thanks, sir."

"Captain Ford?" I ask, feeling a distinct trickle of sweat racing down my dirty face. "What now?"

A fire team of Republic marines runs past us, hurriedly moving toward a waiting assault shuttle. Wraith watches them go, then takes off after them. "Always make 'em pay."

"Hell yeah," Exo says. He puts on his bucket and follows Wraith, who's already overtaking the marines.

I take a deep breath and start running as well.

We move toward the assault shuttle staging area. Big ships like the super-destroyer we're on pack a ton of firepower, but these capital ships—even the relics like the Ohio-class that's slugging it out with us—take tremendous amounts of punishment. The navy can concentrate fire, coordinate bombing runs, you name it. But we're talking layers of durasteel, and redundant airlocks to prevent a ship-wide decompression... It takes hours of non-stop fighting by entire destroyer *groups* to take down a single capital-class ship. A super-destroyer *could* effectively make an Ohio-class cruiser non-operative for combat within six standard minutes. But to blow the thing up completely? Who knows?

The answer? Send in the marines. They aren't legionnaires, but they aren't pushovers, either. Maybe they're a little too proud for their own good, but any leej'll take and deploy a marine squad if the opportunity is presented. They kill what you tell them to, and they won't stop until you give the order. Usually.

What I'm seeing is a textbook battle plan: get on board and conquer the enemy ship from the inside out—like a Corsican water worm. And while part of me wants to sleep for twelve hours straight, secure in the knowledge that no one would hold it against me, the larger part of me is ready to get on an assault shuttle and make the Mid-Core Rebels on board pay for what they did to my brothers down on Kublar.

And they *will* pay.

"Lieutenant Chhun!"

To my surprise, Specialist Kags, the Repub Army basic that crewed our sled gun, comes running up to my side. He's got an N-4 in one hand and fresh charge packs in the other.

"Sir, let me come."

I stop and take his offering of fresh blaster fire. I nod. "KTF."

Kags breaks out into a smile that seems to dissolve the weariness buried in the lines of his face. "Yes, sir."

We reach the assault shuttle at the same time as the marine fire team. Seeing as this *is* a marine op, the fire team climbs on board the cylindrical shuttle without bothering to ask us for permission.

These shuttles are glorified rockets. A pilot stationed at the rear of the craft throttles at full speed until the shuttle's lance-like end punctures the durasteel hull of a capital ship or space station. There are cutting torches around the nose in case the craft needs a little extra boring before reaching that sweet meat inside the starship. But a good shuttle jockey knows where best to impact. Once the shuttle penetrates, the soldiers—usually marines, but also legionnaires—wait for the tech crew to verify seal integrity and pop open the craft for the marines to pour out. That last step is crucial. The last thing you want is to open your assault shuttle and realize that the vacuum of space is doing its best to pull you right outside through a minuscule crevice. Like steak getting sucked through a straw.

Wraith peers into the packed shuttle. "Room for my team, First Sergeant?"

The lantern-jawed hullbuster chews a wad of stim as he takes in the sight of us. "Hell, Leej, looks like you boys've had enough already. Even so, this bird's full."

"Thank you, First Sergeant," Wraith says, looking back at the three of us. "Thing of it is, we may be all that's left of Victory Company, and the scumsacks on that cruiser are the ones responsible. So no, we haven't had enough. Is there any way you can help me?"

This is one of the things I appreciate about Wraith. A lot of officers—especially points—throw their rank around as if it were a golden pass to get whatever they want. I can't tell you the number of rear-echelon basics who made the mistake of thinking it was a good idea to pull rank on the legionnaires keeping them alive on some firebase at galaxy's edge. "*You and your men help load this cargo sled, Sergeant!*" It's a mistake they don't make twice.

The first sergeant lets out a contemplative groan, almost a sigh. He tugs on his chin and looks to the back of his sled. "Tell you what, Leej. We got a nose load of scanners and scrubbers for the tech crew to use once we pop that can open and dust everything inside. What say we forget to load it and let you boys squeeze in?"

Wraith nods and turns his attention to us. "How 'bout it?"

I crack a smile. "Always make 'em pay, sir."

The marines lug the cases of sensor equipment and air scrubbers to the shuttle's ramp while First Sergeant keeps the pilot occupied. Once our nook is carved out, we board, walking single file like we're attempting to find our seat in a crowded holotheater.

"Hold up, Basic." I see a marine lift a halting hand as Kags attempts to board just behind Exo. "This is as far as you're going."

Kags hesitates.

"He's with us," I say. "He needs to see this fight to the finish, too."

JASON ANSPACH & NICK COLE

It's enough. The marine lets Kags on board, and soon he's strapping into the jump seat next to me.

First Sergeant gets off the comm. "Welcome aboard, Basic."

"Thanks," Kags answers. "Don't call me Basic, though."

The marines laugh. "Ain't our fault you signed up for Rep-Army!"

The ramp closes and the lights dim. I feel the ship lift off the ground, the repulsors gently swaying us as we're positioned against the magnetic accelerator launcher. You read that right. It isn't enough for these little bad boy shuttles to fly into enemy capital ships at full throttle. They also get a Gaussian head start. If it weren't for interior velocity dampers, everyone inside would end up one big sheet of goo at the back of the sled.

Pleasant.

"Ready for go…" the pilot announces over the comm, his voice cool.

"Tuck your chin," I instruct Kags. He does.

"Go!" the pilot shouts.

We take off at a snapping speed, enough that even with the artificial stabilizers whining to keep up, I can feel my guts moving to one side of my body.

I have no idea whether the Preyhunters are targeting us, or if we're moving too fast. Modern starfighters like the Republic's complement of tri-fighters have sophisticated enough sensors to take down ultra-high-speed craft with predictive targeting and pulsar missiles or AI-fired blaster cannons. You'd have to ask a flyboy if a Preyhunter has that sort of smarts. I'm hoping they don't.

The pilot's voice comes over the comm once more. Smooth and in control. Pilots are so cocky. "All right, Marines. Strap yourselves in and tighten down. We're breaking this nut open in thirty."

The marines cross their arms and assume crash positioning. Sure, they're strapped in, but slamming into the side of a capital ship at this speed—even in a shuttle designed for the very thing—is a jarring experience. You don't want to get caught with your chin up or your appendages loose. The most common injuries in assault shuttle training are broken arms and noses from some hullbuster who forgets to tuck in.

The pilot counts down from ten, so calm that I might ask Wraith if they're related. Of course, I know the pilot is so tightly packed in the cockpit with heightened velocity dampers, absorption bubble shield, shock absorbers, and impact repulsors that the impending impact won't feel any worse than his speeder bumper getting tapped by an errant repulsor cart in a grocery store parking lot.

We hang on.

"... zero."

Almost to the word, we hear a tremendous boom, accompanied by the shearing and scraping of impervisteel giving away around the nose of our maniacal speed rocket. We come to a halt. The marines keep their eyes on First Sergeant, waiting for the command to disembark.

"All right," the pilot announces from the comm. "We've breached target deck on bridge level. Standby for verification of seal integrity."

The cabin is silent, save for the metallic clink of blaster rifles against kit.

"Seal confirmed. Sensors reading life support go... no hostiles on scope."

"All right, Marines!" First Sergeant shouts. "You heard Johnny Ace! Lock 'em, load 'em, and get ready to chew 'em up!"

The nose of the shuttle opens like the beak of a sea strangler. We remain strapped in, with blaster rifles aimed at the opening maw. This is because until those doors open, we really have no idea what our entry point is. If we went through a ceiling, we could be looking straight down at the deck; if we angled low, we may have to climb. And gravity stabilization will go away as soon as the cabin fully decompresses.

The shuttle opens, and I don't feel any pull. The pilot brought us in at the perfect angle. Marines begin to un-strap and jump out, landing on the deck after a short drop. They sweep out, dropping to knee and belly and securing the area from any potential hostiles. But they're unop-posed and in complete command of the landing site.

Wraith approaches the First Sergeant. "Your op, Sergeant, but do you have an idea of where we are on the ship?"

"I'd say we got a pretty good idea. Decent pilot. We're part of the bridge assault team. We should be a half-click from the main corridor on these relics. That'll lead us to command bridge. Prolly hafta fight our way to it, once we hit the main thoroughfare."

"Which way to the main corridor?" I ask.

First Sergeant nods at a set of sealed blast doors. "Just gotta pop them puppies open."

A pair of marines move to the doors and begin working on them with cutting torches.

"Seriously?" Exo says, his mock disbelief coming through his bucket speaker loud and clear. "Cutting torches?"

"Sorry, Leej," First Sergeant says, spitting a wad of stim onto the deck. "Marines don't get all that fancy equipment you boys in the army and Legion are loaded down with. We got cuttin' torches for doors and N-6s for everything else."

"It's fine," Wraith says. "Exo, Chhun, move to front and prepare to go out with the marines. We've got no idea what's waiting for us on the other side, and your armor'll be able to take what's coming a lot more than their flak vests."

"Yes, sir," Exo and I answer in unison. We hustle to the door.

I hear Kags ask, "What about me?" as we move away.

"You do whatever First Sergeant tells you," Wraith answers.

First Sergeant growls. "And I'm tellin' you to hang back and be ready to bring that nice N-4 into the fight if I call you up. Don't worry, you'll get a chance to shoot some MCR."

The marines cut a circle out of the door and step away. "Time to knock, leejes."

"Ooah!" Exo nods at me to make sure I'm set, then violently kicks the center of the blast doors. The three-inch thick impervisteel pops out and lands with a *ka-thunk* on the other side. If there are any MCR nearby, they heard that.

I jump through, landing in a roll that takes me to the cover of a bulkhead. My N-4 is trained down the corridor. Nothing.

Exo is out, keeping on my heels. He's covering the opposite direction. "Clear," he says as the marines begin to hustle through the rough-cut opening in the blast door, taking care not to burn their combat fatigues on the still-hot metal.

A marine lowers his rifle. "Where is everybody, man?"

I strain to hear over the hum of the ship. Turbo laser batteries are discharging toward the *Mercutio*, and return fire is absorbed by hull and shield. But I don't hear any small-arms fire. No hint of assault parties or MCR crew seeking to repel them.

It's as if we've boarded a ghost ship.

02

"All right, marines." First Sergeant points down the empty corridor. "Just because they ain't here don't mean you can go home. These Mids need killin', so let's find 'em."

I follow the marines down the corridor. Unlike the smooth, mirror-finished decks of Republic battleships, the decks on Ohio-class starships look like they were launched from the orbital shipyard before they were fully finished. There's no under-deck technology—no retractable defense crew turrets, courier tubes, or impact channels. Just grating, a maintenance shaft that includes HVAC, and a deck plate to ensure the area can be properly sealed in the event of a hull breach. And the corridors are constructed from steel—not impervisteel, just *steel*. When these space-whales were built, impervisteel was too precious to be used on anything except the outer hull.

Everything in the corridor I now move through is painted a drab blue-gray that absorbs the artificial light cast from recesses in the ceiling above. I occasionally pass a block number painted in white, displaying the deck and sector.

We move in a straight line until we stand beneath an overhead sign that reads, "Deck 01-C Life Support Rooms." Beneath that is a pair of arrows next to the words, "Bridge Thoroughfare."

"Looks like we're on the right track," Wraith says to First Sergeant.

The first sergeant grunts in acknowledgment. "I want those life support rooms cleared before we move into the main corridor. Don't wanna give the Mids an opportunity to get behind us."

Marines hustle to the doors and storm inside as they slide open. Exo and I move with them, but it's quickly apparent that the rooms are empty. The thrumming of the deck's life support systems is all that greets us.

"All clear, First Sergeant." The marine giving the report seems agitated. Riding an assault shuttle is an adrenaline rush, and that adrenaline is usually put to good use, since it typically isn't long after breaching that a firefight breaks out. But not this time. The ship really does seem abandoned, and I can see the nagging fatigue of disappointment weighing on the hullbusters.

"Let's keep sharp," I call out to my fellow leejes—and Kags. "We've seen this before. Skeleton crew, concentrating forces at a chokepoint. When the shooting starts, it'll be hot and thick."

I say this for the benefit of the marines. They're pros, but the long trek through empty corridors has already given way to inattentive whispers. They need to be ready to get shot at. Ready to KTF.

The corridor ends at a massive blast door that leads into the bridge thoroughfare—a massive corridor large enough for rapid-transport vehicles to move on two lanes, with walkways on the sides where crew and bots can travel four abreast. Think of it as the ship's superhighway. It ends at the bridge, and gives access through subcorridor or speedlift to the entirety of the ship. A capable force could barricade the thoroughfare, even bring up light armored vehicles, and hold off an assault force long enough for the bridge crew to safely deploy escape pods.

Exo slaps the blast door with the flat of his hand. It's like laying down a beat on the side of a mountain; the thing sounds completely solid. "Great," Exo says, his voice thick with sarcasm. "The cutting torches should be through this thing in thirty, forty-five minutes. *That'll* surprise 'em."

"Stow it, Exo," orders Wraith.

The first sergeant sends six marines forward to begin cutting a hole in the massive doors. It takes twenty-two minutes.

"Let's knock 'em down," says First Sergeant.

"Don't think I can mule kick a meter of blast door out onto the next deck," Exo quips.

"We've got det-cord," a marine offers.

Kid sounds like he's trying to be helpful, so I say, "Nice work, Marine."

The kid smiles and begins to adhere the thin coil of explosives around the still-glowing seam created by the cutting torches. The heat won't cause det-cord to detonate. Considered "smart ordnance," it'll explode only in response to an infrared command keyed in specifically to the cord. It's configured to pack just enough punch to blow a maximum of two point five meters of blast door in the opposite direction.

If there are any MCR on the other side, I'm hoping they're standing right where the chunk of metal will land. Save us time.

"Fire in the hole!"

The marines detonate the explosives, and I watch from behind a bulkhead as a massive slab of blast door flies into the next corridor and lands with an enormous thud that must've left a dent in the deck grate.

Exo and I exchange a look.

"Bet you somebody heard *that*," Exo says.

First Sergeant shouts, "Go! Go! Go!" and the marines begin to pour through the opening. Not before Wraith and Exo, though. The two legionnaires established that they would breach first from here on out, trusting their armor to do what marine flak vests aren't quite as capable of: stopping blaster fire.

Sure enough, I see a blaster bolt sizzle past Wraith. Another glances off Exo's shoulder, but it clearly doesn't cause any real damage. The report of the blaster fire tells me that the Mids are shooting at us from a distance, probably the far end of the corridor we're now breaching.

I jump through the gaping hole in the blast door, getting ahead of several marines who are delicately maneuvering over the still-hot metal. As I land, I see that this is *not* the main thoroughfare after all. It appears to be an arterial corridor. Nowhere near wide enough to be our target.

That doesn't matter right now. An assortment of rebels are fighting from partially exposed positions at the opposite end. They have the same cover we do—the rib-like frames that mark each modular piece of corridor. A few are firing from behind the improved cover of an opened bulkhead blast door, but they're too far away to do much with the blaster pistols they're equipped with.

I lay myself flat on the deck, partially covered by a protrusion, and fire my N-4, using its open holosight to add to the body count Wraith and Exo have already racked up. Dead MCRs begin to litter the deck.

My charge pack goes red. "Chhun reloading!" I shout, though I'm not sure anyone hears me over the amplified din of blaster fire. The marines have poured in now, and they're sending down *torrid* streams of blaster fire. I feel like I see more blaster bolts than empty space.

More insurgents are hit, and the bodies of the fallen dance in macabre, rag-doll spasms as blaster fire hits their lifeless bodies. This is a one-sided bloodbath, and the MCRs know it. They turn and break, running pell-mell in the opposite direction.

Even more fall as our intense fire strikes the retreating MCR platoon in the back. We advance, unwilling to let our prey escape until every last fighter is put down like the vicious dogs they are. This may sound harsh to someone who's never been in combat. Someone who looks down from his seat of safety and comfort purchased dearly by the blood of the Legion. Someone who speaks of war as if he knows what the hell he's talking about.

In combat, I am a thinking beast who out-savages the monsters that seek to destroy me.

When the shooting starts, I separate the affable, compassionate part of who I am and give the warrior complete control. These insurgents would kill me as sure as look at me. Their brothers *did* kill the hundreds in Camp Forge and the thousands aboard the *Chiasm*. It is a battle for survival, and I refuse to let them win.

The return fire is sporadic and ill-aimed. We advance in fire teams, keeping up a continual stream of suppressive blaster fire.

As we pass through a bulkhead, I see the blast door up ahead begin to close, its open square ever-shrinking as its four separate panels move to meet at diagonal angles.

"Blast door!" I shout.

"Shut 'em down!" orders First Sergeant.

Wraith drops to a knee and takes careful aim with his N-4. He hits the door's control panel dead center. A shower of sparks flies, and the door's panels freeze in place. For good measure, Exo lines up an insurgent through the opening and drops him with a blaster bolt between the shoulder blades.

It is utterly demoralizing to go up against the Legion. Nearly every shot we send results in a casualty, while return fire seems ineffective. Our enemies feel like children going into battle with their toys.

The MCR is in full retreat. Now it's a matter of catching and destroying them before they have the opportunity to regroup for a counterassault—or physically meet up with another force. I say physically, because their comms are useless. An Ohio doesn't have the sophistication needed to resist the *Mercutio*'s jamming. The insurgents' only hope is to reach a fortified position or get back to the relative safety of their main force.

"Hold up!" Wraith shouts, bringing the pursuit to an abrupt halt.

We've come to the end of our corridor, which opens up into a 'T.' The insurgents have disappeared to either the right or left, maybe both. If I were them, this is where I'd lay an ambush. Hit us as we turn the corner. Wraith must be thinking the same thing.

"Blind corner," he observes, his external comm hushed so that only friendlies can hear him. "This is where it happens if we go in stupid."

"I'm all ears if you've got a plan, Leej." The first sergeant disperses his marines to watch the end of the corridor, ready to shoot should anything pop into the open on our left or right.

"Grenades?" I suggest.

"Out," Exo says.

Wraith checks his belt. "Same."

"Me too," I say, knowing that it ultimately doesn't matter. The marines have two each—one fragger and one ear-popper. A few of them should have smokers, too. I turn to First Sergeant, careful to include him in what I'm about to suggest to Wraith. "With their buckets, Exo and Wraith can see through smoke. First Sergeant, can your marines toss some smokers into the corridor and follow with fraggers? We can move in and dust whoever's left standing before they know we're there."

"Not the ear-poppers?" the first sergeant asks.

Wraith shakes his head. "If we get a chance to take the bridge, we'll be glad to still have those."

First Sergeant nods and produces two smokers from a leg pouch. He hands them to me. I give one to Kags, and the two of us creep toward the end of the corridor, collecting fraggers from the marines as we move our way up. Wraith and Exo are stacked up behind us.

My ears are straining for any hint that the enemy might be rushing around the corner, clanking on the deck grate, but all is quiet. The ship seems to have gone ghost again.

We stop on opposite sides of the corridor, maybe ten meters shy of the T. I set down my fraggers and activate the delay on my smoker to three seconds, holding up three fingers so Kags knows to do the same. I count down from three, silently mouthing the numbers. We both throw the smokers into the corridor at zero.

Billowing clouds of white smoke fill the corridor ahead of us. It's like a cloud got off the speedlift to join us on deck. I hear muffled coughing. They're there. I pick up the fraggers, thumb the activators, and toss them, banking them off the corridor wall and around the left corner. Kags does the same on the right.

Boom! Boom! Boom! Boom!

With the last fragger's detonation, Wraith and Exo sprint into the corridor, trusting the mix of shrapnel, smoke, and their ability to see through it to keep them alive. I hear the familiar sound of N-4 rifles being double-tapped. Each burst means a dead insurgent.

There are a lot of bursts.

And that's not good. It means that either there are more of them around the corner than we figured, or that the fraggers didn't do the damage we'd hoped for. Return fire from the PK-9A blaster rifles and high-capacity low-yield blaster pistols soon answers.

Drrrrt!

My heart sinks. The sound is of a rapid-fire crew-served machine gun sending a flurry of blaster bolts down the hallway. Had the fire team of marines turned the corner blind, there would have been no survivors. If Wraith and Exo were caught flatfooted by that thing...

The two legionnaires leap from the smoke. They land hard on the deck, safe on our side of the intersection.

"Sket, that was close!" Exo cries.

Wraith picks himself up and calls the first sergeant forward as he casually steps over to me. "Fraggers got a couple, but most were farther down the hall. They're dug in like sin-ticks. Barricades and a crew-served KL-5. I'd estimate we dropped ten before they returned fire."

"How many left?" I ask.

"Five, six. But that KL-5 is a big equalizer."

"More fraggers?" First Sergeant asks.

Wraith gives a fractional shake of his head. "No. Too far, and the barricades will absorb most of the impact again."

I watch as the corridor's vent system, already thrumming from working overtime, begins to thin the dissipating smoke. "Well, we need to do something soon. Smoke's clearing."

Wraith straightens up. "Exo, stack up behind me. Chhun, since you still don't have a bucket, stay behind Exo. Prioritize that crew team."

"Hold up," First Sergeant says, grabbing Wraith's armored forearm. "That sounds too much like suicide for my taste."

"I appreciate that, but time is a finite commodity. I expect to see my leejes fill the captain of this ship with blaster bolts within ten minutes, and the clock is ticking."

We stack up, ready to make the best tactical decision available to us, though the odds aren't great. But legionnaires *use* the odds. We *defy* the odds. We don't mindlessly play the odds like some gutless seamball coach. We play to win.

And in this instance, the play to make involves opening ourselves to a crew-served machine gun that will eat through our armor in one terrible burst.

Ooah.

03

Wraith holds up his arm. I watch his fist, waiting for it to open and point, giving the signal to move. My N-4 is set to full-auto, I've got a green charge pack, and if this is how I die... I ain't complainin'.

Though it's only a few seconds, the wait feels interminable. The machine gun team hasn't let up. But it's a sound decision for Wraith to hold us up. They can't fire forever. They'll need to change bolt drums or swap out barrels. Hell, they might even get bored or call a cease-fire, thinking they dusted our entire team, and just wait for the last remnants of smoke to clear.

Just when I think the fire will never let up, it goes full stop. A blizzard of red blaster bolts is going by one second, and then nothing. Nothing save the sound of an N-4 rifle on burst mode. I hear it blasting from around the corridor in controlled, three-round bursts. And then it stops, too.

Silence.

"That a leej?" Exo asks.

"No other leejes on this op beside you, 's'far as I know," First Sergeant says quietly. "They're all gearing up to do an op planetside."

Wraith straightens up and says over the L-comm, "Heartbreaker."

He's giving the Victory company challenge phrase. It should be easy enough for any leej to figure out. He's also assuming the same thing I am, that the frequency we were set to while on Kublar was the *Mercutio*'s standard for the shipboard legionnaires. There's always the possibility that the assumption is incorrect, and a very real leej stationed to the *Mercutio* is just around the corner, unable to hear us over L-comm.

This could also be an MCR trick.

"Lifetaker," comes the reply.

All of us spring up from our positions. It's Masters's voice on the other end.

"Masters," I say, "it's us. We're coming around the corner. Don't shoot us."

"Is Devers with you?" Masters asks. "Because no promises if he is."

He says the last bit on external comm while stepping calmly around the corner. We clamp hands and dole out manly half-hugs. I peer down the corridor. Somehow, Masters approached the MCR from their rear and dusted every last one of them. The crew all have gaping holes in the back of their heads. The barrel of their KL-5 is still smoking.

"You're here, too?" Exo says. "Hell yeah! See, *that's* what I'm talkin' about. They ain't stoppin' us now. Gonna take that bridge, and then y'all can call me *Captain* Exo."

"How'd you get here?" I ask Masters.

"Saw a marine who looked pale. I got him to fake a gut-bug in exchange for my holochit collection. Didn't tell him he'd have to go to Moona Village to collect them."

I smile. "I figured already that you made it on board an assault shuttle. What I mean is, how did you find *us*?"

"Oh, uh, well, I heard from one of the marines I came in with that I wasn't the only leej to make his way onto an assault shuttle. So when they were all hustling to the knockdown drag-out on the main corridor, I moved to where the hullbusters said your shuttle was supposed to hit."

The first sergeant approaches us while his marines carefully make their way past the dead MCRs. "So you've seen what lies ahead? Because I'll be straight. Ain't nothin' looked right since we moved past the deck's life support rooms. We were supposed to be on the main thoroughfare, and this ain't it."

"Yeah," Masters agrees. "It's all clear behind me. I think these guys were a detachment from the main force stationed this way just in case. And it seems the MCR did some reconfig to the usual Ohio-class layout. They obviously didn't have *close* to the necessary crew to man this thing, so they sealed off a lot and made new corridors. I'd guess they had enough crew for battery emplacements, hangar, pilots, bridge, and armed insurgents to help fend off any boarding parties—no koobs, thank Oba. Don't wanna see one of them again unless I'm part of the firing squad."

"Let's push up," Wraith says, nodding for Masters to lead the way. He turns to First Sergeant, but the marine has one hand over his ear, listening to his comm.

"Command wants to talk to you, Leej," the first sergeant tells Wraith. "Looks like our fire team lucked out and got behind the resistance."

"Patch him over to my channel. I'll send you a sync-burst."

"Got it. Coming through."

I can hear only Wraith's side of the conversation that follows. It's a lot of *yessirs*.

"So what do you think they want?" Exo asks, shifting from one foot to another as though he can't wait to pick up the fighting again. "Sneak up behind the main force and wipe 'em out?"

I shrug. "My money's on sending us straight to the bridge."

"Yeah, that's the thing," Masters says, his voice animated. "I'm pretty sure this corridor we're in will take us right up to the bridge's port-side blast doors. It's configured all wacky—bad weld jobs really start to show up further down the line—but I'm pretty sure I passed it. Ohio-tech cameras—not that they're working with the *Mercutio* ghosting them..."

Wraith finishes up his conversation. "Understood, sir. Victory-1 out."

We all look at Wraith expectantly before Exo asks, "What's the word, Captain?"

Wraith speaks loud enough for the marines to hear. "That was *Mercutio*'s legion commander." He pauses and looks to the first sergeant. "I assume he informed you that this is now officially a Legion op and that your fire team is under my command."

First Sergeant nods. "Yep. A little confused why everyone is calling you 'Captain' since you got lieutenant bars on your armor, though."

Masters holds up a hand. "I can answer that. Captain Ford was promoted in the field. And that sergeant," he points to me, "is actually a lieutenant."

"And what are the two of you?"

"Exo and me are still specialists. You had to kill a certain number of koobs to get a field promotion."

Exo shakes his head as if troubled. "Captain Ford and Lieutenant Chhun kept stealing our kills."

"Uh-huh," grunts First Sergeant. "Good luck keepin' your rank once we get back to the ship. Republic is stingy that way. So what's the plan, Captain?"

"The *Mercutio*'s intelligence corps believes the MCRs on the bridge are attempting to dump data before making an exit in the escape pods. Every other marine on this ship is fighting a sizable force farther down the corridor. We're behind all that mess. Our orders are to move to the bridge, infiltrate, and secure it. We are to take the ship's captain and all possible bridge officers alive."

"Be a lot easier to kill 'em all…" Exo mumbles.

"Those aren't our orders," I say.

"Time's wasting," Wraith says. "Let's get to the bridge. Masters, you're on point. First Sergeant, do what you do best with your marines. Kags, you're up with us."

The army basic grins and jogs to catch up with Masters. We've got a bridge to sweep and a ship to capture.

We reach the bridge's port blast doors with zero resistance, but I can clearly hear the frenetic battle happening elsewhere on the main corridor thoroughfare. I can see that the marines are thinking about their buddies; they're eager to bring the hammer down on the MCR and put a stop to the fight. But the truth of it is, if we take the bridge, we take the ship. And surrenders typically stop the enemy much faster than fighting to a total team kill.

A marine pushes against the blast door. "This one's thicker than the one back there."

Exo lets out a sigh. "We'll all die of old age before those torches cut through."

"Well, we gotta do something," says Masters, stating the obvious.

I chew my lip. "If we start cutting, they'll know we're out here, and they'll either send a detachment to engage us or get off the ship before we have a chance to grab them. Even Ohio-class escape pods will jump to hyperspace at launch. Our gunners won't have time to touch 'em."

Wraith nods in agreement. "I'll get *Mercutio*'s Legion command on the comm, see if they have anything shipboard that we might be able to use to blow the door open."

Crouched against the corridor walls, we have teams covering every direction, carefully watching to make sure nothing gets the drop on us.

"It'd be nice if someone from inside the bridge decided to come out on their own," Masters says to me. "Y'know, stretch their legs."

We both look to the door. It stays shut.

"Chhun," Wraith calls over the comm. "Move up to the door panel. Legion command says they have something."

I hear a direct-comm burst over my headset. "Go for Chhun," I say.

"Glad you made it out alive," I hear over the comm.

I know that voice. "Andien?" The scientist. She's back on ship then? Or am I speaking to her via relay from Kublar's surface? There's a mob of questions moving through the streets of my mind. The strongest of them, the one that I express, is, "How's Rook?"

There's a pause.

"Let's... let's focus for now on the task at hand, Lieutenant Chhun."

Dead. Rook is dead. I bury it and him all at once. I look at the panel. It's old tech. Tactile buttons, visible wires behind perforated paneling, and a faded alphanumeric display screen. "What am I doing?"

Andien's voice is steady. "Every Ohio-class battleship has a command override for access to the bridge."

"Okay, what's the code?"

"Not *quite* that easy. The code is dependent on how the access panel is hard-wired. You have to take the panel off. There are four tenor bolts. Unfasten them."

And me without my tool bag. I call out to the first sergeant. "I need a cutting torch up for this panel."

A marine steps forward and lights his torch. A three-inch long flame leaps out of the wand's end.

"Dial it back, pal. I need the panel's tenor bolts *off*, not extra crispy."

The marine dials back the intensity so that a miniature glow is all that the torch emits. He works quickly around each bolt, shearing it off at its head. I grab each hot bolt in my gloved hand as it falls, then snag the panel. I lay all the pieces at my feet—not that anyone on the bridge would hear if they hit the deck.

"Okay, plate's off. What next, Andien?"

"Tell me what you see."

Multicolored wires run from a node into a veritable nest of microcircuitry. The wires are just a little cooked from the torch—scattered black scorch marks mar the blues, greens, and yellows, as if someone held a lighter to them.

"Uh, I see thirteen nodes with different-colored wires hooked into them."

"What color is the first wire?"

"Uh... reddish-brown?"

"It's not black?"

"It doesn't *look* black."

"And you're sure it's not just red?"

I look again, inspecting each of the thirteen wires just to make sure that I'm not missing something. If I had my bucket, it could tell her the exact wavelength of the color. I think about asking Wraith to take a look, but I trust my gut.

"No, it's not red. The red wire is definitely in the seventh node from the left."

"Okay... let me think." Andien breathes into the comm as though she's blowing her hair away from her forehead.

Think? Exactly who is this woman who claims to be a scientist, but seems instead to be an expert on communication tech, both modern and antique?

"There's a blue wire right next to the reddish-brown one, if that helps."

"Thanks," Andien says. "Are the first five wires reddish-brown, blue, white with yellow stripes, black, and then green?"

I mentally check off each wire as she speaks the colors. It's exactly as she describes it. "That's it, yeah."

"Okay. You're going to need to pull out that first wire and replace it with the red one. There's a quick-release tab just above it. Don't yank it out."

"What do I do with the brown one?"

"Brown?" There's mild alarm in Andien's voice.

"Sorry. Reddish-brown."

"Nothing. Just leave it unhooked."

I detach the first wire and then port over the red wire. The display screen for the panel blips for a second, but otherwise everything is as it was. "Made the swap," I announce.

"Well done, Lieutenant Chhun. You're ready to open the door to the bridge. You just need to enter the code."

I motion for the marines and my fellow leejes to prepare themselves. Hands go to N-6 rifles and ear-poppers. Wraith, Exo, and Masters are stacked outside the door, ready to clear the room as soon as the ear-poppers detonate.

Exo looks at the marines. "Better only send in one of those. Confined space; they'll be too deaf for questioning if you cook off more than one."

The marines nod.

"Okay," I say over the comm. "Give me the code."

Andien relays a series of alphanumeric characters. I diligently enter them on the keypad.

"Last character," Andien says, waiting for me to give the go-ahead.

I nod to Wraith, who steels himself.

"Go," I say.

"Six."

I press the corresponding key and bring my N-4 to the ready. The bridge door whooshes open, and I see an ear-popper fly into the room. It drops at the feet of an MCR security ensign.

And fails to detonate.

With no time to toss in another popper, we open fire, dropping the ensign as we storm the bridge. The ship's captain and mates all wear masks of stunned surprise.

"Hands! Hands!" Wraith is on them, his voice amplified and booming. He forces the captain and mates to their knees, his N-4 aimed down at their necks. "On the deck!"

The bridge of an Ohio-class ship has a raised command platform sitting above a crew pit manned by helmsmen, sensor techs, and the like. Kags and I move to the platform to help to secure the command crew, trusting Exo and the marines to lock down the bridge pit. As soon as the crew is ener-chained and disarmed, I look over to Exo to check on his progress—and I see a tech attempting to surreptitiously remove her sidearm.

"Blaster!" I shout in warning.

Exo and Masters swing their N-4s in unison. They find the target and open up in quick bursts. The suddenness of the action causes the marines to open fire into the pit as well. Before my eyes the entire tech crew is laid to waste.

"Cease fire!" I order. The command is echoed by Wraith and First Sergeant.

The shooting dies down, and we're left with shaking MCR officers and a pit full of dead crewmen. The silence hanging over the bridge is interrupted by the chime of the comm announcing a priority message.

"This is Colonel Fitz. We're keeping the Republic at bay. Their marines are suffering heavy casualties. Advise ETA to data dump and jump."

Data dump and jump. They weren't looking to escape, only to hedge their bets. Dump whatever data they don't want discovered should we take over the ship, then jump to safety, effectively stranding whatever marines were on board. The *Mercutio* surprised this ship; they probably figured that with the *Chiasm* gone, there'd be no other Republic vessels in reach. Just a few surviving leejes on the planet's surface to be dealt with by their Preyhunter squadrons. The thought makes me grow hot with anger.

Wraith has tied the ship's captain's arms behind his back with an ener-chain. He hauls the rebel to his feet by his collar and walks him to the bridge's comm relay. "I'm going to need your cooperation, Captain. Is that clear?"

JASON ANSPACH & NICK COLE

The captain, a bearded man somewhere in his fifties, stares back at Wraith defiantly.

Wraith nods at the comm. "Order your men to surrender immediately."

"And should I refuse?" the captain replies.

Wraith answers with a vicious, armored elbow to the man's face. The captain drops unconscious to the deck, a pool of blood forming around his head.

Wraith removes his blaster pistol and calls out to the other officers. "Your captain is incapacitated and unable to command this vessel. Who is next in the command chain?"

A timid hand goes up. "I am." The kid looks much too young to warrant a first mate position, but there he is all the same.

Wraith motions for me to bring the kid to him. I oblige. Roughly.

"Order your men to surrender immediately." Wraith thumbs off his blaster's safety, as if emphasizing the last word.

The first mate looks down at his battered captain and speaks into the comm. "This is First Mate Darehl Lund, speaking on behalf of Captain Entressex. The bridge has been captured by the Republic and you are hereby ordered to lay down arms and surrender immediately. This ship is no longer able to enter hyperspace. Surrender. Repeat, surrender."

"Good," Wraith says. He mockingly pats the cheek of the fresh-faced officer before I take him away.

First Sergeant has his hand to his ear. "Report on the comm is that most of the MCR are comin' out, hands up.

Few pockets of resistance, but they'll get chewed up before long."

Wraith seems preoccupied. Like he's having another conversation over L-comm. Finally, he acknowledges First Sergeant. "Nice work, Marine. It was a pleasure, as always. Lieutenant Chhun, round up the prisoners. Legion Command is sending in a shuttle for retrieval, followed by immediate interrogation. We're gonna find out how the MCR pulled this off."

04

Somewhere at galaxy's edge.
Two months before the Battle of Kublar.

He was known as X.

He was the Director of Operations and the grand pooh-bah of espionage within a small Nether Ops unit known as "The Carnivale."

They got that name because the operations they pulled were often viewed by *other* Nether Ops pooh-bahs as third-rate, showy, all flash, a bit of theater, and of little value in the grand scheme of Republic intel-gathering.

What is Nether Ops?

Most citizens have heard of Dark Ops. It's run by the Legion, and has the best operators from a war fighter perspective. A military check to balance the bureaucracy of the House of Reason and Senate Council. Dark Ops has budgets and offices and it's all very proper and legal.

Nether Ops, on the other hand, is the whisper of a rumor. Even in Dark Ops, few people know what *really* goes on there. Nether Ops does for the Republic what the Legion won't. It's the fulfillment of a dream that died the day General Rex and his Dark Ops legionnaires refused to obey. And so the Republic stopped asking Dark Ops to do what it *really* wanted and formed Nether Ops. A clandestine unit that did what needed doing.

And often... what shouldn't be done.

Because sometimes bad things—downright horrible things, in fact—must be done. For the greater good of the Republic.

The "greater good" is, after all, what the Republic is founded on.

The greater good. *All for all.*

Isn't that what the elites at the top like to say every time they bother to go through the pomp and circumstance of an election? All for all? As they switch seats and positions just often enough to keep the rubes believing it's all a democracy? Or a "modified galactic republic"—that's how they teach it to the younglings.

Emphasis on "modified."

Most citizens, the great unwashed, would be surprised at how "modified" it truly is.

They wouldn't like to know how the steaks get cut.

X knows this better than anyone.

As he walks along the wet streets of the North Sea commons neighborhoods, just beyond Utopion Prime, the weather is fine and misty, some would say gloomy. His destination is the old starship works near the harbor. The Carnivale, an off-off-*off*-book operation, has always liked to be away from the hustle and bustle of the capital, with all their big modern buildings, sprawling conference rooms, high-tech security, agendas, planning committees, power, politics, and hot-potato games. Out here, in a refurbished engine housing manufacturing headquarters, is a nice place to do business and blend in with the locals.

And since anyone who isn't a local is easier to spot, it's much easier to run your ops away from prying eyes. Or at least, that's what X explains to all the junior field officers who get assigned to him. They arrive feeling glum—because some mistake they've made, or indiscretion they've committed, has ruined their career and forced them out here into the gulag of the Carnivale. The Carnivale, truth be told and let's be honest, is the joke of jokes in the Dark Ops community.

But as X likes to tell the other Nether Ops pooh-bahs: "What do they know!" And everyone laughs. Because Dark Ops are like little goblins playing wicked goblin games, and Nether Ops... well, they're actual monsters.

In Nether Ops, you don't just *know* how the steaks are cut—you *cut them*.

After butchering the corpse.

X threaded the maze of the old building, deftly navigating its semi-abandoned darkness and gray skylight lighting. There was a new girl at reception. Pretty. She carried a subcompact blaster and had several decorations that could never be admitted to in open hearings.

Nether Ops was like that. No one ever knew how many times you did something noble enough to get an award.

But they also never found out about the failures.

He passed her and checked in with a few of the juniors, receiving status updates on three ongoing operations in various stages. And then he moved on to his office.

Everything was quiet for a beginning-of-the-week morning.

After last week, of course, it was best that it all be quiet now. Nothing really to crow about. Of course, you could never crow in the first place, even if you won, but especially not after that fiasco.

What was needed now... was a story.

X had sent a man out there to die, and, well... *What'd you expect, old boy?* Now it was time to sit down, collate the reports, and organize some kind of narrative that was mostly true—because of course by week's end he'd be on someone's carpet explaining how everything went so sideways.

So he started the kettle and sank down into his vintage leather chair. He petted the kitten that called his office home and stared out into the rain as he waited for the kettle to boil. Only when all was ready, mug in hand, did he pick up the first document. The one he'd created himself. The one that detailed who the operative was. The recruitment reports. The initial interview. The mission briefing. And of course the bio.

A bright and shining navy officer from a fine family. They'd recruited him to play the fallen-out-of-favor-turned-arms-dealer-rogue they needed to stage their little playlet.

"Our Hamlet," he had told the juniors, for Operation Ghost Hunter.

He read his own briefings once more, moved on to the reports that had come in from the trainers, then picked up the first report from Ankalor. That was where the operation had begun in earnest. Infiltrate the inner circle of the main weapons dealer supplying the Mid-Core Rebellion.

And X began to tell himself a story.

"This is the story of you, Tom..." he murmured as he flipped through the dry reports and incident logs of the watchers who'd been watching their dear boy, that bright and shiny naval officer.

Because the chiefs in Nether Ops didn't do reports. They did *stories*.

And so X began to tell himself the story. The story of Tom. He needed to understand it just as much as they would. And he needed to tell them what they needed to hear, never mind the facts.

"You find yourself staring in the mirror," he began. "And waiting for the contact. Waiting days on end in the heat with the mad and the drunks. Because that's what all spies do, Tom. Especially the ones who are afraid of losing their way. They talk to themselves in the mirror without ever moving their lips. Because they're the only person they can talk to who knows the truth. Who knows who they truly are. And because they can't tell anyone else, and go on living. You're standing in front of the mirror, Tom, in a cheap hotel on dark, dangerous, and violent Ankalor. Waiting for the contact..."

That's you, Tom.

The guy standing in the dim bathroom in the worst hotel on Ankalor.

That's you.

You don't look like a Repub Navy officer. Not anymore. But of course you're not supposed to. You're not even you anymore, Tom. Not now. Maybe later.

But not now.

Right now you're Tom.

You still shave. You still dress smartly. Khaki combat trousers and high-quality safari boots. There's a mostly clean white shirt out in the terribly dark bedroom you've been hiding in for three days. You'll put that on before you go.

It's been six months of being Tom.

And as you stand in front of the mirror in the dim bathroom looking at yourself, you try to remember who, exactly, you used to be.

You lean in close.

You lie to yourself and think something like: "There I am. I still exist. I can be seen. I know the way home."

Except that's a lie.

You've almost completely disappeared from the galaxy.

You pick up the smoldering cigarette, ash it, and continue shaving. Ex-navy officers still shave. It's a habit. Even if they have been thrown out for moral violations. Gambling. Contraband. Smuggling. And a few other things to make you seem just dirty enough to be attractive to all the wrong people. Or at least that was the highest of hopes for your handlers at the Carnivale.

No. You're not you anymore.

But you're not supposed to be.

You pick up the plastic glass the low-range hotel has provided. It's filled with scotch, and you take a drink.

You wince.

Because you want to?

No. Never. You were never a drinker.

Because it helps complete the down-and-out-de-frocked-naval-officer look.

The lying never stops. Tell just one... and then you have to tell them all.

You smile.

Yes. You are still charming.

You always were.

Now you're out among the zhee of this planet, among them and their braying calls to prayer. The zhee are not the original inhabitants of this planet, Ankalor. They murdered whoever those people were about the time the big sublight colony ships were first struggling out into the void.

The zhee are fanatics.

Fanatics about their beliefs.

Fanatics about trade.

Fanatics about weapons.

Fanatics about themselves. Everyone else is just prey.

Y'know... fanatics.

That's what makes this planet the premier weapons market along galaxy's edge. Just beyond the fringe of civilization. That's why freighters are hauling into orbit on the hour to pick up more weapons than anyone can possible know what to do with. Except that, too, is a lie. They know exactly what they can do with them. They're doing it in a hundred brushfire conflicts across the galaxy as of this late hour in the Ankalorian day.

For a hundred years, it's been just the mercs, bounty hunters, pirates, and local warlords availing themselves of the "Night Market"—which is where you buy weapons of all conceivable types to destabilize governments, fight battles, and murder your opponents in their sleep. Whenever someone in the dark underbelly of the galaxy needs to do a big job, they pull into the docking ports that make up the bulk of the city, the closest thing to civilization the zhee have to offer. But now... well, now things are escalating. Now that the Mid-Core Rebellion is working up to really *be* something... there's a whole lot more money being spent. Because everyone is *real* excited to kill each other.

You're not a navy officer anymore.

You've fallen from grace.

That's the role we've crafted for you. You are our Hamlet.

At least, that's the way it's supposed to look to the target.

Frogg is the target's right-hand man. A bistro, as the zhee like to call it, is where you meet him. He looks like a toad. Short. Hunched shoulders. Bulging eyes. He was a major in the Legion until he got thrown out for being a violent sociopath. Except they had it all wrong. He was actually a *psycho*path. Crazy, violent. And utterly callous. The opposite of all you ever were.

Excuse me… once were.

What?

A dashing naval officer. You.

That's what Repub naval officers are supposed to be. Dashing. Handsome. Brave.

You were once all those things.

This man Frogg is the opposite of all that. He is small and dangerous and vicious. He is the opposite of you. Or who you once were.

"So we need a bit of a work?" he whispers as you sit down over thick black coffee in the market on this sweltering day. The zhee press about you, never minding your galactic civ need for personal space. Their grotesque man-donkey bodies are covered by the long black robes they wear. Their low harsh language is frequently cut by a braying donkey laugh that comes from their donkey faces. They would be almost comically sad and hilarious in the same bizarre showbiz moment, if they weren't so violently dangerous.

The zhee are viciously dangerous.

You nod at Frogg, because the cover the Carnivale built for you is the strong silent type. Look a little afraid, X told you, that'll make you seem desperate. And pros see desperate as a form of dangerous.

You are afraid.

"Someone's got to go out there and find out who's supplying the Mid-Core Rebels, my dear boy."

X again.

That someone is you. You are X's "Dear Boy."

And you're not even you anymore.

It's like you never were.

"It's like you never were, mate," says Frogg. "Drummed you right outta the service they did. Like me."

You manage to look uncomfortable about this.

You *are* uncomfortable.

The man with whom you're having this unpleasant but pleasant talk has killed more people than the most...

Well, according to Nether Ops Intel, he's killed a lot of people.

Dangerous and vicious.

"I was ex-Legion. Got kicked out for beating a fag to death. At least that's what I say. Now me, I don't mind the faggotry. I'm not a judgmental lad that way. You'd be surprised if you know what I mean. Nah, I beat him because reasons. Faggy had nothing to do with it. Know what I mean, mate? But my CO caught wind of that little beatdown and out I go. Which was a good thing for me, and it could be a good thing for you, depending on what you can do for me and Scarpia. *Mister* Scarpia that is."

In the Ghost Hunter briefings and at the Carnivale, Scarpia—*Mister* Scarpia—is known as the target.

You clear your throat like the proper gentleman naval officer you are. This part's delicate. This is the pitch. This is how it all gets started. So be careful, Mr. Nobody-Arms-Dealer-Named-Tom. Because there's a real chance you'll never get to be who you once were. Never again. Especially if they smell a rat.

Dangerous and vicious.

"And," you begin, you smooth operator, you. "What exactly can I do for you... and Mr. Scarpia?"

Frogg, whom Mr. Scarpia calls Froggy, watches you like the reptilian he fantasizes himself to be. Except he is just a man. Just like you. On a world full of strange aliens who regard you as barely a life-form and certainly not on their level. They would kill you and experience no more regret then someone butchering a chicken for dinner.

And they still murder each other according to tribal grievances that go back a thousand years.

"Explosives. Big ones. Very, very, big ones," says Frogg like some kid gazing at sweets in a shop and telling the clerk which ones he'd like.

You lean back and watch him because you've got to be on this date, too. Even though you're interviewing, it can't seem that way. It's got to seem the other way. Like they'd be doing you a favor to let you play. Let you provide some stuff to kill with. The rumor is that Scarpia is the dealer for the MCR. Even though they use many, he's considered "Numeral One, my dear boy."

It's got to seem like that.

"Surely..." You throw out an arm to encompass the bazaar and the phenomenal amount of weaponry and explosives on sale here. And this isn't even the Night Market. "Surely you can easily find what you're looking for?"

Basically you're telling them to stop wasting your time. Except that you're flattered they're wasting it with you.

Because you're not scared, Mr. Nobody Tom.

Except you are.

GALAXY'S EDGE: KILL TEAM

Remember when you were looking at yourself on this unbelievably hot morning in that sweltering little dank hotel and wondering if you had gone too far? Wondering if there still wasn't time to go back? Because... you're afraid you've gone too far. This is off the star map. This is uncharted. There are obstacles. There's the edge. The edge of the galaxy.

Don't things, people, fall off edges? If they go too far?

Well, you have no idea how far "too far" is.

"Not this type," says Frogg dreamily as he dismisses some N-50 heavy crew-served blasters with an auto-drone function stacked nearby. "We need something bigger. Real big stuff. Stuff the navy keeps around to crack the occasional asteroid or take out a destroyer. These blokes can't get that real deal apocalyptic stuff, try as they might, Tom. Heard you could. Heard you were connected to the knowing of things and people that deal in such big devices. Or did we hear wrong?"

You have no idea how far "too far" is.

But you will.

05

To meet the man, the man known as Scarpia, the man connected to the MCR, the Mid-Core Rebels, whom the news networks tell you are little more than a nuisance and your handlers tell you are blossoming into a real live threat to the Republic... To do that, well, you'll have to do a few things first.

"Do us a few things first, mate. Then square's square and we do some better deals and cut you in on a big trade that's going to not just make us rich... it's going to put us in charge. Someday."

That's how Frogg puts it.

An explosive powerful enough to knock out a destroyer is the thing you've got to do for them. Except those things are hardened against external explosions rated up to Romula nuclear space mines of the Savage Wars variety.

"Pick up two if you can, mate," says Frogg cheerily.

But internally—as in getting one of those things to go off *inside* the ship—that's a whole different game. You could take out a capital ship with that.

You thread the streets of the bazaar, back to your filthy little room. And later that night, when the air is all hot and swollen with fear, rage, and casual murder, and the streets seem only a little cooler than the stifling heat of your unconditioned room, you think about heading out. To visit

GALAXY'S EDGE: KILL TEAM

your contacts at the Grand Ankalor Bar while all the zhee are crazy from the heat.

They won't mind that you're not staying out of sight now that you've contacted Frogg. They'll understand the need to show up at the bar. Because of the heat.

Why are you making excuses?

"Because they're watching, dear boy."

We've taught you that they will always be watching you, before the first contact, and definitely after. So take the stage, Hamlet, and do everything with a reason they can understand.

You lie in your room and wait to make your next move as the fan barely turns overhead.

You should stay in.

The warm air swirls around and you sip the liquor you'll be nursing all through the night. You have a novel to read, but your mind drifts to the inhabitants of Ankalor.

They say it's the heat that makes the zhee crazy and homicidal and genocidal and weapons-hungry like no other race in the galaxy. So to hell with personal responsibility for collectively being a race of murderous scumbags.

Except the zhee are crazy everywhere they go.

The news networks don't tell you that because the zhee have a powerful lobby in the House of Reason.

So it's the heat. Or economic disparity. Or specism. Or whatever reason they can sell to the masses.

But... your life is on the line. Hard to read when that's going on. Hard to read when you could die at any moment. So you lie there and watch the fan and think about getting out.

You smoke and wish for a gin and tonic in a tall glass with square-cut ice cubes and maybe a lime. Over at the Grand Ankalor with all the journalists. The calls to prayer echo over and off the fat spires and the crawling slums of the zhee.

It'll be more dangerous out, at night.

It's always crazy, but the daytime craziness is just business for the zhee. Nighttime craziness is some kind of pleasure fair of murder and insanity. So best be careful. Everyone is warned that you take your life in your hands when going out at night on Ankalor.

You dress in the one suit you have and again find yourself staring in the mirror, trying to find you again. You've been doing that a lot lately. You wonder if she'll even recognize you if you survive this assignment.

For a brief moment, you imagine returning home when this is all over. She opens the door, and she knows. She knows all the done things that needed doing. Even though you've taken a thousand hot showers to wash off all the blood and stink of where you've been... she knows. It's there. Underneath the cologne. She smells the blood.

Because there are done things that needed doing, darling.

And then she closes the door on your face and you might as well just fade back to Nether Ops because they say, over there at Nether Ops Command, there really is no going back.

They told you that when this all first began.

They did.

But you thought you were different. You volunteered.

You take the needle blaster out of its hiding place in the cruddy, dingy room that shows nothing but religious zhee programming. The silencer goes in your breast pocket. Your blaster in the shoulder holster. And then you leave your hotel for a better one, in search of information to locate powerful explosives in order to blow up a Republic destroyer.

There really is no going back.

Except… you hope there is. Surely at any moment some legionnaire kill team will come sweeping in and clean everything up before it goes too far.

The last-rate hotel you're leaving opens out onto a small alley. And the night. You step over the gutter and decide to stick to the center of the alley until you reach the street up the way.

An old zhee watches you from beneath her hooded shawl. Her donkey face is cracked and leathery, and her dead eyes betray her past. The zhee used to eat anyone they found. Everyone knows that.

It took the early Repub thirteen dead worlds to figure out that the "space locusts" they'd been hearing about… were actually migrating zhee.

They'll eat anything.

That's why it's dangerous out at night.

The Legion wanted to destroy the zhee then and there.

But the House and Senate don't much like the Legion.

You make the main street, and it's alive with zhee cafes and zhee corner markets. You can buy cheap blasters in the corner markets alongside the local fermented drink and the sugary snacks the galaxy sells to them.

It is not uncommon to see zhee children carrying blasters.

There is nothing so fundamentally wrong as a child with a blaster and the worldview that you are not even an intelligent life form. The zhee believe that the Gran Pasha will one day return to lead them to resume their conquest of the stars.

Then they'll eat everyone.

Until then they'll just breed like rats.

A thousand different musicians on a thousand different sound devices compete to achieve the absolute opposite of harmony and orchestration. This too is the zhee, and anyone who comments on anyone else's music will most likely find themselves at knives.

The zhee love knives.

They call their special version the *kankari*.

It's still early, and you make the Grand Republic Hotel, get past the state-of-the-art security bots, and enter the opulent lobby. This place is the opposite of everything else on this stinking, boiling, broiling world. Here everything is charm and elegance and the murmur of polite conversation from discreet corners. The Grand Ankalor Bar— where the journalists and diplomats and the occasional naval attaché come to exchange trade—is where you're headed. It's already busy.

You enter the bar and nod to the usual crowd who know you and will swear under oath that you're a good man and it's just terrible about your luck. You wonder which of them is your minder tonight, because the Carnivale has all its players playing. This is quite a big op, and you are the tip of the spear. So someone is always supposed to be minding you.

Because whoever they are, they'll need to be there if it all goes south.

Do they watch you in the streets where it's most dangerous? That's what you wonder as a reporter named Darringa from *Republica Press and Information* buys you a "G and T, old chappy!" though you are much younger than him.

Or maybe not.

He drinks a lot, so...

You wonder if they watch you as you thread the stinking little alleys filled with murderous zhee who've been told by their clerics that they must resist even if they use only knives and hammers and sleds to mow down any and all unbelievers.

And do they, the minders, watch you while you sleep?

Did they watch the girl you hired and didn't have sex with? Did they watch you through the night as you lay next to her and listened to her sleep so that you could be reminded of someone else breathing in the night? Someone somewhere else in the galaxy?

Did they?

Do they?

You gulp at the gin and tonic with a splash of rosewater, which is how Chuntly, the barman at the Grand Republic, mixes them. You gulp, and you tell yourself it's all part of the act. You gulp your drinks because you're a drinker and you're desperate.

"There's got to be that hint of desperation, my boy," X has told you. "So drink like you're dying of thirst."

All part of the game of espionage.

All part of the game of finding explosives to blow up capital ships. *Republic* capital ships.

You find out from Steadron, who works for Spiral News Network—if you call drinking all day and trying to dig up dirt on who's selling weapons to whom as you crawl from one bar to the next, work—that a Repub Navy officer has been seen over in the Night Market selling some pretty good stuff. He's on leave and doing business with contraband and stolen merchandise.

"Rumor is he's got two, my friend," says the red-eyed Steadron as the hustle of the Bar Utopion grows hot and close in the late of the Ankalorian night. Players in the weapons bazaar, and courtesans who want nothing more than mere credits beyond their ability to spend, wage their wars and make their deals all around you.

Suffering and lust are good friends tonight. Hopefully everyone can walk away a winner.

Except the dead who will get killed on the back end of all these deals.

Except for them.

Someone has to lose. Why else would we need all these weapons?

"Two of what?" you ask Steadron.

"Massive antimatter reaction ordnance. But I hear he's leaving tomorrow, so better make your deal quick before he's gone."

It's dangerous to cross the zhee-infested slums. Night or day, it's dangerous. But two MAROs will do the trick to make sure that Frogg and Scarpia know you can acquire what they want. And hopefully acquisition leads to trust, and trust... well, that should lead straight to betrayal.

And termination. But that'll be some legionnaire's job.

"We merely acquire the intel, my dear boy," said X when this all began. "You won't be pulling any triggers."

Then a medal, and back to that life you once had. No more Tom. You'll be that other guy... what's his name? She knows. Don't worry... she remembers who you are. If you forget, when you get back, you can ask her.

You down the last of the gin and tonic and can't help yourself from checking with a quick pat that your blaster is still under your arm, hidden beneath your light coat.

Then you're out the front of the hotel, and the doorman, dressed like the grandest of Republican admirals, tries to get you a cab.

The man is earnestly trying to save your life, you think. Except you know cabs won't be headed where you're going tonight. Even they know it's too dangerous.

So you cross the busy street and start walking. It's instantly darker here on the other side. But it has to be, because it's the opposite of the glitter and glamour of a grand hotel. This is Ankalor, and it's overrun by the zhee.

They watch you pass the cheap stores, and you can hear them muttering in their guttural tongue. You're sure they're noting, remarking, informing on you.

So switch it up, just like you were taught.

Just like the pack predators they are, they work together at killing. There are no moderate zhee. That's a lie the Repub tries to sell every time the zhee blow themselves up in a crowded café. Never mind the rest of them dancing and braying in the streets, firing off their blasters for their bizarre gods, celebrating the deaths of *other* as some kind of moral victory.

Never mind that, Tom.

And also never mind the irony that you're the one out to find explosives on a night like this to do what they do in the name of freedom. You're doing it for freedom too… right, Tom?

Or a medal.

Or her.

Or the action.

Never mind you're going to provide some explosives for just the same reasons the zhee are going to blow up a transportation terminal on some core world. This is different.

Why?

You make an unexpected turn down an alley. Junk shops and noodle bars line the way. Their weird moaning music blares at you from every stall.

Why is it different?

You pass zhee porn and jade lotus dealers and cheap blasters and all kinds of things that'll ruin lives.

How is it different?

You're walking fast. Switching it up. But roughly making your way to where you want to go—the Night Market and the last chance to catch the dirty naval officer who's rumored to have some really big fireworks.

Your ticket in with Scarpia. The target. *Mister* Scarpia.

How is it different? You answer yourself. Because you'll just be procuring the ordnance. Delivering. And most likely Nether Ops will arrange for Dark Ops to send in a legionnaire kill team to clean everything—every*one*—up. All long before those two big firecrackers actually get lit.

You tell yourself that and keep moving.

You're pretty sure two of them are following you. Two zhee.

Where are your minders?

Except... if the girl in charge of the op, Operation Ghost Hunter, knows that Frogg and his people are watching you, and suddenly you get rescued from two hired zhee killers by men in black who've been tailing you all the way from the Grand Republic... well, then they'll know you're a...

They'll know you're not Tom.

You're someone else.

They'll probably kill you. Just to send a message.

You can't shake the two zhee, and now you're deep and away from the main streets and the illusion of security the Repub tries to create with their never-stopping, always-moving armored sled convoys. That's all it is. An illusion. And the minders won't be saving you this time. You're pretty sure of that.

You're on your own.

You hear their hoofsteps closing in on you. Their snuffling voices that sound like monsters. Because they *are* monsters. Vicious, violent monsters that look like humanoid donkeys.

You take a quick glance back and see them reaching under their shrouds.

Cloaks.

But the cloaks remind you of shrouds.

Coal-dark eyes watch you in the night. Yeah, they're coming for you. It's going down right now in a dark alley on a dangerous planet. Your heart is in your throat. So you make for a smaller, even darker alley, and you start to run.

Fast.

You can hear them behind you. Their hoofs clobber the stone of an alley filled with silvery moonlight and deep dark blue shadows. They've stopped speaking. They're not laughing or shouting, because this is the part they love: running prey to ground. It makes them frenzy.

Except you're leading them to a nice quiet place where you can have it out with them. Because the thing with the zhee is that they're constantly fighting each other, and when they're not fighting one another, they're fighting the rest of the galaxy. And should any one zhee ever fight any other member of all the races and species of the galaxy, then all the other zhee will come and help it.

You can win money on a sure thing like that.

So the thing that must be done next... it must be done as quietly, and as privately, as possible.

You've got your blaster out and you're screwing on the silencer. Slowing. Letting them catch up to you.

You were trained for six months by the handlers at some cottage in the Vindar highlands. Trained to fight in the dark, screw silencers on blasters at a dead run, and all kinds of other nasty tricks. And the whole time you kept telling yourself that you'd never really need to know these terrible things that no decent person should know... except you learned them well, because you were pretty sure you were going to need to know those things.

You knew even then.

You knew you would have to go far in the how far will you go department.

At the next intersection of high docking bay wall and zhee slum, you jag right and throw yourself against a dirty wall.

They're coming at you full tilt now. They'll go wide on the turn.

Their hoods have fallen away from their donkey heads. Massive teeth open wide as they suck at the hot night to reach you.

They have gone too wide on the turn.

You fire and hit the first guy.

The bright blue flash of the blaster cannot be dimmed. It illuminates the intersecting alley, turning it a sudden ghostly bone-white. In that horribly clarified moment, it makes their mad donkey faces somehow even more demonic.

You hit that guy in the chest and the zhee behind him pushes the body forward into you, making you shoot the first guy again.

They both have gleaming curved knives.

Kankari, they call them.

Small. Silver. Curved like a crescent moon. Wicked sharp.

You push the dead zhee off you a moment after his smelly body almost crushes you against the grungy alley wall. You grab at his fur and heave him off.

Except...

Except...

Your blaster's in the wrong position.

The remaining zhee dances forward, his hooves clip-clop-clopping on the stone as he delivers a sharp little cut at your wrist. He's trying to open a vein.

The zhee are excellent cutters.

That's what Mageeio, who taught you knife fighting courtesy of the Carnivale, assured you.

"Dey knows how to bleed a man out," he said. "Dey's savages, but dey's smart savages."

You drop the blaster. You hear it hit the stones of the alley in the night.

The zhee gives a short, snorty laugh and shifts his balance back to gather himself for his next attack.

You react just like you were taught.

Taught by Mageeio.

Taught to fight knives in close-quarters combat when you can't run away, which is just about the smartest thing you can do in a knife fight: run away.

But you can't, so you must do this instead.

You do exactly what you were taught.

You rush the remaining zhee and get in close where he can't cut and dance. You grapple and try to get hold of the knife.

"Control the knife, lad!" Mageeio is screaming in your ear, just like he screamed at you back in the highlands on Vindar.

You pin that massive arm with most of your body, and now you're ramming your knee like a jackhammer into the monster's groin over and over. It brays once, and on the next strike you flex upward, raise your knee, and slam it into the zhee's swollen belly, causing it to lose all its available air.

It lets go of the *kankari*.

And you have it and now you're just slamming it over and over into the thing, anywhere you can. Over and over into its donkey-leather body.

Just like Mageeio told you.

"This ain't the pretty part like in the entertainments, lad. This is for survival. So keep stabbing until dey don't move no more."

You do.

And he doesn't.

Move, that is. Not anymore. Because the zhee's dead.

You get up, shaking.

You do the opposite of everything you're supposed to do next. Everything Mageeio taught you about this situation.

You lean against the wall of the alley and take out a cigarette. You light it. You can hear the streets just a few blocks away. The light, life, and music of the galaxy.

Here in the night, with the two dead zhee at your feet…

It is the opposite of everything known up until now.

06

You make it to the Night Market, and it's not hard to find the Repub Navy officer fencing ordnance for personal gain. The things he's selling are located in a large main hall. The mercs he's hired are watching the crates and the clamshell cases with specialized weapon systems. He, on the other hand, is enjoying the company of two stunning Endurians.

Yeah, they'd probably tell you they were princesses. But here they have another job title.

You're sitting at a dirty table filled with bad scotch and picked-over rice bowls. The Endurians cast long lashes at you when the Repub Navy officer isn't looking.

You try to ignore their obvious charms.

"RepubNet says you're defrocked. Dishonorable discharge." He's wearing a flower-printed shirt and he hasn't shaved in days. There's a small pile of powdery blue H8 in front of him on a silver mirror. "How do I know you're not Dark Ops sent here to find out exactly what I'm doing? Bust me, and my men will shoot you dead."

He holds the H8 out in front of you. You take a pinch and inhale.

It punches you in the brain... which is what H8 does. It'll do other stuff later. But right now you're still cruising on killing two zhee. You're wound tight, and now you're stoned to the gills on H8. Not a great combo.

Which makes you sassy enough to swipe the cheap gutter scotch he's been pouring and take a swig just to get the vile H8 drip out of the back of your mouth. You swallow and it burns, and you fight feeling mean. You fight looking at the Endurians. Both of them. The lines between hate and lust blur when you're rushing on your run.

Or at least that's what the H8 junkies scream in all their shoegazing songs.

"I don't care what you think," you mutter. "I'm here for those MAROs you've got. Deal... or don't waste my time."

The officer who goes by the phony name Abo leans back in his chair and smiles. The name might be fake, but everyone knows he's been selling real live legit legionnaire ordnance. So they know he's a Repub officer on leave.

"Those are very expensive. House of Reason keeps trying to get the military not to use 'em anymore. Pretty soon they'll be a banned weapon galaxy-wide. But until then they are absolutely perfect for taking out a tunnel complex, or any bunker built to capital ship standards. Problem is the delivery system. I don't have those."

You wait and say nothing. Then...

"I'll take two."

"Two's all I got. And like I said, they're expensive."

"How much?"

"Three million apiece. Hard credits. Meaning I actually want to see the credits. And since no one carries that big of wallet around... until I see it, we're just talking, Defrocked."

You smile and taste the bad scotch again. The H8 makes it taste just right.

"Obviously. Six million in hard currency would get you killed on Ankalor."

Abo smiles back at you.

So do the Endurians.

"And bringing the money here would be suicide. The zhee would jihad if they knew they could get their hands on those weapons, or the credits."

"Yeah, I know. And then they'd take that fine piece of Republic tech and probably strap it to a sled, drive it into a market on some capital world, and blow up a dozen noodle bars and nail salons and bray... *Hajeh*!"

Hajeh. Holy smiting.

Abo laughs and does a few more bumps of H8. So do the Endurians. They look tired.

"So you want the credits IRL, and I want the bombs."

"Ordnance," reminds Abo.

"Roger. I want both. Credits, I have."

"Then let's arrange a meet... after you convince me you're not Dark Ops sent in to bust me. I'm sure Dark Ops could fake a records jacket for offenses... moral. Gambling. Contraband. Yeah, all that just screams why you're here to do business with me. Like it was made to look that way for me."

You smile and look away. Dark Ops is nothing compared to Nether Ops. People in the know... *they* don't even know about Nether Ops. It's wacky.

"We like to weaponize our *imaginations*," X said when explaining the Carnivale. "We go about things... *differently* here, my dear boy."

When you come back, you come back with the double-blind story, manufactured for just such an occasion.

"Since you dialed into the RepubNet," you say, "go ahead and look up an Admiral Rulal."

Abo leans forward to a datapad and taps in a few strokes. He's probably using someone's hacked ID from his duty station.

"Says here he got smoked on Zasor six months ago."

"That's right. And I smoked him."

"And…"

"If you'll look through his last command staff structure, you'll see I was one of his staff officers. The admiral was dealing arms. He made you look like a zhee street vendor. We were doing deals with the Kandari, the Brotherhood, and even some outfits supplying the MCR. The admiral got greedy and tried to cut everyone out. Tried to get us all killed, too. Just to clean things up. So I iced him. And then we all got discharged to cover it up."

"I don't see that in here. It's a nice story, but folks've been making up nice stories since the first campfires. And if you iced an admiral, you'd be awaiting execution."

"True. Unless that admiral was directly related to someone in the Council and they wanted it kept quiet. As in, they were on the back end of our profits. Start a summary court-martial on a bunch of staff officers, and your political enemies start asking questions. I was caught. Red-handed. If you can crack Dark Ops, or get someone to talk… they'll tell you it was all covered up. But here's how you can tell all of that without going to any trouble. All six staff officers were given dishonorables. You ever hear of anything like that before? All six of us?"

Abo smiles dumbly, like maybe he has, and maybe he hasn't.

"So go ahead and check it out. And then we meet. Dock ninety-four tomorrow, with credits *and* ordnance. We do the deal, and we both fly away happy."

You get up and you leave, and you're just hoping that someone, some zhee, messes with you on your way back to your terrible hotel. Because you are wired tight on H8 and you're ready to unload on anyone.

But somehow the night senses this and no one comes even close. You make your room and drink scotch in the dark. Smoking and waiting for dawn.

You message Frogg for the six million.

Dock ninety-four.

He says they'll be there.

And...

"Pack your bags."

The shuttle that picks you up is high luxury. You were expecting some kind of freighter. Some crew of part-time pirates and full-time lowlifes. Instead you get the luxury shuttle and Frogg. Former legionnaires of the very professional variety are everywhere. Polite. Friendly. Armed with subcompact light blasters dialed up to eleven. And each one could kill you dead in about a hundred different ways that don't require a blaster.

So there's that.

You watch Ankalor recede as the shuttle races out over the burning deserts, and it's clear from the get-go that this ship is staying in the atmo. No jump to light speed yet.

Not just yet.

No.

An hour later the ship circles a high desert encampment, all white safari tents and high-tech equipment crates. Parked down below is a large starship, and next to that is a small Republic Navy shuttle. A supply shuttle, to be precise.

Yes. You'll want to remember all these details in the report you're no doubt going to give soon if they don't kill you out here. X will want to know all about this, and you're hoping for that opportunity.

But... they're always watching.

Out here in the high desert where even the zhee don't bother to migrate in their ceaseless quest to cause mayhem everywhere. Why, it would be a courtesy if they even buried your body out here. Frogg and Co., that is.

You've been sitting in the passenger section of the lounge. Massive square portholes gaze out into that unending burning wasteland that is the hinterland of Ankalor. But inside the shuttle it's cool and air-conditioned, and you and Frogg have been talking across the aisle while nursing large tumblers of Faldaren scotch.

He's been telling you all about himself. Which is good. Good for that report you hope to be giving soon and then your work is done. Just another sleazy arms dealer, exit stage left. Send in the kill teams. That was all that was asked. Intended. And it has been delivered.

No more Tom.

X said so.

"Dear boy, at the Carnivale we just do the gathering. Not the wetwork. So go in and be a good fellow and find us this Scarpia. You'll need to get real close, so do whatever it takes, because we've got to know the end users. And then the legionnaire boys can go in and dispose of the target. That's all we're asking, and then you'll be back in the navy with some secret commendations no one can ever look at. Get close to this fellow, as close you can, then start to feed us info."

X smiled from behind his desk as he puffed on a pipe he had to keep relighting. Tweed jacket. Spectacles. More academic than spymaster. A desk down in the deep basements of the old sector on Utopion littered with antiques. Fancying himself a living relic of a mostly forgotten history.

But now you're sitting with the murderous Frogg. And he's telling you all about his horrid life.

"Was an orphan. Joined the Youth Legion and got a commission in some no-name little fight you might have heard about called Bunker's Station." His eyes are far away and dreamy.

Bunker's Station was a real slaughterhouse. For both sides. That the man talking to you isn't maimed for life speaks volumes about what kind of soldier you're drinking with.

"Got a taste for it then," he continues. "Killing work. Knives and such."

Not all wounds are visible, of course.

"Was just a way for me to work out my rage."

Everyone knows, and since you're still part of the collective known as everyone, you know, too, that the Legion went native on Bunker's Station. Had to. They were cut off for six months.

They went native and just murdered everyone.

"Was so much easier to solve your problems with a bit of the knife than file reports about it all. Reports no one is going to read when you really get to thinkin' about it all." Frogg takes a big gulp of the scotch, and his bulging eyes fall to half-mast. "Made major before they figured out something wasn't right with me. Psychiatric bot with updated software. Couldn't dupe 'em any longer. So out I went. Six months later I'm in a jail cell on some no-name world, and so is Scarpia. If you can believe that! Well... I knew he was a prince among men, except we weren't in no palace. Raving lunatics and rapists in there, I tell you. I watched his back for three days down in the lower cells where the guards wouldn't even come. We got out together. He'd paid my bail and hired a mouthpiece. Then he offered me a job."

The shuttle settles to the ground, lightly. Barely. Just like the scotch you're holding.

"He's a good man, Tom."

Who's Tom?

You are.

Frogg seems to notice you haven't reacted to the use of your alias. You play it off by continuing to drift dreamily into your scotch. The shuttle is venting. You can hear the soft whine of the boarding ramp.

You glance out the porthole at the wide, burning desert. It's going to be very hot out there. It's a terrible place to die.

"Tom?"

You come back looking slightly goofy. He doesn't notice you've hardly touched your drink. You've just been listening to his tales of horror and mayhem. All told matter-of-factly. The CV of some deranged lunatic laid out for your consideration over scotch.

"It's time to meet the boss, Tom."

After six months of playing the scoundrel, you've finally arrived at the nowhere-end of no-place and now you're going to either meet the person who will kill you, or, most likely, be killed by you. Indirectly, of course. Someday some legionnaire boy all juiced up on Repub glory and ready to add some more trigger time will do the honors.

Not your business. You'll be you again.

"We just do gathering, my dear boy."

Scarpia is an enigma. No one has really ever seen him as far as the intel the Carnivale has acquired is concerned. He's a ghost.

Hence the op name.

Ghost Hunter.

At the bottom of the boarding ramp you meet a rather unexpected fellow. Unexpected because he's not some low-life arms dealer or vicious alien crime lord of the giant squid variety. He's just a man. Slim. Unassuming. Hair thinning to balding. Nice smile. Deep-set eyes that have seen far too much.

They remind you of your own.

"It's good to meet you, Tom," says the arms dealer, who is responsible for at least five million dead, according to Nether Ops intel. "Froggy tells me you're a man to watch. Gin and tonic?"

This is Scarpia.

This is the man in charge.

You follow respectfully as the entourage crosses the little encampment they've set up here in the shadow of the big hauler. The wind crosses the desert and pulls at everyone's clothes. The mercenaries. Frogg. Scarpia. The man in the suit... and the girl. A Cassari. Beautiful green skin. Four slender arms and a body to die for. She has long, luxurious dark hair that falls across her shoulders and chest in curly tresses. She wears the barest of gossamers, and when the wind passes, there's little to discover.

Except that's not all true.

Of course, Cassari have their legendary pheromones. But her smoky eyes are haunting and alluring. Both at the same time. And though she greets you and calls you "Tom" and that's not really your name, it starts a fire inside you that cannot be easily quenched. Because the way she says it... well, the way she says it, you'd *like* to be Tom.

But maybe that's just the pheromones talking.

So you remind yourself that these people are more than likely going to shoot you and not bury you. It's a sobering thought. It helps to focus and remind.

Out here.

In the desert.

They could just shoot you and fly away and no one would ever know.

"Can I get you a drink...? Tom?" Her smoky voice is deep and soft at the same time.

You manage a nod. And then a deferential, "That would be nice, thank you."

You're all in a tent. In the desert. Luxe leather couches surround a holotable.

"Now," begins Scarpia. "Let's talk about how you're going to blow up a nasty little Repub destroyer that's giving my clients a hard time."

You sit down on one of the couches as Scarpia busies himself with the display. It shows the ship, a planet you don't recognize called Kublar, and some legionnaire base. Camp Forge.

You try to act as if everything is just fine as she hands you your drink.

"Here you go... Tom."

Because that's who you are.

07

She was right.

Illuria.

She was very right.

Here you go, Tom. Just pop off and blow that destroyer to high heaven with the MAROs you just acquired for us.

Or at least, that was the gist of how Mr. Scarpia— Scarpia to you now—put it.

What's the plan?

That's what you ask after you make all the usual protestations about just being a supplier. Not a contractor.

"Except you're ex-navy and this perfect!" cries Scarpia like he's just found the lead in his production of *Hamlet*. "And it's really, beyond all the money I'm going to pay you, it really is an opportunity to shove the Repub's face in it for what they've done to you, Tom. Taking out a destroyer says don't mess with Tom Delo. That'll teach 'em! Right, my boy?" Scarpia seems genuinely happy for you to have this opportunity.

Bit of trivia. Both X and Scarpia call you "my boy." That's odd, and it doesn't mean anything. It's just interesting and it's what you're thinking about as they—Frogg, Scarpia, and the man in the suit—go on to tell you how, exactly, you're going to blow a Repub destroyer called the *Chiasm*.

It's a suicidal plan... but you're in, in with Scarpia, if you do it.

Get as close as you can, said X when all this was just talk. Did you ever think you'd get here? You must have.

"After this," says Scarpia as he puts his arm around you and you walk out into the purple desert twilight evening, the smell of grilled meat in the air. "After this I'll have a lot more work for you, Tom."

"Do whatever it takes, my dear boy," said X before all this began.

And... what other choice do you have?

How do you blow up a Republic destroyer?

Not *should* you.

But *how*?

Because you passed "should" a long, long time ago. When X said, "Do whatever it takes, my dear boy." You passed it then.

Scarpia has asked you, mainly because you were, are—no, *were* for intents and purposes of espionage—you were a Repub Navy officer. You've commanded shuttles and small craft. You know the protocol.

To do what?

Rendezvous with a destroyer named the *Chiasm* in orbit around some cruddy little planet called Kublar. Land with parts and spare crew. Detonate the bomb. And deliver another right down on top of Camp Forge. Camp Forge is the legionnaire base on Kublar. You couldn't obtain the special delivery system the MAROs need, but well, that's what the shuttle is for. And gravity will do the rest, with a little help from a glider drone.

Scarpia will arrange for travel. He will have the tech and ordnance ready. He will get the necessary documents and subterfuges in place. You, Tom, will do the rest. This is your baby. Your plan. To destroy a Republic warship and a legionnaire base.

And you can't help but think, as you wait for the necessary components, biding your time with these madmen, that the whole thing is almost simple, really.

The approach to the *Chiasm* is straightforward. You flash the standard codes and impersonate a Repub officer who's less than excited about commanding a shuttle coming out to resupply a big front-line destroyer. There's a long pause during code authentication, but in the end they clear the shuttle for landing along the port-side hangar.

Scarpia's ex-legionnaire mercs are dressed as two pilots and two techs. They're really in charge of the show right now. You, you're just the front man. You're Hamlet in this production, too.

The shuttle passes through the force field and flies out across the deck. Assault transports and support craft assisting in operations below are going through preflight, rearming, and maintenance. It's pretty busy on the deck. Seeing all the techs working, you're suddenly made aware that they're moments from dying.

Because of some operation. Some espionage operation that's trying to stop the deaths of tens of millions. A good seven thousand crew, a couple hundred gunners, and almost a thousand leejes, marines, and other soldiers are going to die today—if you do what you're supposed to do to get close to the target. Mr. Scarpia. *Just call me Scarpia, Tom.*

And another thousand more on the planet below. Don't forget about them. We have to do them too, to make this look legit. The front-line legionnaires running ops and manning Camp Forge... they're going to die in the hours, days, and weeks that follow. They'll die because no one will be able to pull them out of firefights, or provide close air support, or even feed them.

The ones down there are already dead. They'll just die a lot slower.

Whatever it takes, my dear boy.

Scarpia is the biggest of fishes. He must be caught. Never mind the bait we'll need to cut up.

The shuttle sets down and the merc in charge nods at you. Frogg has provided a perfect Repub Navy LT uniform. You pick up your datapad, place it under your arm, adjust your headgear, and saunter down the ramp like any junior grand officer would.

"We weren't expecting you," says the deck officer on duty in the hangar.

Two Lancers are spooling up and heading toward the flight line. Their lift repulsors throb and hum eerily as they head for the massive force field that protects everyone from open and deep space just beyond its invisible barrier. The ground crew salutes, and both pilots give the Tally Ho salute back. Then they're gone off the deck, diving for the planet. Not knowing that they'll never return to the *Chiasm*, a ship that is just two minutes from going boom.

Because right now the mercs are setting the master arming switch and initiating the countdown on the first MARO inside the supply shuttle.

The deck officer checks the manifest and makes a face. He senses something is wrong. He *knows* something is wrong when the mercs come down the boarding ramp in HOLO suits. High-Orbit, Low-Opening. State-of-the-art legionnaire planetary orbital infiltration suits. They look like deep sea divers. Weapons and gear are secured across their bodies. Between the four of them they're pushing a repulsor cart with a large glider drone atop it.

"What the hell are they doing in that gear?" asks the deck officer just before you shoot him with a needle stunner. He's the most important person to take out right now. He's the only one who can get legionnaires here on the double. Everybody else on the hangar deck is unarmed and only responsible for star craft. They have no trigger time. No one can stop you and your team from crossing one hundred yards of open deck to the force field.

After that you need one full minute of drop time to clear the *Chiasm*.

The mercs start to trot. Their bulky HOLO suits slow them down. But they need those suits.

You follow at a run. You feel your legs wanting to give out, because this is as real as it gets. Because you just killed everyone, or because you're about to jump off a starship two hundred thousand feet from the planet's surface, you don't know.

Probably both.

Fifteen yards from the force field, someone starts shooting. One of the mercs goes down. The others keep moving toward the force field and the orbital drop.

Those are the orders.

One of them opens the drone and beckons to you as more blaster fire careens off the deck all around you. One of the mercs returns fire, covering, while the other two keep pushing and beckoning you to climb into the drone. Which you *must* do, because you're not wearing a HOLO suit.

It's a two-stage drone. Stage One is for you. It'll separate from Stage Two. Stage Two is for the second MARO. You'll pilot the drone and glide it right into Camp Forge. But just before it hits… you'll disengage.

Or so you've been told.

What if you don't? What if that's Scarpia's way of getting rid of you? He's left other little greeting cards just like that for other espionage operations that failed to get close to him. That was definitely hinted at all throughout training. Scarpia is a crafty foe. But what can you do? This is the plan.

You climb in, and two of the mercs secure the hatch behind you. The mercs don't need the drone; their HOLO suits will keep them alive during the drop. They'll try to stay with you, keep you safe on Kublar for the few minutes it takes the extraction team to jump in and pull everyone out.

But again, what if they don't? They don't have to. Scarpia could just leave everyone in the clutches of the planet. A wild, hostile, alien environment teeming with counterinsurgents.

The blaster fire recedes and fades to nothing as the two mercs push your craft over the edge of the deck and away from the destroyer. One hundred thousand feet below is Kublar. You may feel like you're floating in space, but you're really falling, and rather quickly, into Kublar's gravitational well.

One minute later, you're orienting yourself once more to the drone's simple control interface when you hear the *Chiasm*'s spine crack in half.

The MARO has detonated in the hangar.

And you're practically straddling another bomb just as big as that one.

You begin reentry, and the drone shakes violently. Then you're outright falling through the barest of atmosphere and locking in a glide slope for Camp Forge.

Only two of the mercs made it off the *Chiasm*. Both are off your wings when atmo begins to take hold. A moment later you've got the glideslope set for the end of the fall, and everything is green.

Far below you see Camp Forge. It's just a tiny little outpost from way up here.

At ten thousand feet, you separate. The smaller glider, with the MARO, streaks straight toward Camp Forge. You drift down gently onto the wastelands of Kublar beyond.

The MARO hits hard, but not at the critical center. It penetrates the garage housing the Republic main battle tanks—and it detonates. In the blink of an eye, it fully destroys more than half the Repub outpost that was Camp Forge. But not all of it.

A hard landing. And now you have two hours of wait time before the extraction ship arrives.

You hear a full-scale battle in the distance. The resounding echoes of too much blaster fire, along with the reports of antique slug throwers. Rebels? Natives? Probably both. An epic defeat of Republic might, all arranged by Scarpia. You realize that you just made the target into a legend. He's now done what others have only bloviated about.

Thanks, Tom.

Where you're going next, you have no idea.

Oh, and you did land in time to watch the *Chiasm* burning reentry in atmo. Both halves of it. So there is that to live with for the rest of your life.

There is that.

You wonder if the stranded legionnaires saw it burn up. You wonder what they're thinking.

08

I'm standing underneath the first hot shower I've had in I don't know how long. My arms are propped against the tiles, and the water is pouring over my head like some never-ending baptismal font. For a brief moment, as the steam rises around me, my mind clears. I'm here, aboard the *Mercutio*, and for a sweet, blessed moment, that's all. Just a guy in the shower. Enjoying how the near-scalding water melts the taut muscles around my neck and back. Heat. Steam. And solitude. Though Exo and Masters are only a few feet away, talking in low tones as they dry off, I feel like a man in his fortress here in this shower stall. I like to think that Kublar—all the dying, the fight on board the Ohio-class; I never caught what the ship was named— that all of that is just circling the drain.

And that's what ultimately brings me back.

I look down at the drain and see a multi-colored swirl. Dirt and grime from Kublar mix in with red—human blood diluted by hot water. I remember the girl, and I think about how this last part of her to ever leave the planet is now going to be sucked through the plumbing for treatment and reuse.

I let the water spray against the side of my face, rinsing off the phosphorescent yellow blood of some koobs that I don't even remember getting splattered by. All of it mixes at my feet and circles the drain like a whirlpool of sorrow.

I tap the tile and shut my eyes as the water gives way to foam cleanser, and then back to clear water to rinse until the scanners built into the wall determine that I am, in fact, cleaned to Republic regulations.

The water gradually moves from hot to warm. I've got about three minutes until it goes ice cold. A luxury afforded to me by a sympathetic sailor who had the access to increase the warm water time.

Because everybody on the ship knows.

And other than a cook that Exo had to threaten with castration in order to get the chow heated, we haven't gotten any flak. We were given a wide berth once we landed from the Ohio-class with our prisoners. Even the sailors who were busy taking selfies in front of the shot-to-hell shuttles and starfighters—some never pass up the chance to look like warfighters to the people on their home worlds—even they grew quiet as we passed by.

Wraith wasn't with us for long. When he transferred the prisoners to the deck officer, he was informed that his presence was necessary, too. Kags is gone as well; he was taken to rejoin his unit. Word is that more basics made it out than legionnaires. But that's to be expected. I'll find out which leejes made it out alive soon enough.

When the shower's done. I'll find out then.

There's a moment where I feel a flood of emotion. I think of the leejes lost on Kublar, a place whose name I couldn't recall just days ago. A place I'll never again forget. I press my forehead against the tiles. In my mind, I can see a version of myself—maybe a better man—releasing this emotion. Silently weeping for all that was lost. For Pappy and the others.

But the tears won't come. I feel hollow inside. No, that's not right. Not hollow. Resigned. I feel resigned. It was their time. Someday it'll be mine.

And so it goes.

I swipe the backlit control square, bringing my finger from top to bottom to shut off the shower. The white noise of the water cascading around me is replaced by the ringing in my ears from too much war without a bucket. With the steam still thick around me, I step out.

Masters and Exo are out before me. They're each half dressed, wearing pairs of black training shorts.

I wick away excess water with an absorption cloth. It sucks up the beads of water resting on my face and neck. I begin to dry off my chest, then halt at the sight of myself in a mirror. My face is peppered with cuts and scrapes. There's a gash across the bridge of my nose, and I have a yellowish bruise beneath my left eye. A piece of my ear is missing—just the tip, maybe a centimeter of flesh. It seems that every part of me that wasn't protected by armor has some sort of wound.

I guess it was more than hot water that caused the stinging in the shower. I stare at my reflection. Lost.

"Lieutenant!" Exo shouts. "Put some clothes on, for Oba's sake!" He fans himself. "You're gettin' me all hot, standing there buck naked."

Masters lets out a belly laugh. I crack a smile before toweling off my immodest places and pulling on a pair of my own training shorts, neatly folded and waiting for me on the sink counter beside an array of cleansers, balms, and all the other objects for personal hygiene available on a capital-class battleship. I toss my absorption cloth into a hamper, which beeps and then moves on a magnetic track to ferry the garment to the ship's laundry conveyor.

"There," I say to Exo. "Now can you control yourself?"

Exo makes like he's about to faint. "Those abs, sir. Too much. Cover yourself before Masters switches teams. It's him I'm most worried about. He's drooling, sir."

Masters throws his absorption cloth into the back of Exo's head. The leejes laugh as the bot controlling the hamper moves in to pick up the discarded article.

The truth is, we're all outstanding physical specimens of humanity. Being in the Legion breeds maximum conditioning. Masters, with his shirt off, looks like an underwear model. Exo is every bit as cut, just thicker and more compact. He's the sort of leej who looks like he could run through a duracrete wall without noticing it. Of course, no amount of abdominal muscles will stop a blaster bolt.

"There's no pleasing you, Exo." I grab the black T-shirt set out for me. It's surplus from a squad of legionnaires stationed on the ship. I pull it over my head and slip on a pair of shower shoes emblazoned with the *Mercutio*'s name and hull number. "Any word on who else made it out from Victory?"

"No." Masters shakes his head. Both he and Exo lose their mirthful expressions. I've killed the mood. "There's an aide waiting for us outside who says he'll take us to the barracks where the survivors are. He didn't have any answers, though. Said he'd try and scrounge up a med list, but couldn't promise anything."

"I'll see if Captain Ford can swing us something whenever he gets back from prisoner exchange."

I unwrap an ora-tab, toss it in my mouth, and bite down, sending a wave of deffevmint across my palate. Yech. Not my favorite flavor. Tastes like a mix of tar and one of the heirloom mints. Smells good, though. My breath is immediately fresh, and the thick, rank taste in my mouth from too many days in combat operations leaves, while millions of nanite bots released from the ora-tab stay behind to clean my teeth and gums.

Wraith enters the refresher room. "Lieutenant Chhun, I need you to come with me."

I nod at Exo and Masters, trusting them to make it all right to our barracks. *We're on board a Republic battleship,* I remind myself. *Your men are safe now.*

Wraith walks at rapid pace, moving gracefully in spite of still being in his armor. I feel anything but graceful. With my gear off, and my muscles heated by the shower, my body is telling me just how banged up it got down on Kublar. I'm struggling to keep up. Walking with a pronounced limp. Alternating pains in my right foot and left hamstring with each step. My back feels pinched and totally out of alignment. There's a trickle of water coming out of my ear that I missed. I wipe it away, rubbing the fluid off on my shorts. Wraith must see me struggling to keep up. He slows down, but doesn't mention it.

"So where we going?" I ask.

"Legion Commander Keller," he says, as though it were the most mundane thing in the world. *Oh, we'll just stop in to see Dad at work. No big deal.*

It's a huge deal. The legion commander has direct authority over the entirety of the 4th Legion. Up until a few days ago, that included the 131st Legionnaire Corps—of which I'm among the few survivors. He's a battle-hardened leej sent by Legion Command to oversee operations on board the flagship of this sector of galaxy's edge. And I'm on my way to see him wearing a kelhorned pair of shorts, a T-shirt a size too small, and a pair of shower shoes. Not to mention I haven't shaved in days.

"I can't report to the legion commander like this!"

Wraith looks me up and down. "You look fine. Besides, he didn't want to wait. You think I would have left without getting in a shower if I didn't have to? The purifiers in my helmet are struggling to keep up. Or starting to fail. I can almost smell myself. It's that bad in here, Chhun."

We stop at a speedlift. Wraith presses the button and we step inside. He keys for the bridge deck. The speedlift's shaft fills with a soft, violet light as we're scanned. I'm certainly not authorized for the bridge deck, but it looks like Wraith has some new privileges. There's a ding, and the lights revert to their usual, daylight glow. A sailor attempts to join us, but Wraith waves him off. The lift's door closes in front of us.

"So the smell is what keeps the helmet on?" I ask Wraith. I would have *never* talked to him like this before Kublar. But... we fought side by side through hell. And we're both officers now—though I fully expect the loss of my battlefield promotion to be part of this meeting. Probably a simple debrief. I'd ask Wraith, but I know that he'd have already mentioned the reason for our trip if he was supposed to.

"You got me," Wraith says. "I'm doing everyone on the ship a favor keeping my bucket on."

The legion commander's personal quarters were *not* where I was expecting we'd end up. The room is like a core-world studio apartment. It's spacious; only the admiral's and captain's are larger. There's an entryway with an overhead light shining like a spotlight onto a Legion crest woven into the carpet. To one side stand a miniature galley and a sitting room, and in the back, deeper in, is the commander's bed, neatly made to drill instructor standards. I stand to the right of the entryway, before the commander's desk.

Bald, with a crooked nose and a granite jaw, Legion Commander Keller stares at me from behind fiery blue eyes. I stand at ease, eyes forward to the Legion crest, the sword stabbing through the deci-number four, for 4th Legion.

"You boys," Keller begins, his voice deep and full of the confidence of someone who's been there, "did one hell of a job down there."

"Thank you, sir," Wraith and I answer in unison.

"The Republic," Keller points to a datapad on his desk, "wants to control the narrative here. Hearts and minds. Right now, every citizen in the Republic is glued to their holos soaking up the details of what happened. Wondering how in God's name an entire corps of legionnaires and the ship they flew in on are just lost"—he snaps his fingers—"like that.

"They'll hear their reports. Families will grieve while the rest go on thinking... if it could happen out there, could it happen here? Only it damn well didn't happen out there. Those backward-ass koobs threw in with the insurgents and the Legion made them *howl*. The Republic wants the heroes of the battle, the legionnaires who fought through hell and survived—sacrificed themselves so the basics could get out on the drop shuttles—they want those heroes back on Utopion so the citizens of the galaxy can say, 'Look at what the Legion did. So few against so many.' And feel safe again."

He pauses. I start to feel uncomfortable. "Yes, sir," I say, instantly regretting it. *Stupid. Keep your mouth shut.*

Keller smiles. "Hearts and minds. That's what the House of Reason and Senate Council want right now. The killing's done, and hearts and minds need to be won." He stares at his hands, which rest atop his desk. "If there are heroes worthy of commendation, it's the two of you."

He looks up at us. "But I won't make you those heroes."

I shift—imperceptibly, I hope. Where is he going with this?

"There's a leej point—Devers—who'll do the job. If he survives. Looks like he will." Keller stands and clasps his arms behind his back. He stares at us, but it's not a malevolent gaze. He looks at us like a proud father. "I know you leejes aren't fond of points. Necessary evil. And I can still take it all back. Hand you fortune and glory and parades. But I don't think I'm wrong. I know a pair of *real* leejes when I see them. Captain Owens."

A legionnaire in black armor materializes from the shadows of the room. He moves to the legion commander's side. This guy is Dark Ops. A legionnaire serving at the most elite level the Legion has to offer. The greatest tests of concentration and endurance, both mental and physical, the highest-priority ops… they all happen to those serving on a Dark Ops kill team. No doubt, this is a badass leej standing before Wraith and me.

I could have done without the theatrics, though.

Captain Owens pulls off his bucket and places it gently on the legion commander's desk. He has a thick red beard. His hair hangs loose, almost to his shoulders. A far cry from Legion regulations, but Dark Ops have special exceptions. It would drive me nuts to have that much hair under my bucket.

The captain holds out his hand. "*Captain* Ford and *Lieutenant* Chhun, if I understand correctly?"

That surprises me. I figured Pappy's field promotions wouldn't last any longer than the time it took to leave Kublar's atmosphere. We shake hands.

"No matter what, those ranks stay," Keller says. "Colonel Hilbert was one of the best legionnaires to ever put on the armor."

I nod. "Thank you, sir."

Owens stares at us. "Sorry about coming in from the shadows. I'm a believer in first impressions. I wanted the opportunity to watch the two of you up close for a while. Make sure I liked the impression I got."

"Sir, I'm confused about the purpose of this meeting."

I'm a little taken aback by Wraith's forwardness. But I'm thinking the same thing. The 4th Legion commander and a Dark Ops commander are standing before us on a part of a ship I'm not cleared to even *walk* through unless I'm on assignment. I feel tired and sore. I want to go to sleep. And Wraith—he probably hasn't even had the chance to get a bite to eat, unless there was one last ration pack in his kit.

A smile rustles from behind Captain Owens's beard. "I need a Dark Ops kill team. Right now. *Mercutio* has four teams. I'm all that's left of one. The other three kill teams are operating in the Ryori Cluster. Had to jump without them when we intercepted the distress beacon."

Commander Keller takes over. "We need a team to head back to the planet. That's as much as you can know and as far this discussion goes—unless you're willing to leave the lives you know behind in order to commit to Dark Ops."

"Sorry about the high-pressure sales," Owens says, scratching his chin through his beard, "but this is too hot for you to sleep on it. We need more leejes like you in D-O."

This is a *lot* to think about. Physically, mentally, I'm prepared for Dark Ops. Virtually every legionnaire is. There's no special school. New operators are pulled directly from the Legion. If the Legion is reserved for the one percent of the one percent, Dark Ops is the one percent of the Legion. Still, I have a family back home—Mom and Dad, my brother Satteeah—and they probably think I'm dead already. They're *sure* to believe that if I go into Dark Ops now. I won't even bother asking for access to a ship-board comm to call home first. And what about my guys? The survivors. And then there's Devers. It doesn't sit well with me that a guy like him will be *rewarded* for getting so many good men killed.

"I'm in," Wraith says. "But a kill team is seven. We're three. I'd like to have input over which legionnaires will fill the team. That's assuming Lieutenant Chhun is in."

I can't quite believe what I'm hearing come out of Wraith's mouth. No pressure or anything.

Keller and Owens communicate in raised eyebrows and downturned lips.

"Fine with me," Owens answers, crossing his massive arms at his chest. "*After* the op. If you're in, along with Chhun, here," he stares at me intently, "then our next stop is to get you both kitted out in Dark Ops black and report to the ghost shuttle. So what do you say, Chhun? Leak or leave."

I don't know how to answer. I feel like I'm being pulled by combat sleds in a half dozen different directions.

Commander Keller must recognize this. He puts his fists on his desk and leans forward, piercing my soul with his gaze. "Son, this is the opportunity to avenge what happened to the rest of the 131st. I can assure you that no finer opportunity will ever present itself for the rest of your life. You want to KTF? To make sure no nux-groping MCR *ever* thinks to try something like this again? You say 'yes.'"

"Yes, sir." I answer. The words seem to come out involuntarily. "I'm in."

Owens claps his hands together. "Good. Here's the plan. Ditch the dirty leej suit." He looks me up and down. "Or in your case the shorts and flip-flops—way to dress up to meet the legion commander—and we'll meet up with our fourth. Debrief on the way down. You can pick your team if you make it back."

I incline my head. "I thought you said three."

Without missing a beat, Owens answers, "Yeah, but that was before I could tell you the truth. Welcome to Dark Ops."

09

The interior of a stealth shuttle is a lot like the inside of a combat sled. Jump seats are lined against the walls, enough for a kill team plus one. Two repulsor bikes are strapped to the cargo deck between the jump seats. There's a third bike in the cargo bay underneath.

The three of us are kitted out in the black armor of Dark Ops. The Legion armorer fitted my bucket in under thirty minutes. I wish I'd had him a few days ago. Would have saved me from a wealth of future hearing trouble, I'm sure.

I examine the bikes. They look like typical repulsor bikes. No weapon systems I can see, and the sensor panels look to have limited comm-jamming and life-scanners.

I have a pretty good idea how we're going to reach the *Chiasm*.

That's where we're headed. Orbital scans from satellites released from the *Mercutio* found the wreckage of the capital destroyer that I've jumped all over galaxy's edge in.

Captain Owens's briefing was fairly straightforward. All hell broke out on Kublar once the MCR and the Moona tribe made their big move. For us, that meant being overrun, nearly dying to the last man. For the rest of the planet it meant civil war. The delicate balance and alliances achieved through Republic-steered diplomacy and

Kublaren-arranged marriages died with the senator. The tribes were now engaging in full-scale, total war against each other.

Genocide is the word of the day.

The Republic has vowed not to interfere. This will ingratiate them with whatever tribe emerges victorious, and then they can begin their plans for Kublar anew. But the Republic also needs data from the *Chiasm*. Emphasis on *needs*. It's not a matter of keeping the tech and data out of enemy hands; an orbital bombardment on the crash site could have accomplished that. Something needs retrieving.

And down to the planet goes Dark Ops.

And down *I* go, with Wraith and Captain Owens, and one more.

I saw Andien, the "scientist" from Kublar, access the cockpit from the pilot's ramp shortly before our shuttle took off from the *Mercutio*. I probably shouldn't have been surprised—her skill set was setting off alarm bells long before our rescue—but I am. I ride out the shuddering reentry into Kublar's atmosphere thinking about her.

These shuttles are thin, light, and all but undetectable. You won't know that one is approaching unless you happen to spot it with the naked eye. It's invisible to virtually every sort of monitoring technology. The closest the galaxy has come to true stealth invisibility. You can fold light and make a ship invisible to the naked eye, but scanners picked up that trick ages ago. Republic stealth shuttles got around the scanners, at least. Not that the koobs have the tech to pick up a cloaked starcraft anyway. Come to think of it, they're *more* likely to spot us coming down in one of these than a cloak. And given how easily high-density blaster fire will chew through this shuttle's hull... I'm feeling a lot less safe than I was when first leaving the docking bay.

At least we have the cover of night. That's when Dark Ops does its best work. When the galaxy sleeps. And hopefully the koobs with it.

As the shuttle's reverberations from reentry subside and we glide smoothly—stealth shuttles move so quietly that over seventy-eight percent all known species can't hear them—I decide to test out how much Captain Owens will share about Andien.

"Captain Owens," I say over L-comm. "Who was that woman who boarded the shuttle prior to departure?"

"You saw her? That'll be a burr up her butt. Those types think they're Dark Ops. Her name's Andien Broxin. At least, that's the name she'll share."

"We know her," Wraith says, joining the conversation. "Pulled her out of a bad spot on planet. She's the one who helped us hail the *Mercutio*."

"Not surprised," replies Owens. "She's good in a jam. Nether Ops."

I exchange looks with Wraith. "What's Nether Ops?"

Owens lets out a sigh over his L-comm. "Take Dark Ops, remove the leejes and any sense of honor, and you've got a good idea."

Doesn't sound like the captain has a high opinion of Nether Ops. My curiosity is piqued. "Why haven't I heard of them?"

"You're not *supposed* to hear of them. If Dark Ops is the black sword that vanquishes the enemies of the Republic in blackest night, Nether Ops is the poison dagger. And they construe the word 'enemy' in the loosest way imaginable."

"But *you* know about them," Wraith observes.

"Yeah. I do. You stay in the game long enough, you're bound to get tangled up with them. On one side or the other."

I rest my N-4 against the inside of my knee. "So what's she coming down with us for?"

"She knows how to get whatever it is we're after."

"Wait," Wraith interjects. "We don't know what our target is?"

Owens shakes his head. "Our job is to get her into the ship and kill any koobs that get in the way. Nether Ops won't actually tell us why."

Wraith leans back in his jump seat. "You mean *she* won't actually tell us why."

"Nice to see Nether Ops doing all it can to promote harmony within the Republic," I say.

"Yeah," Owens says, the hint of a smile coming through the L-comm. "They suck."

The shuttle drifts to a noiseless stop, its landing struts touching down on Kublaren dirt with barely a sound.

These stealth shuttle pilots are something else. I haven't had such a smooth ride since I've been in the Legion.

"We landed six kilometers east of the crash site," the pilot informs us over the ship's comm. "Sensors aren't picking up any hostiles within three clicks—for whatever that's worth in Kublar's atmo."

The shuttle's ramp begins to lower. Like everything else on this bird, it does so quietly, if a little slowly.

"We'll keep the engines warm for when you get back. Dust off is thirty minutes before sunrise, max, so don't lollygag, leejes."

Owens pounds against the cockpit door. "Hey!" he shouts over the comm. "You featherheads take off without us and I promise I'll remote-det the blast bricks I stowed in the cargo hold."

I laugh. And then stop. It dawns on me that I have no idea whether Captain Owens is serious.

We push the repulsor bikes, painted matte black for minimum visibility in the night, out of the shuttle. Wraith and Owens open the under-cargo hatch and pull out the third bike while I watch the perimeter. It's sort of nice having a bucket again. A few days ago, I was squinting into the darkness, trying to see by starlight. The day-clear night vision now showing through my visor is *much* better. And a whole lot crisper than what I'm used to. Dark Ops seems to have higher-end kits.

So that's nice.

I hear the soft imprint of Andien's boots before I see her emerge from beneath the port wing of the shuttle. She walks right up to me and pulls back a loose strand of hair, caught in the wind and blowing across her face.

"Back on Kublar," she says.

Maybe to me. Maybe to the galaxy.

I reply, on the chance that she's talking to me. She's standing right next to me, after all. "Yeah, well, I forgot my squad challenge coin. Had to come back down to get it."

She smiles.

I press her. "So you're a secret agent for some government program I never even heard of. That's great, good for you. I don't care that you didn't tell me when we were escaping certain death. In fact, you getting us into the outpost probably saved all our lives. But... you were on Kublar for a reason."

I stop there, allowing the sentence to work as a question.

Andien shakes her head, letting the wind carry away the strands of hair that continually flap across her eyes and forehead. "I was. Yes."

"I'm sure you can't tell—classified, Division X, all that—but I need to know: are you the type who allows legionnaires to die if it means catching your target, or were you here for something else?"

Who am I to ask questions like this? And what am I going to do if she tells me to space off? Kill her? I realize I'm relying on whatever camaraderie our dual survival through fire and rescue might have built up. There's no reason for her to give me the time of day otherwise. If anything, she probably has instructions *not* to talk about this with a lowly leej—Dark Ops or otherwise.

She braces her arms against the chill of the night. A chill I don't feel thanks to my new kit, but I damn sure did the last time I was on this dustball of a planet. "I was here to *stop* what happened," she says. "No, that's not entirely accurate. We didn't know what would happen, only that the MCR took an interest in Kublar and some unknown tribal chieftains reciprocated. But... I know how your ship exploded."

I stand in the darkness, waiting to see if that's all she's going to say. Not wanting to squeeze off the information she's providing me. Talking has a way of messing things up. Let the silence do the heavy lifting.

"Massive antimatter reaction ordnance." She names the explosive almost clinically, like a doc telling you the name of the terminal disease that has your number. "Two of them were stolen and we believe this is where they ended up."

"Massive antimatter reaction ordnances," I repeat. Wow. I've seen what those things can do. Bad guys dig in under a mountain, MARO brings the whole mountain down. For even one to explode inside the *Chiasm*, it's a wonder there's even a ship left to salvage.

"What about them?" The voice, whisper-soft over the external comm, belongs to Captain Owens. He and Wraith join us with the third bike.

"That's what blew the *Chiasm*," I say, wondering if I'm betraying some secret trust Andien was providing.

Owens's reply is over L-comm. "She must have her panties all twisted for you, Chhun, because she wouldn't tell me shit. She can ride with you."

Andien looks at the three of us. "If you're done with your little L-comm conversation, we should go."

My stomach turns at the thought that she just *heard* what Captain Owens said. But Owens isn't buying it. "She can't listen in on L-comm," he says. "Just a Nether Ops mind-screw."

Andien doesn't give a hint that she heard this over our secure comm, and I rest a little easier.

Owens, Wraith, and I each get on a bike and fire them up. Before I can motion for Andien to join me, she's already approaching. I feel less secure in the privacy of my L-comm and decide that the prudent course of action is to avoid saying anything over the L-comm that I wouldn't say to her face. Momma would be proud.

The bike hums, its repulsors every bit as quiet as the shuttle. Andien reaches into a saddlebag and pulls out a pair of augmented goggles. We speed away the moment she puts them on.

It's dark, and we're running with no lights, relying on our buckets to give us a clear field of vision. I imagine that for Andien, this ride must be like riding while blind. You just hope the driver knows what they're doing. I use our private comm channel to see about continuing the conversation.

"So if you know what did the job, what are we down here for?"

In spite of all sorts of audio bafflers, I can still pick up the rushing wind mixed with her reply. "I can triangulate the manufacture of the MAROs with particle sensors— Republic ordnance always leaves behind a trace signature.

Part of the fairness in combat statutes to better prosecute war criminals. We can trace a misfired mortar back to the bot that popped it off. But I need to hook into whatever's left of the ship's local registry. If there's a clue about how the MARO got on board, that's where to find it."

"Can't you just check the registry from the *Mercutio*? I thought everything runs through the sector flag ship for redundancy."

Andien leans her head into my armor's back plate, shielding her face from the wind. "What the *Mercutio* received is clearly falsified. But I can dig deeper with a local source-holo."

"Assuming that anything is still intact. I've seen what one MARO can do. Let alone two in a confined space." Technically, when I think about it, I guess I *have* seen what two do in a confined space. I saw the *Chiasm* erupt and heard the sky crack open. It wasn't pretty.

"You leejes aren't the only ones with highly specialized skill sets. All I need is an intact terminal port to run a ghost hunter through."

That all went entirely over my head. I'm about to tell her that when I see Wraith and Owens swerve. Three humanoids have come up an embankment onto the tract of scrub land we're using as a road.

They're koobs.

10

Wraith and Owens brake past the trio of koobs. I have more time to react and halt aggressively, whipping the bike sideways and placing myself in the path of the bewildered koobs. My N-4 is up before the first alarmed croaks escape their air sacs.

"Hands!" I scream. I don't speak koob, but enough of them seem to grasp Standard. The N-4 probably conveys my meaning just as effectively. "Let me see your hands!"

The koobs just stand there looking dumbfounded. It's dark, but not so dark that they're blind to what's in front of them. The stars are out, and obviously they saw well enough to travel. All three of them have old slug throwers slung across their backs. I hear the clanking of bells coming from behind them, and catch a glimpse of a couple dozen reptilian livestock. Koob shepherds. Great. I fill in Wraith and Owens over the L-comm.

One of the koobs, probably the eldest, takes a step toward me.

"Back up!" I shout. "Back up and put your hands on your head!"

The koob stops in mid-stride. He doesn't raise his hands, but he also doesn't go for his weapon. "Lee-jah!" the koob croaks out, followed by a series of clicks before returning to broken Standard. "Lee-jah. Republeek... big gud!"

Oh, man. Middle of the night, an entire planet, and we run right into a trio of herders. Leej luck. Never easy. And who knows where these koobs stand? Republic is big good now, while a leej has an N-4 pointed at your face, but if we move on... how many more koobs are out there? And how fast can they warn the koobs around the *Chiasm*'s wreckage that we're coming?

My L-comm chimes and I attempt to split my focus between the koob's prattling and Captain Owens.

"We don't have time for this, Chhun," Owens says. "Dust 'em."

Three suppressed blaster shots erupt from behind me. *Deet! Deet! Deet!*

The koobs drop, and the ground licks up their phosphorescent blood as the last death rattles gurgle from their air sacs. Andien took the shots. Apparently she has low-light vision in her goggles. That or some sort of Nether Ops implants. Her eyes *are* an odd shade of blue. Whether she heard the L-comm or not, who knows. But she KTF'd. And she did it faster than me. And honestly, I don't know if she's that quick, or if there was a glitch in my mind that kept me from pulling the trigger the moment Cap said, "Dust 'em."

I make a mental note. This is Kublar, koobs are savage, KTF. If it was a brain-glitch. It ain't happening again.

Owens chuckles over the comm. My HUD tells me it's on our four-person private channel, so Andien can hear it, too. "Chhun, kindly hand over your nuts to the woman sitting directly behind you. Because she just out-leejed you."

Wraith doesn't say anything, but then, he's not much of a talker. There's still that by-the-book officer vibe. Of course, he's not solely a legionnaire captain. There's a man in that armor. But I've got no good idea of who the man is when I think about it. Wraith doesn't let his personal side show through his commission. Captain Owens, on the other hand, seems to allow his personality to carry over entirely. Maybe it's because he's taken me on as Lieutenant Chhun instead of as a sergeant. There's never been that NCO-CO divide with him.

I tell the captain where he can shove his suggestion. With all due respect, of course. We move on and I don't give it a second thought. Exo would have given it to me a lot worse. He still brings up the time I lost my footing going down a sand dune on Renoy and slid, unable to stop myself, three hundred feet to the bottom like a kid on a playground. I had to hear about it from Exo and the entire squad as I lumbered back up, picking up stray pieces of equipment on the way. That was over a standard rotation ago and I'm *still* not convinced that I cleaned out all the sand.

As the kilometers pass, a soft glow appears ahead—a few still-smoldering fires burning inside the *Chiasm*. We're about there. As the superstructure of the battleship grows, we begin to speed past obstacles that dispersed from the point of impact with the planet. Charred and twisted blaster battery cannons. Comm dishes. Twisted impervisteel. And thousands of tiny pieces of who-knows-what, all waiting to be buried by time. Because the koobs won't care.

We're moving too quickly for me to fully grasp what I'm seeing. To get my mind around a ship this size exploding from dual MARO blasts and burning down onto the planet.

All these little pieces were people, Chhun. They're your shipmates. And they're all dead.

I shake the thought away, look past this nightmarish landscape of burnt-up bones and body parts, skulls and buckets, all lying exposed beneath the sweltering Kublaren sun.

Focus on the op.

Most of the ship is half-buried at the bottom of a huge impact crater. The bikes allow us to get closer than I would have imagined possible—maybe two hundred and fifty meters. We stop behind the remains of a massive HK-PP mech—or at least, its upper torso; no idea where the rest of it is. It serves as an excellent shield for our speeders. Anyone looking in the direction of our parked bikes would have a hard time picking them out from the other mechanical detritus.

Crouching in the shadows, I listen while scanning for koobs. A few sentries mill about, old automatic-fire slug throwers from the Savage Wars resting lazily in their arms. Whatever tribe this is, they care more about lookouts than Moona did.

"Time to earn that Dark Ops pay," Owens says over the joint comm. "I need one leej with me to find and secure the nearest terminal port so Miss Nether Ops can do her thing. The other is on overwatch."

"I'll go with you," Wraith says. For as long as I've known him, he's hated overwatch. Not the type of guy who can stand much watching and waiting if he doesn't absolutely have to.

"Good. Settled." Owens creeps to the edge of the shadow enveloping us. "Chhun, start painting hostiles for the HUD."

I pull out my field macros and begin tagging all the koobs I can see. My visor's HUD adds a red dot for each koob I spot. Mostly I'm finding pockets of sleeping koobs, but there's also the occasional sentry. I tag the sentries as high priority, which makes a miniature exclamation mark appear above their dot on the HUD.

While I'm doing this, Owens continues edging his way out of our cover. "This is knife work. Don't discharge your N-4, suppressed or not, unless you have to."

N-4s have the ability to fire suppressed rounds through a toggle near the charge pack. This holds the blaster bolt in a chamber, vents the blaster bolt's gases in a low hiss, and then releases a slowed-down shot. It won't do as much damage, and it's a much slower rate of fire, and despite all this, you can still hear the distinct noise of the thing. But still, the hiss is better than the usual report of blaster rifle fired full-on, and it's enough to kill an unarmored foe at medium range.

Wraith and Owens creep slowly forward. They disappear from my view, but my bucket continues to predict the movement as green dots on my HUD.

"Hey, Chhun." It's Wraith. "We're seeing a few more koobs down this way, beneath the lip of the crater. Think you can get someplace higher and spot them for us?"

I look up to the broken peak of the ruined HK-PP. "Yeah, sure thing."

Andien is alert, her small holdout blaster pistol at the ready. "Hey," I tell her, "I'm climbing up for a better view. You good down here?"

She nods.

I make my way up, finding hand and footholds in the battered and pockmarked remains of the mech's armor. I find a nice little nook to sink into, cradled by the giant war machine like a baby in the crook of its arm, the only one still attached. My HUD guides my field macros right to the last known position of Wraith and Cap Owens. They stand at the ready, vibroknives in hand, with a pair of dead koobs at their feet.

"Okay, I have visual. Nice work." I begin to scan from my higher vantage point. Red dots show up. A lot of them. "You guys seeing this?"

"Yeah," answers Wraith, his tone not defeated, but clearly indicating that this isn't the Kublar getaway vacation he'd been dreaming of. "Most of those asleep?"

"A lot of them," I answer, tagging the sentries as I scroll through my feed. "Just about done tagging. Your best bet is to weave your way around the wreckage of your current position. It looks like you'll come to a section of the ship that was blown wide open. Maybe the leisure deck. It's hard to tell because everything looks so busted up."

"Copy," Owens acknowledges. "Nether Ops, can you pull what you need from a leisure deck?"

"I should be able to, yes."

"Good," Owens replies. "Chhun, how's her path to join us?"

I shift my position, look down to Andien, and follow the path in front of her. "All clear. She should have an uneventful walk."

"On my way," Andien says. I think I detect a flutter in her voice. Nerves.

She moves with her blaster pistol at the low ready, scurrying from cover to cover as she crosses ground and moves down into the impact crater. She ducks beneath some sort of structural beam and then hops up over a meter-high object—maybe a hangar barge. I can't tell. I'm impressed with the way she moves. Cool, smooth, almost elegant. She knows what she's doing. Hardly the awkward and angry scientist who gave Wraith and me an earful on our combat sled.

I wonder if that other scientist, the guy whose wife died... I wonder if he made it. I start to think of him. And then I realize I'm not aware of my situation.

Focus, Chhun.

I take everything in at once. Andien is still in position. Wraith and Owens are waiting for her arrival. The koobs pretty much haven't left their positions.

And I'm lying down, feeling warm. My legs and arms are heavy.

Sleep. I need sleep. Much as I'm loath to admit it, the past few days' events have caught up with me. Legionnaire training takes you to your ultimate limits. We spend weeks barely sleeping, an hour here or there before a drill instructor douses us with water in phase one, or kicks us as hard as he can in our buckets in phase two. We sleep while marching. While crawling. I can operate without sleep. But not optimally. If this keeps up, my bucket is going to detect my slowing pulse and alert my CO. I'm assuming that's Captain Owens instead of Captain Ford, but I suppose I don't really know. Either way, I'm not keen on my first day in Dark Ops being the day I fall asleep on the job. I bite down on my tongue, focusing on the pain and hoping it drives away the drowsiness.

It doesn't. I'm having to force my eyes open, like I'm trying to stare at the sun and have to resist the natural urge to squint. To shut my eyes. I decide to call it in. "Hey," I announce over the L-comm. "I've barely slept in days and it's awfully comfy up here. I'm just talkin' to keep from dozing off. Ooah?"

"Ooah," Wraith replies.

But Owens takes a different approach. "Nah, it's cool, Chhun. Go ahead and grab some Z's. We're good."

What? No... just, no.

"No thanks, Cap," I reply. Is this guy serious?

"No, really. Shut your eyes for a while and see. That's an order."

He's ordering me to go to sleep on overwatch. This can't be right. I fight to stay in the battle against slumber, but it's gaining ground. I feel my eyelids droop and... zap! A jolt of electricity surges through my skull. I feel like someone punched me in the lip. My heart is racing and I'm just glad I didn't fall off the mech I'm perched on. What was that?

My yelp must have been transmitted on the L-comm, because Owens is stifling a laugh. "That'll be standard in

all buckets soon enough, but we get it first. New tech senses when you're in danger of dozing, gives you a jolt to keep
you awake. It's actually better not to fight it so the wakeup
call comes in sooner. If you know the menus you can call
it down on yourself, but it hurts so damn much I've never
had the guts for it."

Well, that sucked. But it worked. I'm awake.

"So what do you see?" Cap asks.

I scan the field. "Nothing. A few of the sentries have
taken seats. No movement around the perimeter or in
your sector."

"All right," Owens says. "Sounds good."

Andien closes in on their position. I call out her ETA.

"Copy," Wraith says, his voice calm. "We have visual on her."

I swear he was born for Dark Ops. I'm not so sure about
Cap. He's not what I expected. I always figured the Dark
Ops guys were the serious, deadly type. Captain Owens
seems anything but.

Andien and the leejes disappear from my view, moving together inside the torn-up deck of the *Chiasm*. It takes
thirty minutes for Andien to run whatever program she
has in the terminal ports on the recreation deck. I don't
get jolted again during that time. That one zap triggered
enough adrenaline to keep me alert.

The trio re-emerges.

"Eyes on anything special?" Owens asks.

"Nothing. Koobs aren't even moving. Most of the sentries are asleep."

"Good. We're coming in."

They send Andien ahead, moving at an even pace but keeping some separation. I watch Andien dart past a battered blast door that's sticking straight up out of the Kublaren soil. A moment later three koobs, each armed with a blaster rifle, step between Andien and her leej protection.

"Andien, stop!" I call into the comm.

She freezes. Wraith and Owens don't move either. I describe the situation. "Three armed koobs got between you all. I don't think they can see you, but the way they're holding themselves, I think they know Andien moved by."

Andien turns slowly. I'm sure she can see the koobs through the darkness thanks to her goggles. She raises her blaster pistol, but unlike the koobs on the road, these have their rifles at the ready.

"Hold up," I say. "If you dust one, another is going to get a croak or a shot off and alert the whole area."

"So what do I do?" Andien asks, her voice a little hot. Easy for me to call her to wait while I'm back here and pretty much out of harm's way. "Just hope they keep on walking?"

"They definitely know something's out there," Wraith observes. "You got a shot, Chhun?"

"I do, but same problem. It'll be heard." I think up a plan on the fly. "Andien, train your blaster on the middle koob. Wraith, Cap, think you can get close enough behind the other two for knife work?"

"On our way," whispers Owens.

The two legionnaires creep up behind the shifting koobs like twin ghosts. They could reach out and caress the back of the aliens' heads if they wanted to.

"Andien, take the shot on three," I say. "One... two... three."

A silenced flash from her blaster pistol. Her target falls to the ground in an awkward heap. In the milliseconds of confusion before the other two koobs have a chance to react, the legionnaires bury their knives deep. Air sacs are split and the blades are pulled upward, piercing brain stems. Wraith and Owens slowly lay the koobs, blood pouring from their fatal wounds, to the ground.

Obstacle clear. No one the wiser. At least, not for a while.

As soon as my team gets close enough to the bikes, I climb down. I find that it's my turn to ride, so I jump behind Andien and we're gone. Silently speeding through the night.

Sunrise is ninety minutes off, easily. We'll make our cutoff and keep the featherheads happy.

"Hey," I say over the comm. "You didn't really leave a charge in that shuttle, did you?"

"Hell no," comes Owens's reply. "If I've got extra blast bricks, I want them with me. But if a pilot's gonna give us crap and threaten to leave us standing at the altar 'cause they got cold feet... I don't mind making them spend their wait time searching for a bomb that ain't there."

We don't run into any more koobs. The shuttle is waiting for us when we arrive. My first Dark Ops mission is over. I didn't even dust anybody.

Not how I figured it would go.

11

The debrief room seems too nice for the likes of us. The conference table is polished to a mirror shine, enhancing the glow of the overhead lights and showing us warbling, mirage-like reflections of ourselves whenever we stand over it. Carpet is pristine, except for the dusty footprints from all the Kublar dust caked on our boots. The ride back to the shuttle on our bikes managed to dry up the koob blood that had drenched the arms of Wraith and Owens. The yellow blood was pushed farther up their arms in delicate streams from the windy ride, making it look a bit like a couple of badass tattoos.

We're waiting for the legion commander. If I was underdressed when I met him the first time, now I just look like hell. We all do. A far cry from the spit-shined, clean-shaven standard that's usually expected when you meet a leej this important. I'm not kidding. I've been in situations where we just rotated in from some week-long fighting, clearing out city blocks of entrenched MCR—armor is dirty, bloody, full of carbon scoring—and my squad is lying around our base, thankful to just be still, when some point officer comes up and demands we shine up, remove our helmets, groom to standard, and prepare to meet General Who-Gives-A-Damn. And the best part is, the whole time everyone's acting like they're doing *us* a favor.

"Aren't you boys proud? You'll always remember the day you met General I-Got-Here-Because-My-Aunt-Is-On-the-Senate-Council."

Something to tell my grandkids about. Sweet!

There's no time to clean up now. Debrief is supposed to start in five. And from what I've gathered in my short time with the legion commander, he's not the type to swear at our appearance. He fought his way to the top. Earned his rank and the respect of his fellow leejes. He's been where we've been. Knows the score.

Cap Owens pulls off his bucket and drops it onto the table. Dirt and grime mar the beautifully maintained surface. More work for the bots—like they care. He flops into a seat. I half expect him to kick up his feet and lay his dirty boots across the table, but he doesn't.

Following his lead, I remove my helmet and place it down—a bit more gently. Having fought for days without a functioning bucket, I guess I'm a little more appreciative of them now that I've got one back. I take a seat. So does Wraith. He doesn't remove his helmet. I know what Captain Ford looks like when he isn't Wraith, but at the moment, I can't remember his face.

I need sleep.

Andien is standing in a corner, wrapping herself in her arms like she feels a chill. She hasn't talked much since we left in the shuttle. But then, none of us have. It was a quiet ride. Probably all she wants to do is analyze the data she has, but she's seeing the op to its end with us. I appreciate that.

I look over to her, catch her eye, and nod. She smiles faintly, warmly, and nods back. It dawns on me that this is probably the last time I'll ever see her. She'll go on and do spy shit, and I'll KTF. I start to feel... sad about this. Only for a second, though.

The emotion evaporates like sweat beneath the Kublaren sun as the door whooshes open and the legion commander steps in. There's another leej with him, with a lieutenant colonel's dragon painted on his armor. We all jump up to salute.

The commander quickly returns our salutes and motions for us to sit back down. "Stay in your seats, men. You've earned some time off your feet." Keller gestures to the lieutenant colonel. "This is Lieutenant Colonel Bergh. He's here to see if his boys need to take any follow-up action based on your report. Captain Owens?"

I figured Owens would stand to give his report, but he doesn't. He just sort of swivels in his chair as he relays the basics. Times. Encounters. Enemy killed. The state of the *Chiasm*.

Legion Commander Keller interrupts. "That crash site looks like an absolute disaster from orbit. You saw it first-hand. The Republic wants us to stay out of Kublar, but if there's the slightest possibility of survivors..."

"No possibility, sir," Owens answers, his voice sounding heavy. "It's a graveyard. The only living things there are koobs and some scavengers picking at bones. They're all dead."

Lieutenant Colonel Bergh speaks up for the first time. "I don't like the idea of koobs or vultures picking over our dead. I'll see about arranging for an orbital bombardment. Shouldn't be a problem as long as we have what we need."

Commander Keller looks at Andien, still in the corner. "How about it, Miss Broxin? Did you get what you need to find the bastards who did this?"

Andien steps forward. "It's too early to say if I've got exactly what we'll need to find them, but I *can* say that we've recovered all that the *Chiasm* has to tell us."

"Good." Keller turns back to Bergh. "No sense waiting around. Get Captain Avery to start the bombardment. Patch me in directly to the bridge comm if he gives you the slightest hint of reluctance. Not that he will. Good man, that Avery."

The lieutenant colonel excuses himself and leaves the conference room.

Andien addresses the commander. "I need to start digging into this. Time is of the essence."

"Dismissed, Miss Broxin."

The room is left with only legionnaires.

"Captain Owens," Keller says, waking a datapad in front of him. "Were you satisfied with the performance of Captain Ford and Lieutenant Chhun?" The commander turns to us. "Those ranks have been made official now, by the way. I got that much done while you were on Kublar."

"Thank you, sir," we answer in unison.

Owens nods at Keller. "Yes, sir. Both performed at Dark Ops standards. They're good leejes."

I feel relief. I guess I didn't realize it, but the stress of Andien dusting those herders before I did was weighing on me. Owens must have felt she was just a little faster to pull the trigger is all.

"Excellent." Keller slides the datapad toward us. "Here's a list of the survivors from Victory Company. Dark Ops team is six plus your command officer. That would be Captain Owens. As agreed, you pick the rest of your team. I'm going to warn you now, there's not much to choose from. Most didn't survive, and of the few who did, the wounds suffered are substantial. You need a team that's ready to go now, because we've got work to do."

I pull my chair next to Wraith's, and we begin to look over the list with Cap Owens standing behind us. It's a full roster, listing KIAs, MIAs, casualties unfit for service... we have to scroll for some time before we reach someone deemed fit for duty. And it's my name, so that doesn't really help.

I see Twenties's name: Denino, Baeus.

My heart jumps to see a buddy that made it. The list says he's medically unfit for combat, but I'm hoping it's just his eyes. That should be fine in a day.

"That's one," I say. "Twenties. Specialist Denino."

"Yeah," agrees Wraith.

Keller enters the name on another datapad. He looks up. "Says he was in the infirmary for an eye infection, released to quarters."

"He'll be fine," I say. "Best sniper I've ever seen."

"Sounds good," Owens says. "If it's something that pills can clear up, let's take him. Who else?"

"Masters and Exo," I say.

Wraith relays their Legion numbers for entry.

I scroll, looking for more.

Doc Quigs is dead. So is Rook. Maldorn. Clauderro. All dead.

Devers is still alive, medically inoperative. But screw him anyway. I'd sooner ask a koob to join the team.

Sergeant Powell is listed as inoperative: medical. But maybe it'll be like Twenties, something he can heal up from between jumps. "How about Sergeant Powell? He was Captain Ford's right-hand man."

"Don't think so," Wraith says, shaking his head. "He went down hard during the fight. I dragged him to a transport, but I have to think he's out of the fight. Maybe for good."

Commander Keller confirms with a few swipes of his datapad. "He's undergoing extensive bionic reconstruction right now."

"Need one more," Owens says. He hasn't argued at all. The trust he's showing us in selecting this team is remarkable, but I guess that's because he knows we'll be the ones rubbing shoulders on breaches and in combat. His job is to plan and join the fight when needed. "If there aren't any more, I can ask for recommendations from among the legionnaires on board the ship. I'm sure there are more than a few qualified."

I nod, ready to agree to just that if Wraith is of the same mind. Then a name pops into my head. I blurt it out without thinking. "Kags."

"Yeah," Wraith says. "Kid can fight. Performed well alongside us."

Keller checks the name against his list. "I don't see a Kags anywhere on here."

"He's Republic Army," Wraith says. "But he's good. Fought as fierce as any leej. He's fit. Mentally tough. Helped us take the Ohio-class... he'll be an asset. Kid should've started in the Legion to begin with."

The legion commander sighs. "Very unorthodox. Captain Owens?"

"Let's do it. Having someone who can blend in easily with the basics could help. This whole thing with the *Chiasm* and Camp Forge was inside. I say go."

Rubbing his face, Keller agrees. "He'll need to stay behind for two weeks. I want him up to speed on Legion protocol and familiarized with the armor. Lieutenant Colonel Bergh was a DI. He'll get him where he needs to be."

"Great," Owens says, clapping his hands together. "We've got a team. You two clean up and get some sleep. I'll find out if we're staying on the *Mercutio* or shuttle-jumping somewhere else. Be ready for hell at a moment's notice from now on."

"No..." Keller says, his brow furrowed almost to a scowl. "You're a man short."

I list the names in my head. Ford. Chhun. Exo. Masters. Kags. Twenties. That's six. "Who?" I ask.

"Exo—Specialist Gutierrez—is no longer aboard the ship."

"Sir?" Wraith asks. "He was with us right before I brought Lieutenant Chhun to our meeting."

"He's been shuttled off-ship for immediate court-martial on Utopion."

"On whose orders?" I know I shouldn't be talking to a legion commander like that. A case could be made that I'm on the fence straddling familiarity and insubordination.

Keller doesn't seem to mind. He looks at me and raises an eyebrow. "Who do you think?"

We burst into the medical bay as if we're clearing a house. I'm on point, followed by Wraith and Owens. We're all in our armor and we're all hot. The first thing Devers must have done once the docs got him patched up was go after Exo. And one thing you have going for you as a point on a ship full of people looking to impress, is quick action. The shuttle jumped with Exo on board while we were killing koobs by the light of the silvery stars.

A bot regards us from behind a reception desk. "How may I help you?" it asks in a sweet, synthesized voice. Totally oblivious to the fact that three big, pissed-off leejes are practically foaming at the mouth in front of it.

"We need to see Captain Devers," Wraith says. "Immediately."

The bot pretends to look down at a datapad. They do things like this just to appear more human. In reality it's running Devers's name through its own connection to the ship's network. "I'm sorry," the bot says, programmed to sound compassionate. "Captain Silas Devers is recovering and unable to see visitors except during normal visiting hours: 0900 to 1500, *Mercutio* standard time."

"What room is he in, for when we come back?" Owens asks.

The bot makes another show of looking that up. "Med-bay six, recovery room 14-A."

"Thanks," Owens says, completely insincere. "Boys, let's go visit. Break down the door if you have to, damn point."

The bot stands up. "I'm sorry, you are not allowed to—"

"Shut up, bot." Owens palms the bot's head and pushes it away, causing the machine to tip over into the wall with a metallic clang.

"I am required to report this incident to ship security." The bot isn't done yet.

Owens keeps walking. "Command override: Foresight Six. And shut up."

The bot sits down. "Override acknowledged. Shutting up, sir."

We move down the hallway to Devers's recovery room, passing confused nurses and orderlies, human and bot alike. They probably think we're here to visit a friend, just a couple of leejes seeing a wounded buddy. Truth is, I really don't know *what* I'm here for. Get Exo out of trouble, I guess. Devers got what was coming to him.

In fact, he got off easy.

When the door slides open, Devers actually cracks a smile at seeing us. "Oh, hey, Ford," he says, somewhat weakly. "Hey, Chhun. It's nice of you to drop by. Did you hear? They're giving me a medal on Utopion."

I get the distinct sense that Devers is still a little loopy from meds. I don't care. I go right after him. "Did you arrange for Exo to be court-martialed?"

Devers sits up in his bed, looking at Wraith and Owens, who I assume he's never seen before. He gets the hint that this is the question all of us want to know. "Yes, I did. Of *course* I did. Chhun, you're new to the officer corps, so your NCO brain may still be catching up, but that sort of behavior is unacceptable. He assaulted a superior officer. That type of infraction cannot stand. You need to think beyond emotion and imagine the morale loss, seeing that sort of insubordination among the rank and file. To be honest, I was a little shocked neither of you made the report while I was under the bots."

"We had unfinished business on Kublar," Wraith says. "Call it off, Silas. We're alive, and Exo is a big part of the reason. We barely survived your screw-ups."

"My... *my* screw-ups! I'm getting a *medal*, Ford. A medal! Order of the Centurion!"

This guy... I don't punch his teeth in. It's probably the most restraint I've ever showed in my life. I keep telling myself, he's loopy from meds. He's an idiot, but not this big of an idiot.

"Fine," Wraith says. "Whatever. Congratulations. But call it off so the legion commander doesn't have to, because he will."

"What do you mean he will?"

"It's twarg crap and you know it," I say. "You were conducting yourself in a manner unbecoming an officer.

Take your medal, have your career, leave Exo alone. We need him."

Devers looks my armor up and down. "Yeah. I see you're in Dark Ops now. That was quick. But the answer is no. The Legion has rules, and the rules need to be obeyed."

Sure. Just like the way you obeyed the rules for exiting a combat sled. I keep it inside.

"So that's it?" Wraith says, disbelief coming through his usually calm and steady voice. "You're willing to throw away your prestige just to get back at Exo?"

"I'm not throwing away anything, and Exo deserved to be shot on sight. A court-martial is lenient."

"You're wrong," I say, hoping to hammer home the point Wraith subtly tried to make. "Legion Commander Keller wants Exo on our team. He files a counter-petition to your request for court-martial, people start asking questions about why a decorated Legion officer isn't being trusted. They start asking questions. Word gets out from the survivors left alive, the basics and a few leejes—that you messed up. That your decisions caused men and women to die without need or gain."

Devers waves it all away. "You're delusional. I was appointed by *Orrin Kaar*. He's one of the most respected men in the House of Reason. If Keller wants to make a big deal out of this, it's his career you should be worried about."

"All right," Owens says, approaching Devers. "Screw this." He wraps a massive arm around Devers's neck and clamps down in a rear naked choke.

Devers's eyes bulge, and the veins in his head begin to swell. He's turns red, then purple. Support machines start to beep.

"Chhun, go watch for nurses. Keep them outside if they come near," Owens orders.

I move to the door and look down the empty corridor. From the corner of my eye I see Owens bringing his mouth close to Devers's ear. Cap doesn't lower his voice. He's making sure his every word is clear. "Listen up, you point space-rat. You're gonna rescind everything about Exo. You understand? You're going to blame it on a hallucination brought on by pain meds. And you're going to do it the moment I let you go. Tap your fingers if that sounds good. If not... you won't live long enough to collect your shiny medals."

Devers frantically taps in agreement.

"Good," Owens says, but he doesn't let go. "You know I'm Dark Ops. You know what I do. This matter is settled. You bring this up again, give any of my men even a hint of trouble, and I don't care how far down the line we're talking, you're going to wake up one night from your comfortable bed to see me standing above you. And I will kill you. That's an oath."

Owens lets Devers go, and the captain gasps for air.

A nurse comes running down the hall. I motion for him to come inside.

Wraith takes control of the situation. "Hey, you need to get a deck officer in here right away. Our buddy gave false information while under the effects of medication."

The nurse hesitates.

"Lives are at stake," Owens barks. "Move your ass!"

Devers manages to nod in agreement. The nurse takes off.

We stick around until Devers has called off the entire thing. As I prepare to leave, I tell him I hope this is the last time I'll ever see him.

Wraith stops at the door. "Silas, when you look at that medal they give you, remember how many leejes had to die so you could *pretend* to be a warrior."

Owens cracks his knuckles. "Also remember the part about how I'll kill you if you ever cross us again."

I think I'm in love with Dark Ops.

12

You're Tom. This is Pthalo.

Pthalo is a world of blue oceans, dry brown coasts, and golden sunlight. Massive floating luxury estates migrate from one party to the next. Only the best and brightest maintain a residence on secret, tax-free Pthalo. The House of Reason likes it that way. It's a reward for those who give so much to the Republic.

Arms dealers.

Drug dealers.

Crooked lawyers.

Syndicate financiers.

Everybody who pitches in and does all the stuff that needs doing but can't actually be done—legally speaking, that is.

Pthalo is the place of hoard and pleasure.

And as the freighter *Hoplyte*—which you've been sleeping on for three days now as it hurtles through the void known as hyperspace—drops out of faster-than-light travel and picks up an intercept course for the surface, you begin to pack. Organizing things that have followed you to the freighter berth where you find yourself this morning. That novel you finished as best you could to keep your mind off all the ways you could disappear forever. And the *Chiasm*. And Camp Forge. And... And... And...

You don't see the approach, you're merely walking forward to the boarding area when the ship sets down. You hear the repulsors throb and the engines flare and then all is silent.

The crew has kept their distance throughout the journey, and you get the distinct impression it's because they don't want to know you, as opposed to they don't like you. They don't want to know you because knowing is dangerous. The crew is hustling about as you arrive.

The news you pick up on your data comm as the boarding ramp lowers to the deck says nothing about Kublar. Nothing about a destroyer cracked in half and burnt up in the atmo. Nothing about a camp full of the Republic's finest who got hit by a massive bomb you piloted right into their midst.

Checking the news feeds, it's as if those terrible things never happened.

Wouldn't that be nice?

If they had never happened. Because now that you've had to live with them, you'd like to have never had them happen.

But they did.

The warm blast of air from sweet-smelling Pthalo hits you. You smell bougainvillea and salt water. The two mercs follow you, hauling their oversized bags full of weapons and gear. You've still got that blaster. The one with the silencer.

Beyond the boarding ramp and out from underneath the venting freighter you see the dazzle of sun on sea glittering like a thousand million tiny diamonds. The ship has landed on the aft platform of a massive estate gliding across the blue waters between two distant peninsulas.

Lizard-like dragons the size of eagles dance and swirl in the suns above. The estate rises away toward the rest of the ship in sleek white ceramic and tinted portholes. High above, a tower, rounded and rectangular, juts out. The bridge, most likely. All kinds of toys adorn the deck. You take interest in those as though those things are interesting.

Why?

Because you're sure the fear is showing on your face. And Scarpia, Frogg, Illuria, and the lawyer are waiting for you at platform's edge. Smiling. Beaming. Looking at you like hungry wolves, or celebrating. The line between the two blurs.

So you watch all the toys around the platform. Small submersibles. Water jet craft. The latest in sail speeders. The promised pleasures seem unlimited.

"There's our boy," says Scarpia triumphantly, like a father welcoming home his son from university on some distant core world. "Fine job, my boy. Fine job."

Frogg smiles. The smile is genuine, and the look in the eyes of the killer is winsome. As though something of value has been lost, and whatever it was, it is still oddly longed for. Ached for.

And then there is Illuria, who hands you a cold flute of cryopagne. Ice-cold wine that tastes like peach and effervesces like an undersea volcano. Her smile is genuine. Model perfect. She probably was one. Could still be. Her green skin screams lust and commerce while her four slender arms beckon and invite to some kind of hoped-for oblivion beyond dead starships and stranded legionnaires.

But that could merely be the pheromones talking.

"Let's get below. We've got a whole fine dinner planned and then an evening you won't forget." Mr. Scarpia ushers everyone into the wide tunnel that descends below the ship. The two mercs peel off, and it's just you and the target and his entourage. You're keenly aware that you should make contact with your minders. The Carnivale.

Who?

But now is not the time to think of such things.

Instead you're walking along a curving hall that twirls down around the massive ship. You pass staterooms and lounges with the latest in comfort and entertainment. The party pauses beside a wide viewing wall that looks out into the shallow coral depths below.

"Oh, look," moans Illuria in her deep velvet voice. She dances toward the window. "They've come out for you, Tom."

Tom.

Tom.

Your name is Tom. Even when she says it.

Beyond the window, the murria have come out. Undersea humanoids that inhabit this world. Children, really. Even you've heard of them. They want nothing to do with the Repub. Instead they swim among the coral and sunken ruins of some ancient civilization, cracking shellfish and sunning on the rocks. Singing their haunting songs in the twilight.

They are aliens, and yet there is something so primal and ancient about them. Like some glimpse into a past one cannot remember.

They come up into the central column beneath the passing ship, somersaulting and twilling in the bubbles from the engines, only to return to the white sandy depths and pink coral below. They are beautiful. Especially the females. Innocent and childlike. Their narrow features and elven eyes cast that knowing look you saw in the Planetary DataNet when you looked them up on the way here.

Their eyes unsettled you then—the way their pictures looked out at you from the datapad. As though they knew your secrets. It unsettles you now as they come close to the windows and watch the party. Watch you.

"I wonder what they taste like," murmurs Frogg at your elbow, face pressed up to the glass. He watches them like a dead-eyed shark.

Scarpia laughs and tousles the short man's hair. The violent psychopath's hair. Scarpia is the kind of man who makes pets and playthings, and even friends, of such monsters. He is that kind of man. He is that kind of monster.

This is the lesson you learn as you watch the murria play, hoping they don't signal Scarpia somehow and tell him they've looked inside your soul and seen nothing. Hoping they don't rat you out.

But they're right.

Your soul, or whatever you want to call it, it's gone. It's *been* gone. Lost or taken. Started disappearing on Ankalor, and finally up and left on Kublar. So if they did, if the elven swimming children beyond the glass suddenly told on you... well, you'd agree. And Scarpia would say...

... We already knew that, children. That's why we chose him for the job.

That's the first disconnect.

The first moment when you feel... disconnected from who you are, were, and Operation Ghost Hunter. When you feel like that other guy you've been becoming all along.

The first moment when you really are Tom. Doer of dirty deeds done for profit. Snuffer-out of the innocent if the price is right.

That's the moment of disconnect, when you're confronted by the innocent children beyond the glass. The moment when you could slip away and just be Tom forever and never go back.

"It's like they can see right inside us," croons Illuria.

And did you just feel one of her four hands on your shoulder? It was electric.

The days that follow on Pthalo are days of sun and sea as Scarpia's estate—he calls it *Smuggler's End*—drifts through the outer banks of a chain of desert islands. On some days you arrive over old ruins unlike anything the Ancients left anywhere across the galaxy. These are not enigmatic pyramids set high in the hinterlands and nigh-unreachable wastes of all those other planets. No, these are like strange sunken cities just below the waterline. Ten to twenty feet down sometimes. Tall columns and sculpted angular roofs wait just beneath the seafoam green waters that are clearer than any color at all. The water is pleasant and tastes of salt, and it's warm to swim in, even in the dark.

Gorgeous multicolored fish swim in and out of the ruins, and so do you. Occasionally you spear one and haul it back up onto the floating estate where Chef Tyrol prepares it, often raw with just a bit of citrus and some coarse Malasian fire salt. Frogg accompanies you, and of course he always wears a wicked, jagged-edged diving knife, but that's because Scarpia's woman, as he calls Illuria, like to dive too. You try not to watch her in her barest of bathing suits, but it's hard not to, even for Frogg, whose loyalty to the man known as Scarpia is like nothing you've ever seen. Scarpia, who does not dive, but always waits above and greets you like returning heroes with flutes of cryopagne and listens enraptured as Illuria gushes about what has been discovered in the translucent dreamy depths just below.

"Did you see any monsters down there, my dear?" Scarpia always asks her, tongue in cheek.

She turns a brighter shade of green, rolls her languid eyes, and replies. "You and always with your monsters. No, my love," she teases him. "The only monster we saw was the one we saw when we came back on board."

And then Scarpia makes horns on his head and growls as he lumbers about the firepit where sometimes Chef Tyrol roasts the fish on fragrant planks and serves them with succulent fruit or roasted potatoes crusted with salt and strange herbs.

Sometimes.

Those are some days.

Other days are spent wandering the coast and lonely foothills of the small islands you pass. Taking thermogliders off the deck of the estate, and "a survival pack"— which is what Scarpia calls a knapsack with wine, cheese, and a crusty sourdough batard— you all soar out in the two-seaters toward the small island you've chosen for the day's adventure. The gliders repulsor-assist the water landing in the small coves, and the craft are so light you're able to beach and then drag them into the soft white sand.

Then explore.

What are you hoping to find here among the dry grass, red rocks, and strange small lizards? Sometimes arrowheads. Sometimes some strange array of stones left by that other lost civilization that lived beneath the waves. Sometimes those things in the vast yawning silence that is this world.

And sometimes, toward the end of the day, as the winds began to sweep in from the sea and you top the ridge of the hilly island you've been threading your way toward all day... sometimes it's not what you're trying to find... it's what you're trying to lose.

It starts out as a game you play.

Lose yourself in this role of Tom.

Why?

Because if this role bombs, gets even one bad review... well, then... they'll just space you somewhere along the way. Won't they?

So it starts out as losing yourself in someone you aren't. It starts out that way. Except... what's the old saying? Tell a lie long enough, begin to believe it.

And so those disconnects happen on the happy, lazy, indolent days of exploration and luxury. The disconnect of never again having to be yourself. That scared, frightened man who's been gone too long and done too many "done" things in the name of the Republic doesn't have to be here anymore. You never have to be him again.

You can be Tom now.

Everybody loves Tom.

Scarpia treats Tom as a kind of son. Tom is good-looking and athletic. Kind and friendly. Everything a father could ever want of a son. And it's clear, as the next operation is being discussed over those wine and cheese lunches of indolence and luxury on lost desert isles, it's clear that Scarpia has high hopes for Tom. He has inside tips for Tom. Dreams Tom should consider if all goes well.

And Frogg loves Tom, even though Tom is oft-plagued by visions of nasty little Frogg, small bad teeth bared, pinning him and raising that wicked diving knife before plunging it down and down again and again because that's surely where this is heading. You see that, right, Tom? You see Frogg, you see he's a psychopath. And not just a "Hey, that guy's a psycho" psychopath. But a real live nightmare diagnosed as such by the Legion and subsequently drummed out because he was too violent, deranged, and murderous.

Too violent for the Legion. That's really saying something.

No. Frogg is nothing but friendship. He tells horrible stories of the things he's done and seen, and at times, when your skin is crawling and you're doing everything within your power not to run shrieking from his presence and subsequently blow your role as Tom, at times Frogg shows insightful moments of incredible and brilliant self-diagnosis.

And this makes you love him. Pity him. Try to question your own findings and make a friend of him. Because a psychotic killer like the unlovable Frogg would be a great ally if you were ever to take up full-time Tom.

Think about that, won't you?

You do.

And Illuria...

There's this moment. This moment when you've reached cliff's edge of some small and nameless desert island. It's on the other side, away from Scarpia's floating pleasure estate. This view looks out onto nothing but the wide empty ocean that stretches toward every corner of this world.

That might seem boring. But for some reason it's not. You see her standing at cliff's edge as the day begins to fade. Far out to sea, the east surrenders to the coming purple of twilight. The first star comes out. Everyone is there. This is not some silly moment just the two of you have. Frogg is there, searching for rocks to toss into the sea. Scarpia has stepped away to do some business comm. Stepped to the other side of the hilltop because he is doing business and though you are part of that business you cannot know all the business. You're not that inner circle. Not yet.

But promises have definitely been hinted at.

Tom is going places, my dear boy.

But there is this moment when you see her staring out to sea. Her perfect chin lifted. Her chest forward. The very essence of her life force seeming to search for something out there. Some other thing the constant happiness and sultry inherent sexuality have never confessed to wanting in all your firepit conversations and island adventuring. This other part makes you think of a lost little girl, searching for something she knows she'll never find.

And you want to go to her and comfort her... as Tom.

13

I'm sitting on a shuttle bound for Utopion, capital world of the Republic. The name seems to have stuck. Utopion. I remember it was called Liberinthine for a while when I was a kid. They'd change it all the time, naming it after just about anyone so long as they were famous and agreed with the ruling class on all points deemed essential. I don't think the planet was ever named for a leej. At least, not that I've ever heard. It's not exactly my field of study. And if they did, you'd think it would have been after General Rex, seeing as how he was responsible for ending the Savage Wars.

But... Rex didn't exactly do what the Republic wanted once he formed Dark Ops.

Anyway, he's dead and gone now, and the Legion is the one branch of the military that won't identify him as a traitor. He did it right, though. Him and everyone who served with him. There was a rumor once that Pappy knew Rex. Pappy said all that traitor stuff was crap, which was enough for us.

Anyway, ooah for faithful leejes.

The Legion came into being a long time ago. Not long after the Savage Wars broke out. That was, what?—two thousand years ago? Anyway, the Legion was formed because people were dying all across the galaxy. And the Legion got strong. Strong enough to win the fight. So strong, that the Senate and House—it was just the House back then, it didn't become the House of Reason until later, when it absorbed the High Court—they were afraid the Legion would take control of the galaxy. The Legion could have, back then. Probably not now, though we'd put up a hell of a fight. It would be close.

So the Legion's commander at the time made a deal for the peace of the galaxy, while maintaining the Legion as an independent military body. The Legion would work under the House and Senate but was free to serve as a check and balance should someone take power over those fine—and by fine I mean scummy—institutions that posed a threat to the Republic's constitution. That was the deal. The Legion will protect the galaxy so long as the House and Senate don't try to assume command of the Legion. Some of us feel like that deal's getting strained more and more with each new point that comes in. I'm one of those somebodies.

That's some history, but a school lesson isn't why I'm on the shuttle. We're finally on our way to add Exo to the team... after one more op. Because there's always one more op.

Getting the okay to get Exo took longer than we hoped for. Exo spent a good three weeks in a brig near the Republic Strategic Command compound. He's out now, but he doesn't know he's wanted for Dark Ops, doesn't know we're coming. Cap Owens has a guy keeping an eye on him, though. Word is that Exo's visiting the pubs, and I don't blame him. What happened to him sucks.

We wanted to be there sooner, it just didn't work out that way. There was a Dark Ops team pulling sniper over-watch for the legionnaires in some hellhole called Pory Bory. I'd never heard of it, either—just another place where idiots arm themselves with stims and blaster rifles and attempt to bring down the galaxy. One of those places always engulfed in war, where your enemy has probably seen more combat than you, but isn't as well trained.

Dark Ops there couldn't kill the bad guys fast enough, and they needed a break. Cap volunteered us, said he wanted an opportunity to watch how our entire squad worked. We impressed him. Twenties was a machine. Nineteen confirmed kills in the week we were there. Ooah. Badass. We rotated out and left for Utopion after picking up Kags from his advanced Legion training. I think he likes his new spot in the Republic's war machine.

So I'm in the shuttle. Triple-checking my breaching gear. That's my station now: breacher. I blow, splice, or otherwise open the door so our shooters can storm a room, kill the bad guys, or snatch our target. It's stuff we've all done as leejes in the past, but we're crazy methodical about it. If we're not fighting, we're training to fight. I was close to these guys before, but we're reading each other's minds now.

We're all waiting for Cap Owens to give us our briefing. We have one op to snatch a high-value target, HVT, on Utopion. Then we get to have our family reunion with Exo.

Wraith is fiddling with his blaster pistol. He loves that thing. Loves it. I think he'd use only a pistol, just for the challenge, if our lives weren't on the line with every op.

Kags is alternating between pushups and squats on the deck. Kid is a bundle of endless energy, and this is how he deals when he starts to get too amped. Masters and Twenties are in the middle of a conversation that just got interesting, so I listen in.

"No, no, no," Masters says. "See, that's the crap they teach in the schools. But let's consider: the schools *also* teach that the House of Reason and Senate are interested in more than looking the other way so each branch can get mutually rich, right?"

"Yeah, but—" begins Twenties, but Masters cuts him off.

"Right. And they talk about the need for appointed officers to join the Legion so our 'outdated' warrior code can be adapted to meet 'modern galactic sensibilities.'"

Twenties shakes his head. "Right, sure, but that's not the point. What you're saying is—"

Masters holds up a finger. "No, no. Don't jump to conclusions yet. It only *sounds* crazy. But my dad would tell me this growing up, and I heard it from more than one chick at a cantina, girls from all over the galaxy. And they know what they're talking about. They have *wombs*."

"Some of 'em don't," I say. "Egg-layers."

Masters gives me a stay-out-of-it look. "*Most* of them do. And that's also the point. Women know things, man. They understand stuff to be true at a foundational level."

"You sound like someone who's never met a woman," Kags calls out from in between reps.

"I've met plenty. Ask your mom if you need a reference."

Twenties takes a deep breath. "Masters, two things. First, you're an idiot. You fight like a wild drusic, but you're still an idiot. You cannot tell me that you believe every sentient being in the galaxy comes from a common ancestry."

I smile, eager to hear Masters's response. The kid is full of two things: impure thoughts about the opposite sex, and conspiracy theories.

"I'm not saying *all*," Masters says, holding up a hand in an attempt to show his reasonableness. "I'm saying *most*. I'll prove it to you."

Twenties folds his arms. "Fine. Let's hear it."

Masters begins an interrogation of sorts. "What is the name of our species?"

"Humans."

"Correct. Who first discovered hyperspace?"

"Humans."

"Yes. And who colonized the galaxy?"

"Humans again?"

"Yes!"

I stand up to stretch. "I'm not seeing where this is going, Masters."

Masters looks up, wounded, at me. "You're killing my moment, Lieutenant. Now, what do we call a species that, while not human, *looks* human?"

"Humanoid?" guesses Twenties.

"Exactly." Masters leans back as if he's just scored the winning stroke. When he sees that we're not following, he rolls his eyes. "C'mon, guys. *Humanoids*? It's not because humans are terrible specists who use ourselves as the model of how life should be, like the government tries to guilt-trip you into thinking. It's because almost every species is part human."

"How?"

"Humans discover hyperspace. The exploration starts after that. Who goes on the exploration? Humans. But what kind of humans? Okay, men. Right. Men. And when these ships full of men—because, statistically, the women did not leave on these trips at nearly the same level, and the number of males to females was incredibly lopsided, that's a fact—these ships were full of men, and those men arrived on planets and built their shelters and got tired of waiting for ships with women to show up and got lonely and..."

I stare at Masters blankly. "You're saying that almost every species in the galaxy as we know exists because lonely men started sleeping with whatever native animal was on the planet they landed on?"

"Exactly." He interlocks his fingers behind his head and leans back. "And some of these species—surprise!—were sexually compatible. Now when the other dudes saw that nasty Nate had a kid that looked pretty much human, they followed suit. Well, in a few generations, all that was left was the new species, right? And by the time the next human ship arrives—when our exploration really got going—you've got all these humanoid populations. And no one knows that humans started it because they were all breeded out."

No one says anything, and Masters is grinning like a kid who won first prize.

I turn to Wraith. "You hearing this, Captain Ford?"

He looks up from polishing his blaster, answers, "Sounds plausible," and goes back to his work.

"No," Twenties says, shaking his head in big, exaggerated arcs. "No way. Species evolved with humanoid characteristics because those are the characteristics that allow those species to survive in the widest array of environments. And *that's* why we see so many today."

Masters is undeterred. "Then how do you explain how ridiculously hot Sataars are, even if they're full-breeds? Their planet sucks. No self-respecting species would evolve to be that hot to humans on a lousy planet like that."

Just before the argument can pick up any more momentum, the door opens and Cap Owens steps through. A holobot follows him, projecting a holographic image of a middle-aged man on the deck in front of us.

"This is your target, leejes." Owens points to the holofigure. The man is well-dressed, a solid upper-middle class type for Utopion. "Name's Cantrell Saan. Mr. Saan works for a low-level Senator's aide. He saw how things worked on Utopion and figured, since no one was paying attention, he'd make some extra money on the side arranging for Republic weapons to be sold where they'd be in highest demand. He may not look like much, but he's the head of a smugglers' cell that diverts all sorts of tech out of Legion and Republic armories and into the hands of the enemy. Supply clerks and corrupt quartermasters skim from inventory, Saan tells them where to get the best price, and no one ever knows the difference. Except the Legion. We know."

The holoprojection shifts to an apartment building. A high-rise that looks like every other high-rise around it. The view zooms in and focuses on the eighth floor from the top.

The image becomes static, and Owens continues. "As you can see, our target is living much closer to the top floor than the bottom. There are questions about whether the roof can handle a shuttle's weight, so we'll get on the roof with quick-drop ropes. Secure the roof, move down the stairwell, and storm the target's apartment. We've got a strong feeling that this guy will be a talker, so try not to kill him."

Twenties raises a hand. "Is there a clear view of the apartment windows from an adjacent building?"

"Yes," says Owens with a nod. "We'll stop to drop you on the roof of the building across the street. You'll have an unobstructed view of the apartment's window."

I raise my hand. "We cutting power or is that arranged?"

"It's arranged."

"How 'bout security?" Wraith asks.

"Was just about to get to that, yes." Owens brings up another holo of the target. This time he's flanked by a pair of ornery-looking humans. "Our observer saw these two men enter the apartment with the target this morning. Neither of them has been seen leaving, so we assume they're in there. And probably not to play a friendly game of trexxo. Any other questions?"

We shake our heads. It's fairly standard, stuff we've all done out on the edge. Bringing in cell leaders for the joint purpose of taking them out of the fight and getting intel that might keep our guys alive. Only this time, instead of storming a compound on Grevulo, we're on the Republic's capital world. But I guess, when I consider what happened to us and the *Chiasm*, it makes sense for the problem to have started in the core. That's the only place where trouble this big *could* begin.

I swear, the Republic is its own worst enemy.

14

We had Kags set up with Twenties on the overwatch roof. This was his first live op in leej armor, and he was desperate to storm the apartment, but Cap made the call.

"This is just as essential to the op. You'll get plenty of chances to kill bad guys. Don't worry. Ooah?"

Ooah.

Our shuttle is hovering over the top of the target building. Doors open and quick-drop ropes uncoil to the rooftop like spasmodic serpents. I'm queued up to move first. I hear Wraith, our team leader, give the order to go, and I feel the squeeze from Masters behind me. I jump from the shuttle, slide down thirty feet, and land in a squat position on the roof. We cleared the area visually from the air, and Twenties and Kags are guardians watching over us.

Before Masters has a chance to follow, all the power goes out in a four-block radius. This will keep our targets in the dark, and make us a bit harder to see should someone other than Twenties be watching us from another building. It would have been preferable for the lights to be out *before* we started dropping, but my focus is on what's in front of me.

I move at the low ready toward the freestanding box where the service speedlift and stairs have their end. Both the speedlift and the stairway door are locked, but that won't be a problem. I stack up next to the stairway door. Speedlifts are faster, but if we were to get trapped inside one...

I'm crouched underneath the access pad. Across from me is Masters, covering the door. That way if someone carrying a blaster rifle swings this door open, Masters will have a clear shot through the opening. Makes me feel all safe and warm, seeing him there.

Wraith is stacked behind me, and Owens is behind Masters. Under normal circumstances, Cap would do the planning and then monitor the op. But we're still short one Exo, and Cap *really* doesn't mind getting in the fight.

I feel Wraith squeeze the back of my arm, in between the body armor. That's my signal to breach.

A door like this could probably be kicked in. It could certainly be blown in. But it's a good bet that the target doesn't know we're here yet, and making a lot of noise might just change that. So I pull out a roll of slice-tape. It's a programmed micro-carrier with an adhesive. You stick it to a basic lockbox, like an optical scanner, print detector, facial recognition cam, or even a non-military grade pass key console. The strip boots, connects to the host, and works its little restricted-AI brain off until access is granted. It takes all of five seconds for most locks.

This door takes two. I push it open, and instantly a ringing alarm sounds. Masters storms inside. Wraith rushes past me to follow. Then Owens. Then me. The alarm shuts off the moment the door closes behind me. It probably sounded only in the stairwell, so I don't give it much thought.

Emergency lights are glowing a soft red, and runway lights are built into the stairs, showing arrows for roof in one direction and the floor below in the other direction. We practically fly down the stairs, our weapons at the ready. I'm using an NK-4 for this op, same as Wraith and Masters. It's basically an N-4 with a slightly shorter barrel. You lose some range, but can get on target a split second faster, which can make the difference between dusting someone or praying that your armor holds. It's an ideal blaster rifle for close quarters. Owens has a surge shotgun, which is technically *more* ideal for close quarters combat because you barely have to aim the thing and anything it hits will be very dead.

"Twenties, do you have visual on the target?" Wraith asks over L-comm.

"Negative. I haven't seen any motion inside the target window."

"Copy."

We reach the target's floor and move hard into the hall, counting off doors as we go. As luck would have it, this guy is at the extreme end of the hall. A neighbor opens his door and comes out to take a peek. As I stop to get him to go back inside, I nearly piss myself. He's a vuline. Looks like a werewolf. Red eyes, sharp teeth. They're actually a pretty friendly species, more like dogs than savage wolves— good friends to have—but, damn, they're scary when you run into one in the dark. I push the vuline back into his apartment, my gloved palm sinking into the thick fur of his chest. He takes a few steps back, and I hold an index finger up to my bucket, the universal sign for "Shh."

His red eyes widen as the situation dawns on him. *Holy strokes, there's a kill team of legionnaires in my apartment complex. I'd better get back inside.*

He shuts the door and locks it tight. Good boy.

My team is stacked outside of the target's door. Waiting for me to show up and decide how to open it. I get in position and decide that more slice-tape should do the trick. Only it doesn't. We wait something like fifteen seconds, and the access panel hasn't given a green light. If it hasn't worked by then, it's not going to. Our target must have upgraded his door security. Smart move.

By now Wraith has called in to Twenties to say that we're getting set to breach and clear. Our suits should stand out clearly as friendly targets in his scope, but the information is just another layer of precaution. Stuff gets crazy too fast, he doesn't know we're in the room, fires a shot off... it happens. And it's a leej's worst nightmare. It takes four seconds to communicate over L-comm. It's worth the time.

"Slice-tape's not working," I say to my team. "Target upgraded his locks."

"No worries, bro," Cap Owens says, "take your time and get us in there in the next thirty seconds."

He's not kidding, and he's not wrong. Guys get killed hanging outside a doorway for too long. I have my bucket analyze the lock panel because I don't see any distinctive branding. My bucket quickly brings up the info.

Manufacturer: Premafortress, Inc.
Model: Protector 89E
Planet of Origin: Ellepses

Registration: Cantrell Saan
MSRP: 549 Republic credits or local equivalent
Display Owner's Manual? Y/N

The target registered it to his own name. I guess I can rest easy that we're stacked outside the right door. I decline the option to see the owner's manual. I know this make and model from the instruction portions of my breacher's courses. It's the stuff I read when I'm not training. You know, reading for fun. So this model has better than standard encryption protection, which is why the slice-tape didn't work, but it's still a budget model. A true lockdown device would cost about five times what the target paid. This one can be circumvented by cutting off its link to the door's drive motivators.

"Cap, gimme your shotgun."

Owens and I switch weapons. I stand up and aim the shotgun directly above the lock device. A surge shotgun at range will leave a dent in the hull of a Republic corvette. It'll blast right through the impervisteel reinforcing this residential lock.

Boom!

The lock goes dead and the door slides open. They never show you that part in the product demonstration videos.

Masters rolls in an ear-popper...

...

... and nothing happens. Dud.

We hear footsteps inside. "Who's out there?"

Crap.

"Go!" Owens shouts. This all took seconds.

Masters bolts inside and goes right. I follow with the shotgun and take the left. A human armed with a knockoff N-16 comes charging out of a door just in front of me. It's not the target, just one of his friends. I squeeze the trigger, and he spins and pirouettes as he crashes to the floor. "Dusted one," I call into the comm.

Masters's NK-4 barks. "Dusted the other guy," he reports.

I've moved past the guy I dusted and into a hall that leads to a kitchen. I clear a small bathroom on the way and call it out on the comm.

"Bedroom clear," reports Masters.

"Second bedroom clear," calls in Wraith.

Owens is behind me, and we move through a kitchen. It's empty too. "Kitchen clear," I call.

All that's left is a sunken living room. If our target isn't in there, we'll go back through, checking for hidey-holes. Owens leads the way, barging into the room like a caged agro-bear just let loose. Keep in mind, this entire process has taken us less than sixty seconds.

We see the target on his knees in the middle of the living room, his hands on his head. "Surprise, kelhorn!" Owens rushes the guy and kicks him square in the chest. "Stay down."

The man cowers fearfully at Owens's feet.

Owens holds a hand out to me. "Gimme my shotgun. I didn't get to dust anybody, and it's this guy's turn."

I hand it over. Cap isn't actually going to blast the guy, but this is part of how kill teams work. Most people think that if a kill team shows up, that's it. You're dead. It's a common misconception, and given that we're called *kill* teams, I get that. But the truth is we capture as often as we kill. Interrogations can often lead to more bad guys getting dusted.

Owens aims the shotgun at the target's head.

"No! I didn't know!" the target yells.

"Didn't know what?" Owens asks.

"I didn't know that's what the MAROs would be used for!" Tears are streaming down the dude's face. That's how these types are. They become sniveling cowards the moment you take the fight to them. "It was just out there to try and reel in some big buyers."

"Cap," I say to Owens, "this guy is a piece of garbage. Dust him."

"No!" the guy pleads, desperate for a few more minutes of life. Anything. "I... we thought if people knew we could get MAROs, they might sniff around. But then when we told them the price, they'd just settle for the other stuff. Aero-precision missiles and N-18s. But someone had the credits. Look, please don't kill me. Please."

Owens lowers his shotgun, and this encourages the target. "I'll tell you everything. I know the supply clerk who made the sale. Where the deal happened, the amount, everything up to the transaction itself."

"Chhun," Owens says, "pick him up and detain him."

"Oh, thank you," the target says.

Owens answers with a kick to the face that splits the man's lip. "You should be dead for what you did. You still might end up that way. Shut up."

I put ener-chains around the target's wrists, making them tight and uncomfortable behind his back, then drape an isolation hood over his head. He won't see or hear anything until we lift it back off. Being cut off from most of your senses for an extended period of time can break a man faster than you'd think, unless he's been trained to resist it. Most haven't. A lot of guys start talking the moment we allow them to re-enter the real world.

We turn over the apartment looking for intel. We find a hidden safe, some records, take the guy's datapad and holodrives. Photos, anything. Each piece is bagged with a unique serial number, and our buckets record 360-degree holo-renders of the room it's found in. That makes intel processing happen a lot faster. With the goods in hand, we turn the scene over to some basics who were set up in the lobby. They'll deal with the neighbors until the Utopion police arrive.

We climb back to the roof with our target, hurrying him along. It hasn't yet been fifteen minutes. The shuttle crew drop hand and footholds down along the quick-ropes. We clamp these tightly to the ropes, hang on, and are pulled up into the shuttle as the ropes are winched in. I'm still babysitting the target, and I'm pretty sure he's screaming at the sudden sensation of being sucked upward from a windy rooftop. Not that anyone can hear him.

When we reach the shuttle deck, I toss the target down hard onto the middle of it. With everyone on board, we leave to retrieve Kags and Twenties.

I'm feeling good about this op. In debrief tonight we'll review the whole thing, giving brutally honest but constructive criticism where it's warranted. I plan on carrying a surge shotgun with me from now on, because if Cap didn't bring his, that door would have needed det-charges to open. Something we all wanted to avoid in a Utopion apartment building.

But we got the guy. And I'm feeling confident he'll lead us to whoever gave the MCR those MAROs. And then...

... we'll make 'em pay.

15

You're Tom. You're in paradise.

The big reveal, as X would have called it, finally comes. It comes one lazy golden sunlit afternoon in one of the many lounges high atop the central conning tower of *Smuggler's End*.

It's time for you to find out the details and exit stage left. Once you know everything that needs to be known, you can disappear, Hamlet.

Can you?

Can Tom?

Yes, you tell yourself as you lie there in the night, the night before the big reveal, trying not think about her.

Who?

Of course... the one you're going back to. The mother of your child.

But as the moon crosses the sea beyond your open windows, as *Smuggler's End* sails on toward its next destination, it's Illuria you're thinking of in the night. Illuria with Scarpia. Illuria alone.

Illuria with you.

You get up and light a cigarette and stand on the balcony high above the main deck. You tell yourself that's just Tom. Tom's that kind of guy. The kind of guy who tries for the boss's wife. Girl. Whatever. Tom's a taker. And he takes.

And for all intents and purposes ... you are Tom. You've got to think like Tom. This is just Tom thinking.

You know she's up there, with Scarpia. Above you on his private floors. So you push those thoughts away.

The big reveal comes the next day.

"So here's our little game, Tom," says Scarpia. He's relaxing with a whiskey, ensconced on a wide couch. Frogg wanders the room, circling and always investigating but really just listening. Of course he has that knife. Lately he's always got that knife.

The writer who took all those creative writing courses at university before you joined the Repub Navy thinks... *The knife has been introduced into the plot. And so it is important.*

"We've managed to secure a real live Repub corvette we hijacked from the shipyards at Tantaar. She's a beaut, Tom."

You smile and try to look impressed, bewildered. That's a very Tom thing to do. To be charmingly bewildered. I mean weapons, blasters, armor, and military-grade hardware for rebels is all very fine and dandy. Even man-portable torpedo launchers. The occasional surface-to-space anti-ship missile system. Yes. Those are the kinds of things arms dealers and smugglers deal in. That Scarpia deals in bulk in these items was known. It's why you were aimed at him, directly. Of course.

So you behave as if you're charmingly bewildered, impressed even, by the man who hijacked a Repub corvette out of a shipyard.

But the game was to know the end user. To let the weapons arrive where they need to arrive. Then the kill teams, the legionnaire divisions, they could all arrive with the big warships, and everything could be had out in man-to-man combat and you'd be done with this op. You were only supposed to pass on the info. That's what was promised when this all began.

But a military naval vessel... that's a whole different animal. That's actually quite a big deal. Possibly bigger than anything X and the Carnivale were anticipating. Or were they hoping? It's all getting very blurry. The lines are shifting.

"That's... impressive," you manage. Because it is.

Scarpia allows a smug little smile to cross his face below the ever-calculating dead eyes he cannot hide.

You wonder if the eyes change when he's with Illuria. Or does he regard even her so coldly? Does she see something the rest of the galaxy cannot? Is that her special gift?

It's just the pheromones, you tell yourself. You can take something for that. Frogg probably does.

"And that's where you come in, Tom. We need to get this corvette deep inside the MCR zone of influence and linked up with a pathetic little ragtag 'fleet' they've put together. Believe me, it's all rather underwhelming." Scarpia's voice is dry, his manner droll. He takes a sip of the whiskey in the cut crystal tumbler he holds lightly in his manicured hand. "You being a navy man, you can manage the crew and get the ship there and delivered. Except you've got make a stop to pick up some serious armaments."

You agree to this, because what else can you do? But you do manage to probe. Gently. But you do. That's what spies do. That's what the Carnivale wants. That's what the *Chiasm*, and Camp Forge, and all the dead legionnaires were for. This end-user moment, never mind the casualties.

"And what is the MCR planning on doing with the corvette once I hand it over? If I'm handing it over?" you prompt in a very Tom-like way. Totally ever figuring the odds in your favor.

"Ah... well... thankfully we don't have to be a part of that, Tom. But it's going to be pretty big. The plan is, as I understand it, and now that you're in... why not. Now that you're one of us... The plan is to jump into Utopion with a suicide fleet, and then smash the corvette right into the House of Reason. She'll be loaded with a crustbuster, so there's a good chance we'll get a planetary crack out of this. In a hundred years, after the rads die down, whoever's in charge will have a nice mine on what was once the galactic capital."

Never mind, you think, the seven billion you'll kill doing something like that, Scarpia.

You do allow yourself to be shocked. You lean back into the sumptuous overstuffed chair you've settled into. It would be absolutely phony to seem blasé about all this death and mayhem. For Frogg, yes, that's his default setting. For you... no. You've got to have a little bit of self-preservation. A little of a *this-is-going-too-far* reaction. Got to.

"Oh, come now, Tom," says Scarpia after a sip of whiskey. After watching and gauging your reaction. "It's not like they're actually going to get away with it. Are you kidding? A fleet getting through Utopion's orbital automated defense network? Impossible."

"Then why even try?"

"Because they want to." He sighs in exasperation. "And they're willing to pay us a lot of money to help them. That's what we do. We provide the fireworks. Who cares if the customer blows their toe off? Or tentacle, in some cases. Not our business. We'll be well clear and living on our own planet after this. And I do mean the *entire* planet, Tom. That's how much we're making on this one."

You feel like you've blown it with all this concern for Utopion and the seven billion who live there. Scarpia was watching you. Watching for your reaction. Did he see Tom the guy who's out for himself and all the money he can steal? Or did he see the other you?

You lean forward. "I'm in."

"That's good, Tom. Really good. And oh, by the way... on the way out there I'm going to need you to take care of something. A *loose end* has come undone."

You nod as though there's nothing you'd like more than to do this because you're really excited to get to that corvette and the planet you've been promised on the other side of this little deal. That's what Tom would do. That's what Tom would want.

To keep up the character, to not throw up like you *really* want to, you think of Illuria. She's out there, lying under the lazy sun in the barest of bikinis. You think of her skin. Her lips. The husky sound of her voice when she says "Tom."

"I need you," says Scarpia. "To take care of the contact who sold you those wonderful bombs that took out that destroyer and killed all those leejes. Seems there's a kill team on his trail. Can't have it leading back to you." Scarpia pats your knee. "Do that little thing for me, and then we'll go pick up that corvette, Tom."

16

Our team finally has the all-clear to bring in Exo. So we put on our civilian clothes and take to the streets.

The sun is out. It's beautiful, actually. But the weather isn't doing anything for my mood. The last thing I said to Captain Devers was that I hoped I'd never have to see him again. Well, today was Silas Devers Day on Utopion. The "hero of Kublar" has returned to Utopion to receive his medal. The Order of the Centurion. That's the highest honor the Republic hands out. Ninety percent of its recipients are awarded it posthumously.

So of course it makes perfect sense to give it to Devers.

I don't get it. I mean, I *do*… I get what Legion Commander Keller said. The Republic needs a hero to make its citizens feel safe as word of what happened to us spreads across the galaxy. The real heroes are dead, or in Dark Ops, and you can't exactly tour Dark Ops leejes throughout the Republic. You can do that with Devers, and from the early press photos of him shaking hands with senators and representatives, he's set to be the Republic's golden boy for the rest of his military career. Which will probably last just long enough for him to be assured a place on the Council.

I weep for our future.

The silvene lining, if there is one, is that Devers is out of the Legion. Of course, even the way that was handled ticked us all off. The official statement was that the House of Reason felt their Legion appointee had done all he could do for the Legion, and thought the Republic Navy needed him most.

So they made him a commander.

Yeah.

Know the right people and you just get to skip right over lieutenant commander, apparently.

Twenties reads the holostatement. "Guys, listen to this crap. 'Commander Devers's heroic exploits on Kublar, where he led the battered remnants of Victory Company of the 131st Legion (officially decommissioned), were critical in saving the Republic Army support staff and other military personnel from an overwhelming force. Devers, who began the action with the rank of captain, was awarded a field promotion to major by his senior officer, Major Jorleth Hilbert, when Hilbert was wounded in an ambush of nearly five hundred hostiles.'"

"One hundred and fifty," Masters corrects.

"Two hundred tops," chimes in Kags.

Twenties continues. "'Once in command, Major Devers's tactical brilliance and staunch determination to keep his men alive saw him lead a campaign of evasion and destruction on the Mid-Core Rebellion and their allies...' Blah, blah, blah. It goes on like this for a while, and now he gets to get sailors and marines killed instead of just legionnaires."

"A hundred credits says he makes admiral before I make sergeant," Kags says. "I'm not telling you guys anything new, but outside the Legion, merit and service are a distant third behind connections and power when it comes to career advancement."

"You sure our spotter saw Exo at this bar?" I say. "Because I've gotta imagine he's in a sniper hide somewhere by the ceremony waiting to pop Devers in the brain."

Owens digs for wax in his ear, his massive bicep swiveling, making the tattoos on his arm dance and jiggle. "I should have popped that point's head off when I had the chance."

"This is the cost," Ford says. I can't bring myself to call him Wraith right now. It's odd seeing him without his bucket. He seems taller, somehow. "No one's ever going to know the sacrifices made by Pappy, Rook, and Maldorn... not really. They can get medals. They can have holofilms and books written about them. But nobody will really know. Except us. *We* know. And like Legion Commander Keller said, this is how we stay in the fight. Let Devers soak up the fame. It would be a loss to the Republic to have any real leej in his place instead."

We continue our walk, considering what Ford said.

"I heard they're making a movie about Devers," Masters finally says. "I wonder who'll play me?"

"There are a number of plus-sized actresses available for that part, I'm sure," Kags says.

"You take that back." Masters stops in the middle of the street. He raises his shirt, revealing a concealed blaster pistol, but we all know he's just showing off his abs. "I should be playing myself, looking like this. Captain Owens, I'm requesting leave now for when the studios start filming."

Owens calls back over his shoulder, "Just waiting for them to call and you got it, bro."

The levity brings back our spirits—plus we're all pretty excited to see Exo again. Kublar was some heavy rocks, and he's had to deal with it by himself.

I can sense our swagger as we walk down the streets of Utopion—which are not made of gold, because all the gold lines the politician's pockets. The sun is shining, we're all wearing Eclipse-Martin shades, and Masters is right: we look like movie stars. We're the fittest guys on the street, and we've got that leej confidence just exuding from us with every step. No, better than that. Leej plus one. We've got *Dark Ops* confidence. And it's confirmed with every look and smile that catches us on our way.

Cap nods at a cantina just up ahead. "That's the one. Remember the plan. I get to talk with him first. You picked him, but I need to feel good about him."

I'm sort of dreading that. If Exo is in a funk, I wouldn't put it past him to try and pick a fight with Cap. Just to make himself feel better.

A kid, maybe fourteen or fifteen years old, seems to recognize Owens. He runs up to him, and Owens gives him a credit chit. The kid runs off. Cap looks at me and says, "That was our spotter. Cheaper and more discreet than anyone we have on base."

Shortly before we reach the door, it swings open. An old man comes stumbling out. He walks right in the midst of us, we're all so close together, and sort of squints at the intensity of the light. Then he straightens up. He has the swagger, too, and I can tell right away that this is an old leej. Apparently he recognizes the same in us. He winks at us and says, "When did this turn into a leej bar?"

We laugh and go our separate ways.

Ooah. I love the old leejes. And if we didn't come to this bar for business, I'd ask him inside for a drink and a story.

I remember once, when I had just gotten my Legion crest, I was at a graduation ceremony and there was this banquet with former legionnaires. Kind of a big deal on the planet where my Legion academy was located. I was part of the first class to have to pass a low-oxygen assault course. Basically, they put you in a room with a fairly standard assault and obstacle course and then thin the oxygen to the point where you feel like you're running around on the peaks of Mount Witomco. It was awful, but I made it.

So that night at the ceremony I see an old leej. He's just sitting in a repulsor chair. That's a thing about the old leejes. A lot of them won't go for cybernetics. They don't want to be half-bot. They've got a thing about the war bots used with and against them in the old campaigns. So I saunter up and say, in a friendly way, "Hey, old-timer, ever see this before?" And I show him my course certification pin. "You never got one of these, did you?"

I was trying to be funny.

He looked straight at me and said, "You're wrong, Leej. I did get one."

Well, that couldn't be right because this course was brand new, and the leej in front of me was old enough to have fought the Savage Wars from beginning to end.

"When?" I said.

"Junico, 1980, RSE."

I felt like a fool. Junico, one of the final large-scale battles of the Savage Wars. Legionnaires dug into dizzying high mountain peaks fighting relentless Savage marines that just kept coming. And this old-timer was there. Yeah, he earned his low-ox pin that day. Anyway, I learned a lesson. It's great to be a leej now, and it was great to a leej then. You get old, but you're still a leej. Ooah.

We walk inside the bar. This place is dark, and the light from the outside stabs at the darkness like a solar dagger then fades from view as the door closes behind us. I can see Exo at the bar, nursing a drink, his back to us. We all stay back while Captain Owens saunters up. It's barely lit in this place, but Owens still has his shades on. He takes the stool right next to Exo and orders a bottle of beer.

The guys all keep to the shadows, but I move forward, watching everything from the side, because I want to hear what they have to say. I'm in the shadows, too, and even though Exo is looking in my direction, he can't see me.

But I see him. Exo looks at Owens as if he's in an empty bathroom and the dude took the urinal right next to him.

Owens doesn't say anything. He just wraps a paw around the beer and takes a long pull. When he brings it back down, he's bulging out his bicep like he wants to arm wrestle. Exo, even though he's wearing a spacer's jacket, can't let that go. I see him bring his own thick arms onto the table. Owens grins from behind his beard.

"That ceremony today was funk vapor."

Exo nods at this. "Yeah, it was. But I think that sort of thing's been happening for a long time."

Lifting up his beer, Owens says, "I'll drink to that." He drains the bottle and signals for another.

"You in the Legion?" Exo asks.

Owens pulls up his shirt sleeve to reveal a Legion tattoo. "Yep. You?"

"I'm done with the Legion."

"Why's that?" Owens asks, taking a sip from the newly served bottle.

Exo shrugs. "Just... buddies are all dead or stationed who-knows-where. Barely avoided a court-martial because of the point who got a false medal today—I think they lost the paperwork about me. I've got two months left on my enlistment. Gonna run down the clock. See what the galaxy has for me."

"Sounds like a good excuse to drink." Owens puts his beer down and looks Exo straight in the eyes. "But what if what the galaxy has for you is the bastards who blew up the *Chiasm*?"

Exo was about to take a drink, but he stops halfway up. The glass just hangs there loosely, like it could slip out of his fingers at any moment. He puts it down and swivels in his seat to face Owens. "Say again?"

Owens repeats himself, more slowly. "What if what the galaxy has for you is the bastards who blew up the *Chiasm*?"

Exo squints. "Who are you? Because I *know* you're not coming in here to mess with me like that."

Cap holds out his hand. "Captain Ellek Owens. You've been selected for Dark Ops."

Exo stares at the hand in disbelief. "By who?"

"My team."

And with that we step out from the shadows and greet our wayward brother. Happy to have him back.

Twenties shakes his hand, followed by Masters.

I pull him in close for a hug. "Hey, man, let the point stay where he can't interfere with the Legion any longer. Let's make these MCRs pay for what they did. The galaxy's gonna hear them howl."

"Yeah," Exo says, pounding me on my shoulder. "I hear *that*, Sarge."

"Actually, they let me keep my field promotion. So that's *Lieutenant* Chhun, soldier."

Exo smiles. "Well, if the lieutenant remembers, he owes Exo a drink for the time Exo blew up a tank before it could blow *him* up. So... make good, L-T."

I order a round for everyone, and then Kags comes in. "Hey," he says to Exo, "glad to see you."

Exo stares blankly at Kags. "Are you kidding me? A *basic* made Dark Ops before me? That's it, I'm out."

Everyone laughs, but I can tell that Kags still feels like he's not quite part of the team. I catch Exo and dart my eyes so he can see the spot the kid is in.

"Hey," Exo says, grabbing Kags and bringing him under his arm. "You fight like a demon dog. I'll go to war with you any day."

Kags smiles sheepishly as the bartender delivers a round of beers. I see Cap go for his comm as Twenties makes a toast.

"To Victory Company! Their sacrifice was not in vain."

We lustily repeat the toast and throw our drinks back, only to see Cap with his arms crossed. "Interrogators rolled our target already. We've got our supplier. Shuttle leaves in two hours."

17

There's absolutely no way.

That's what you tell Scarpia. Not Mr. Scarpia. He told you to call him Scarpia.

So you do.

You're inner circle now.

Which everyone already knew, and for the most part that was okay. Except you manage to see Frogg watching you. Like you've somehow trespassed on sacred ground, or robbed a child of his most favorite prize. Or... come between a pit monster and its prey.

You did.

And you catch that look from the psychopath that thinks he's your friend. So there's that.

But never mind. You tell Scarpia there's absolutely no way anyone, right now, and especially after what happened on Kublar... there's no way anyone is getting onto a Repub Navy base. Or supply depot. No way to take out a supply officer, dirty or not. Security protocols after Kublar have got to be incredible.

"Of course not," Scarpia dryly remarks as he holds his cut crystal tumbler up for Frogg to freshen. The glance of casual murder Frogg casts your way is enough to make you shiver. Except you can't. Not in front of these killers. These cutthroats. These pirates.

Shiver your timbers and they'll know you're not Tom. You scream this at yourself as you listen to Scarpia's insane plan to "tie up a loose end" on a locked-down Repub supply depot.

That's what he calls taking out the dirty supply officer. Tying up a loose end.

And there's some distant part of you, even though you are, were, *are* a naval officer, and you've commanded battery fire on unseen enemies, there's something you should feel about "tying up a loose end."

Outrage?

Nope.

Indignation?

Nope.

Nothing?

Check.

You feel nothing about casually arranging someone's murder. You even provide a nuance to Scarpia's plan. Yes, not to put too fine a point on it... you provide a nuance. To a kill.

Lovely.

And once again you try to tell yourself that you're almost clear of this mess and then the kill team full of big bad legionnaires can come rolling in to clean things up.

Keep telling yourself that, Tom.

The plan Scarpia wants to pull is to run a distress call from a disabled freighter that needs to dock at Supply Station Ootani somewhere out in the Jack Taar Nebula. That's where the guy operates from.

When he's not selling out his fellow Republic servicemen by providing the MCR with the bombs that will kill them.

But you don't care about that. No, you do. Tom doesn't. So you don't. Because Tom wouldn't.

Scarpia just wants to fly one of the old bulk freighters in there and blow it up on the hangar deck. You fly it in, and get off just moments before detonation. Just like the *Chiasm*.

Except they'll be all over that. Or at least, that's what you tell Scarpia. After what happened to the *Chiasm*, they'll be double-checking everybody trying to dock, declared emergency or not. No unauthorized landings allowed, and if there *has* to be one, it'll be watched like observation bots. Only by squads of legionnaires. If there's the slightest hint of trouble, they'll blow your ship to pieces. They'll blow any ship to pieces that seems even vaguely suspicious.

And, you add, do this same little plan again and it'll be a pattern. Dark Ops gets real interested in plans. Dark Ops knows too much of the plan already. And knowing more, of course, will draw more intelligence assets later in the operation. Whereas going unnoticed might make a difference. Could make it a success or a failure. The end game, in particular.

Scarpia listens in silence, and you're pretty sure he doesn't like being told that he's not always brilliant. That his plan is actually uninspired and bad. He enjoys praise and adoration. Not phony versions of such, of course. He enjoys genuine praise for his honest efforts. That might be what he would call supplying rebels with illegal arms and creating terror, destruction, and loss of life: *honest efforts*.

But who's to say what's wrong? Isn't that what the Repub House of Reason is always going on about in its constant march toward Social Perfection?

What's wrong with anything?

Well, point of order here, you think. Blowing up an entire supply base to get one guy is… well, it's wrong.

But so was blowing up the *Chiasm* and Camp Forge. And that didn't stop you.

So are you reluctant because this is wrong? Or because you feel bad about the wrong you've already done? Even though Tom does not feel bad.

So maybe that's why you're casual about getting only the supply officer. Maybe that's the win in this situation. Just get the one dirty guy, and everyone else on the base— what, what maybe about five hundred, give or take?—get to go on living.

"So what are we gonna do about this scumbag then, mate?" Frogg asks you. He enjoys this little play of yours only because it might cause you, golden boy, to fall from favor in Scarpia's eyes.

Hopes are high.

"You," I say.

"Me?" says Frogg with comically wide eyes.

"You and I are going to go in as freighter pilots. On a ship that's legitimately broken. We need rescue. We go through all the procedures. And yeah… we make it pretty clear we're down-and-out ex-military doing arms deals out that way. We've even got our own junky freighter.

Except we're not carrying anything we can get busted for. Then once we're past security, it's knife work. And we get off the station with a ship that suddenly works."

Frogg likes that because... well... two reasons.

The killing.

And it makes him the star.

He smiles at you.

You thought so.

Like a shark might.

Don't let them see you shake.

You're going in hot. The freighter that Scarpia has put together for you—or torn apart, really—drops from hyperspace in an uncontrolled jump. Never mind all the systems alarms and collision alerts. You're just barely trying to keep this tug from flying apart.

Frogg stares impassively out the front of the cockpit, studying the supply depot that hangs, as though suspended in the clouds, somewhere deep in the Jack Taar Nebula.

The main engines suddenly go offline, and you're steering by small bursts from the maneuver thrusters and maintaining forward momentum inbound for approach to Ootani Station.

"This is freighter *Hoplyte* calling Ootani Approach. Mayday. Mayday. We've lost our engines and have a reactor leak. Need emergency repairs immediately."

No answer.

The ship is shaking itself to pieces as the floating diamond-shaped station with the long docking tail looms larger and larger against the swirling maelstrom of the nebula. Luckily there's no traffic in the area.

And no reply from Ootani Station.

Other than that, most everything's going according to plan, and though you aren't much of a pilot, you've managed not to kill yourself and Frogg. Yet. Portside thrusters go offline after a circuit bus shorts out across the rear of the flight deck.

Frogg pans his head to look at you as you engage the inertial dampeners to slow your approach. His look is deadpan. His delivery the epitome of droll.

"Fun, huh?"

"Ootani Station, this is—"

"We read you, *Hoplyte*. This is a restricted station. Jump to Dulataar Reef. They have repair facilities to accommodate most ships. Good luck."

The inertial dampener batteries max out at that moment and explode across the rear hull. Just like they're supposed to. This too is part of the plan. Part of the show.

The next seconds are tense because all you can do is drift. Once you drift far enough to violate their space, all you can do is hope they don't turn the auto-turrets on you. And if they let you drift on by, all you can hope is that they come out to retrieve you.

Any other action is mission failure.

You're supposed to be a desperate crew flying a piece of junk. So of course you've actually got to be desperate and flying a piece of junk. Sensors rarely lie.

Frogg jerks his head to the side quickly. A quirky little maneuver that seems to say, "Well, that's that."

You reach over and flick the masters to flood the life support generator with space. This is normally done only in the event of a fire. There's no fire. But deep space has a way of frying those generators, and the station's sensors will no doubt detect a fried life support system.

A moment later the generator goes offline and the station looms larger. You try not to look at the auto-turrets tracking you.

"Ootani Station, we've just lost our—"

"Yeah, we see. Stand by for tractor beam. We're bringing you in, *Hoplyte*."

A moment later the powerful yet invisible tractor beam from the station grabs the freighter. Our ship reacts as though it's being strangled and rattled apart at the same time. The beam draws us into the gaping maw of the now-massive station docks.

Frogg pulls out the small blaster he's brought, wipes it once with a cloth, then pushes it under the seat. He stands as the upper decks of the dock loom over the freighter. Deep shadows fall across the cockpit, and the only light that remains comes from the few working instruments.

"I'll get 1D-20 ready. Meet you at the boarding ramp," Frogg says as you finish lowering the landing gear and shutting down the ship.

Out on the deck, three squads of legionnaires—all on station duty—hustle on the double to meet the arriving freighter. The Repub isn't taking any chances after Kublar.

At the bottom of the boarding ramp stands a Repub Navy officer, bored and uninterested. Because he can afford to be. Because he's got thirty elite killers backing him.

He holds out his hand for your manifest.

You hand him the data comm.

After a moment he looks up from the screen.

"Really, you're not carrying anything?"

You shrug and smile and do your best to act like you've been caught for something.

Like a *real* arms smuggler shouldn't. But you do.

"We came out of the cluster with a load of rice. Sold it all and we're heading back to Denku."

"*Rice?*" the officer repeats, not even trying to mask his disbelief. "Sensors indicate your ship has holds standard and hidden. None of which are large enough for rice to be transported in sufficient bulk to generate profit."

He says the word "profit" like it's something that leaves a bad taste in his mouth. Obviously you realize this guy is a point. Came from a made family and never had to do an honest day's work in his life. You hated guys like that. You got your commission the old-fashioned way. Tom hated guys like that, too.

And you're Tom. So it's okay to hate this guy. Because Tom hates this guy.

But these guys were always the ones in charge, and you learned the game a long time ago. Act like they're as smart as they think they are. Let them believe the lie for you.

"I won't dispute that," you say. That's step one: Admit that he's caught you. "It was specialty rice." That's step two: Try a lame excuse for him to see through so he can feel superior about taking the bait you're dangling in front of him.

He snaps his fingers, and a legionnaire NCO steps up quickly.

"Sir?" the legionnaire sounds off smartly.

"Bring in a scanning team and go over this ship. Use long-chain carbon detection. I'm interested in knowing how *special* this rice is. Or was, as it were."

You know the legionnaire just wants to execute the order, but most points can't help but keep talking. So that everyone can know how special they are. This one continues. "My guess is it wasn't rice. *My* guess is they were hauling blasters and other ordnance for MCR scum. We'll see if I guessed right in a couple of hours."

The officer turns back to you. "Until then… the two of you and your bot can enjoy holding."

18

Holding is a large room with minimal station services and some ancient bolted crash seats. This is where they send people to wait out the time it takes for the Repub Navy to get a scanner team down to the hangar and go through an entire ship. But of course you knew that. You were counting on it.

Frogg goes to check station access and begins hacking into the local network while you deal with the bot.

1D-20 is a standard maintenance servitor that specializes in ship systems. It would be an obvious choice for any freighter crew. And of course, a trundling bot like this shouldn't arouse suspicions. It didn't.

"Gimme the package, D20," you order the thing.

"Wot package, sire?"

For some reason it's coded to respond this way. With the accent. It was an annoyance the entire jump out, just not enough to get you to dig up a manual on its programming language and reset the parameters. Instead you decided to live with it. And possibly, if any Repub personnel get interested in this bot, they'll focus on the language and not a deeper, actually useful interest that wouldn't be so great for your plan.

"The one I gave you before the jump," you remind the bolt-headed bot.

Its visual systems light up in a programmed attempt to facilitate non-verbal interaction. Once, long ago, that had all been very important to the people who made bots. Humanizing them. Now no one cares, right?

A moment later a concealed compartment slides open from its grease-covered trash can torso. It wobbles back and forth, approximating some sort of low-bar joy.

"Shall I reactivate the ship now, sire?"

You sigh and ignore the poor stupid thing as you inventory the tools you've brought to do the job.

Two knives. A lock breaker. And two Repub maintenance tech uniforms.

"Sire?" persists the bot. "Shall I reactivate the ship now?"

You know the bot isn't capable of picking up your non-verbal cues. So instead of sighing again you say, "Not yet. Stand by."

"Very good, sire."

"I'm into the net," whispers Frogg.

You begin to dress in your maintenance uniform. Quickly. It's just a coverall. A moment later you roll out the folded hat and don it. You check yourself in the reflection provided by the viewing port that stares out into the swirling red and purple nebula—then you reach over, swipe some grease off the junky little bot, and apply it to the uniform, brushing some across your cheek for good measure. It helps complete the look of a tech who's spent a shift doing the pedestrian maintenance work that passes so invisibly on any given station.

"Where is he?" you ask Frogg as you slide the carbon-forged, diamond-edged knife into your boot. Are you really going to stab this supply officer to death? Of course. It's better than Scarpia's plan to ram the station with a suicide freighter. This way... some people live. And, you justify, this guy's selling Repub equipment to criminals and insurgents who'll kill Republic soldiers.

Killed Republic soldiers.

What?

Killed them. It's already done. And you helped. So it's just a bit of unofficial justice. But when do you come to justice? Is it when Frogg discovers that you're not Tom? Does justice come then?

You shake away the thoughts. Reasons. Excuses. You don't need them. And you're fine that you don't. Or at least Tom doesn't need those reasons. Tom just sees the end of things. To Tom, the big planet-sized payout after the arms deal is the end of things.

But that's not what you're interested in, is it?

"Level thirty-six, right now," murmurs Frogg, giving the location of the guy the two of you are going to kill. "Supplies shop fourteen."

You do the route in your head. Reach the core access system and go seventeen levels down. No one hangs out down there. No legionnaires. No blasters. Do the guy and get back to the hangar. 1D-20 should have the ship up and running, because the ship isn't really all that broken once a few things are set right.

As a former deck officer, you know there will probably be only two legionnaires on duty watching the scan.

Maybe not even that. Sometimes the leejes get called away and navy troopers take over security. Barely. Station duty is as boring as it gets.

And no one suspects the bots. Especially not a 1D-20. Especially not *this* 1D-20. It's a moving trash can with an annoying vocal interface and an oddly hopeful demeanor that only comes off as bothersome.

The ship's emergency takeoff will catch the Repubs by surprise, and the jump is already computed. It's not *super* safe given the gravitational field of the station... but it's been done before. The margins are enough to take the chance.

Or at least that's the plan.

When Frogg is dressed, he picks up the lock breaker hacking tool, and two minutes later you're beyond the blast door. The station won't know about it for another twenty minutes when it conducts a redundancy scan. Asynchronous readings will be caught then. So time, as they say...

You set your smartwatches as 1D-20 rolls off on his mission.

A minute later you've reached the main core's transportation hub, where a speedlift arrives. Another long minute passes as you watch the floor slide by. Then the door opens, and you've got eighteen minutes before the watch officer is alerted that holding is empty of her guests.

You exit the lift into what should be a duty station for cargo techs. You expect to see a bored tech, most likely napping. As a navy officer you've been to enough supply depots, retrieving ship's stores, to know what to expect. Instead you find three legionnaires.

And yeah, you freeze—because you're not really a killer. More of an assassin, you suppose. But even that is more theory than fact. Still, you know that you need the jump. The shadows. The rooftop with the long-range blaster rifle.

You need distance.

Up close and personal is more Frogg's game.

The legionnaires turn and dismiss you as just two more techs. They seem to be down here waiting to pick up something for the squads back on their decks. Maybe new neoprene suits, or calibrated targeting crystals for this week's skill maintenance training on personal sidearms. Who knows?

Frogg kills all three of them.

Like that.

Their first mistake is turning their backs on him. What they perceive as a small, chubby little maintenance sergeant is actually one of them. *Was* one of them? Yes. Was. He was too violent. A major. Gifted in hand-to-hand combat and knives. If they knew that above the dishonorable discharge digital stamp in his file there was a citation recommendation—Order of the Centurion no less, no award though, for the tunnels of Murlon—well... they never would've turned their backs on him.

Of course, if they knew all that, we would be dead. Not them. But they don't. So we live on.

The first one he attacks by breaking the man's knee from forcing it the wrong direction with a sudden and vicious kick. Legionnaire armor can't do much about that.

That guy goes down screaming to his other knee for the moment. At the same time Frogg reaches up and pulls, very gently, the center legionnaire, most likely a corporal who's probably seen combat all across the galaxy. Frogg just gently tugs on the back of this guy's helmet. The legionnaires call it a bucket.

You remember that little detail as the grim and sudden slaughter unfolds before your eyes. You remember that as Frogg moves through these men like a sudden storm of vicious energy.

As Frogg tugs on the legionnaire's bucket, the legionnaire—the corporal—instinctively fights it. His reflexes take over, and he forces his torso and head away from the gentle pull, fighting it. Which is exactly what Frogg wanted him to do. Frogg slams his open palm forward atop the helmet, forcing the corporal's head down toward the edge of the maintenance counter where the supply tech should have been napping. The downward force is so sudden and violent that the helmet, the bucket, makes a dull thump, but doesn't crack. But the guy is stunned. Frogg leans on the armor with all his weight while using the desk as a fulcrum to keep the bucket stable. Half a second later there's a small crack. A crunch really. That's what a broken neck sounds like.

You think that.

You think... that's what a broken neck sounds like.

The last legionnaire standing takes two steps back and pulls his sidearm. The standard legionnaire blaster they carry when not in a combat zone. This blaster is smaller, lighter, a little bit bigger than a pistol.

The legionnaire pulls it as Frogg falls to the floor and rolls straight at him. A moment later as the kid—it's most definitely a kid—tries to target and fire, Frogg surges upward and slips the knife between the small gap in the armor between utility belt and chest guard. There's just neoprene there. Black, thin neoprene.

One move... one quick move with that wicked little blade that was supposed to be only for the supply officer... and the legionnaire just lost all his guts.

As he falls to the deck, Frogg pulls the blaster from the kid's hands. Hands now reaching for spilled guts.

You can hear him moaning inside his armor.

Just like the guy with the broken knee is screaming within his. But they'll go to their comms soon. All of this happened fast. Unbelievably fast. But they're still legionnaires. Frogg needs to finish this. He has to hurry, or we'll be discovered.

With the small, still bloody knife leading the way, a little smile across his grim little face, Frogg finds the gap between the kid's helmet, they call it a bucket, and the chest guard. Then the throat is severed and the kid bleeds out, gurgling horribly.

You have seen many terrible things in your time.

Radiation burns.

Blaster wounds.

Torn limbs.

But somehow this little tableau with Frogg standing above two of the Repub's elite killing machines, this is somehow much worse.

Because it's your plan?

Tom?

But it's falling apart. Because Frogg left a loose end. He left the legionnaire with the broken knee to scream. And the training will eventually win out over the pain. Has won out. Because those legionnaires have comms in their buckets.

Tom would step in. Tom would help Frogg, because Tom would want these legionnaires dead. Because that meant mission success.

A blaster fires. The legionnaire drops, a black hole in his helmet. Execution-style. You look at your hands and see the smoking blaster. You didn't do this. Tom did this.

Not you.

Tom.

Frogg chuckles at your handiwork.

Frogg is the savageness the galaxy breeds.

Frogg is the reason there's a Legion.

Kicking him out was their biggest mistake.

Not because they needed him. Because they should have killed him. Put him down like the rabid animal he is.

He wipes the knife on his thigh and nods toward the access hatch that leads to the supply stores.

The target awaits.

The alarm sounds, because Tom wasn't quick enough in killing that first—last—legionnaire. And that legionnaire did work his comms. And the deck officer just got an alert.

So there's that.

19

Frogg still wants to find the guy. The supply officer. He's somewhere deep in the stores of the station as klaxons are beginning to wail.

"Is there another way out of here?" Frogg asks you. "Because we need to find one, fast. Two squads of leejes would be here in two minutes if I was in command." Then he dashes off into the darkness of the warehouse and you know the supply officer is as good as dead. All you have to do is look at the three dead legionnaires on the floor.

So... plan's out the door. They know you're here. There's one option left, and you kept it in your back pocket because you're that kind of guy. The kind of guy who's been looking for an out since this whole thing began.

That kind of guy.

Tom.

You access the supply administration panel and hope all the protocols are working. Because there's a lot of ordnance down here. And of course you've done this duty. You were once briefed on worst-case scenarios in the boring world of supply. And one of these terrible nightmares is an ordnance explosion. An explosion that has the potential to set off more explosions. In deep space, even with atmospheric force fields and star cruiser–rated bulkheads... it's all still quite dangerous once things start blowing up.

You manage an old override code that's still in use. Seconds later you're setting off the automated fire control systems and logging a report of live ordnance "cooking off."

That should stop the legionnaires dead in their tracks from storming supply. Damage control teams will need to clear the area first.

But that's not the main goal of this little maneuver. If the system goes through all its checks, it'll seal the emergency blast doors and activate the escape pods on this deck. Most escape pods have a one-jump capability, pre-programmed to the nearest base or friendly port in the event of the total destruction of the station. Since it's automated, it's tricky. Because what's the use in jumping right back into Repub hands?

Except you *are* Repub, screams some non-Tom part of your brain that's been starving to death. You're just a snitch, a spy, a plant, a mole. This is a deep cover operation and you're not really playing pirates with Scarpia, Mr. Scarpia.

You're not really you.

Blast doors slide shut across the yawning deck. You can hear them sealing in place. You pull your comm and try to raise Frogg, but he comes rushing back into the supply desk area just before the blast door to this section seals you in.

"It's done," he says breathlessly, ignoring the fact that you almost cut him off. You're sure he would've found a way out of this. He survives, at whatever cost. "How much time?"

You tap in a few more commands, telling the system you're trapped. The station AI will now attempt to save you.

You look up from the console to Frogg. "Legionnaires are stalled but someone has to be watching the holocams. They see us, they'll know what's going on and override protocols."

Frogg turns and begins to shoot any holocams he can find. The blaster whines as shots smash into walls and leave behind burning cameras. You've got to hand it to him: he hasn't lost his cool despite everything going sideways. You, on the other hand...

Your heart is racing.

Your hands are shaking as they fly across the console.

There's a real chance the legionnaires will breach and clear this room. Which means shoot anyone armed with a blaster first and ask questions later.

"I'm not Tom!" you'll scream just before some kid in legionnaire armor blasts you in the chest.

It won't mean a thing.

You think of the other pleas that might save your life. "I'm a deep cover agent for the Carnivale! For Nether Ops. I'm one of you..."

Sure you are.

To them, all you look like is a pirate. An assassin. An arms dealer.

Tom.

On screen, you receive urgent directions to the nearest escape pod. The directions are accompanied by repeating flashing arrows in standard Repub gold graphics.

A message tells you to make your way to the escape pod.

Down the corridor, a panel slides open.

Then the system screen locks, and your heart catches in your throat because if this doesn't work, that blaster bolt to the chest becomes reality.

Sorry... I wasn't really Tom. But you didn't know that.

Goodnight, Tom.

"C'mon!" you yell at Frogg, who's literally watching the speedlift. Half of you wonders if he's not hoping to blast it out with the first leejes to show up.

Half of you hopes that they *do* show up.

He follows you reluctantly and then skips ahead of you in a ferocious burst of speed. He makes the escape pod access corridor before you do.

You peer in. The narrow catwalk threads the internal guts of the station. It passes flashing maintenance panels and machinery meant only for tech access. But way back in, there's a pod powering up for escape.

Standard Repub protocol is for it to disengage from the station and then jump to the nearest friendly port. That's if the survivors indicate it's not a maintenance failure or a temporary situation.

Two minutes is all you'll have to tell it to do something else.

What are you going to tell it?

"In," you command Frogg and follow him toward the pod. The heavy security door is raised in the up position. It's a three-person pod. That doesn't make it roomy. It'll be tight.

Frogg throws himself in and you follow, finding an open gravity couch. The pod says, "Confirm there are no further personnel to commence launch."

"Launch!" you scream.

The door slides down. All around you circuits and systems come to life; the pod has begun the build toward launch. Venting operations hiss as the disconnect happens, and the pod lurches forward into the launcher.

"Hang on," murmurs Frogg with a sick smile. "Never liked this bit."

Then the pod shoots away, spinning into deep space faster than the inertial dampeners can compensate. Some loose gear goes flying around the interior. Something smacks you in the face.

You wonder if your knife is bouncing around. If fate is going to make you pay for what you've done. While you escape, because fate loves irony.

If the station launches fighters, you're cooked. You lean forward, fighting the gees and looking out the rear port-hole at the spinning station now receding into the swirling depths of the nebula.

"Protocol Alpha," the pod announces. "Life support operational. Broadcasting rescue beacon. Powering up for emergency jump to Republic Station Starlyte."

"We can't go there," Frogg growls through gritted teeth.

You pull yourself out of the couch as the pod continues its violent revolutions. Thrusters engage to compensate, but's it's having little effect. You're on the floor and pulling off an access panel because you've got to change your destination.

"One minute to jump," announces the pod. The voice is programmed to be optimistic because, if you were using this pod for its intended purposes, you'd want to get out of there as soon as possible. But one minute might not be enough...

You reach around blindly and find the main navigational computer housing in the darkness below the opened access panel. You run your fingers along its edge, looking for the data connect, but you can't find it. You try another edge. Nothing.

Your mind darkly imagines that it's not the model you're familiar with. That it's some direct interface that can't be disconnected from the pod.

You stop your fear-running mind as cold sweat runs down into your eyes. You again begin searching the surface of the housing by touch alone.

"Whatever you're doing..." growls Frogg, still gripping his blaster like it's some kind of safety blanket, "do it fast, or this thing jumps right into the biggest naval base this side of Antaris."

You find the data connector.

And just like that you pull it out of the housing. And suddenly you're not going anywhere.

"Navigational malfunction," the pod announces.

You roll over onto your back. Sweat runs in rivulets off your body as fear and adrenaline compete to peg out your heartbeat at its max do-not-exceed setting.

"Override," you gasp.

A long moment passes.

You know the pod's trying an emergency redundancy check. Hoping the navigational computer will start talking to the jump drive battery.

The next bit's tricky.

Waiting.

Waiting.

The base could be launching fighters. You'll never know. They'll just target and—

"C'mon," you whisper.

"Override accepted. Standing by."

"Set course for Gypsus V."

Waiting.

"Searching memory database..."

Waiting.

Visions of Lancer search patrols and trigger-happy pilots fill your mind.

I'm not Tom. Don't shoot.

"Warning! This navigational data may not be complete for current stellar minimum jump conditions," the pod reports emphatically.

"Accepted."

"An uncontrolled jump?" Frogg shrieks. This is the first time you've ever seen him display fear. "Are you crazy?"

You nod. "Not technically. But close enough."

"This is your plan?"

"No," you gasp. "My plan was to leave quietly. But then you killed those legionnaires. So... this is our only chance."

"You had a hand in that, too. And if it were a quicker shot..." Frogg watches you with cold murder in his eyes. Then, like some prehistoric lizard, he closes them and leans his head back, letting his blaster go to the seat of the couch.

You strap back in and realize now the blaster was pointed vaguely in your direction the whole time. Which is kind of worse than actually pointing it directly at you.

"Execute jump now," you speak into the ether of the pod. And a moment later the pod leaps away across inconceivable stellar distances. Never mind that you could be killed at any moment by some uncalculated obstacle.

Never mind instant death.

20

We're on Ankalor. Home of the zhee. One of their homes, anyway. They've got four. Most of the time those four worlds engage one another in open warfare, because only one world is the true origin world of that species, and each world claims to hold that high distinction. It's the opinion of scholars that the zhee originated on yet another planet and conquered their four current home worlds not long after the Great Exploration began. But saying so out loud is a good way to get knifed.

So I'm two minutes from dropping via stealth shuttle outside a zhee compound on the nasty side of Ankalor. Not because the supply officer who sold the MCR the MAROs is here. He's on some space station dreaming about what to do with his money when his time in the navy comes to an end. We can get him any time. In fact, we probably won't pick him up at all. A couple of masters-at-arms will do the job when the call is made.

I bet the dude cries the moment they show up to his office.

This raid isn't about him, the supply officer. He'll give us a name, and whether or not it's the real one he was given when he sold the MAROs, it'll be fake. And intel will trace it, looking for leads while we cool our heels for a few weeks, or rotate on another deployment.

This raid is a chance to short-circuit all that. Our friend Andien, of Nether Ops, says there's a zhee militia leader on Ankalor who knows the whole story. Knows our supply officer. Knows the buyer, who the buyer got the tip from, and who made the link and paid the bill in the MCR.

Dude knows a lot.

But Nether Ops hasn't had any luck getting him to roll over. The zhee they've paid to talk with him only report back that he'll talk when the Republic offers sufficient credits. And Andien's undercover zhee ask for more money on top of that, because after tribe and family, money is what matters most to the majority of zhee. There are the fanatics, sure. But you'd be surprised how quickly even they can be flipped if you wave around enough credits. A zhee can always use his knife on the neck of an infidel to win his salvation later on down the road.

I think back to my past encounters with them. Pretty basic control and urban warfare situations. Being inserted from the *Chiasm* to keep a new colony within the lawful confines of their approved state on whatever planet they've identified as a potential home world five. They're a lot like koobs, only more adept with technology. Though no amount of tech will replace the primacy of their knives. Holy weapons for an unholy species. But again, don't tell *them* that.

So this militia leader wants money. We're talking billions. A stupid amount, but at the same time, not outside the realm of possibility when you're dealing with the Republic. Still, that amount isn't exactly something that most agents have tucked away between the seats of their couches. The Senate Council or House would need to okay something like that, and by the time they really got to it, word would leak and the guy with the info would be dead. And Dark Ops can't authorize or deliver that sort of payday, either—not that we'd want to. Our preference would be to break the guy's doors down and go in so hard that he offered to pay *us* to talk. Which, incidentally, is exactly what Andien asked us to come out and do.

The shuttle is hovering high above our target compound, just to the south. The doors open, and I can hear the wind fluttering through, pushing around a few scraps of packaging from someone's discarded ration pack. Probably Masters. The kid always eats on the way to an op. My stomach couldn't handle it. It always rolls and skips until things actually start, and things get real. I'm fine after that.

"Okay, I see two armed zhee on the rooftop."

With a full team, Cap Owens is watching our progress from a combat sled positioned to serve as a quick reaction force. Just in case we run into trouble. It's part of a three-sled team loaded down with legionnaires. He's got eyes on us through a TT-16 observation bot that's flying somewhere above us.

Our HUDs show the two red dots, and we get a visual on them through the open doors while the stealth shuttle quietly hovers in place. I can't imagine how much it costs to make repulsors this quiet. A Repub accountant must shed a tear every time one of these is shot down. Thankfully that's a pretty rare occurrence.

Wraith answers Owens. "Copy."

We're all communicating over the squad channel of our L-comm. We don't have a name for our kill team, but we did have Twenties paint us a new team logo on our armor: a koob skull resting on two bolts of lightning. Let the koobs fear the survivors of Victory Company until their species dies out, replaced by something that will better serve the galaxy. Like parasitic flesh-flies.

"Twenties," Wraith says, "these guys are going to make running around inside the compound difficult. I'm thinking we take them out now and insert you and Kags on the roof."

"I can make that shot," Twenties says. "Probably best if someone else lines up target number two. I think I can get 'em both, but I wouldn't want one of them to go running down the stairs to tell their friends that we're here."

"Chhun," Wraith calls out. "You're up."

I pull out a secondary N-18 and lie down on the deck of the shuttle, the muzzle of my long rifle sticking out of the open door like the quill of a ryhnocine. I find my target and watch through the gentle bobs of the shuttle as it hovers in place.

Twenties, for his part, takes a seated shooting position. That's technically more difficult, but it's really about how the shooter is most comfortable. If this is how Twenties feels the shot needs to be made, no one's going to argue with him. The guy could probably stand on his head and still make the shot. He's that good.

Our targets might be chatting, it's tough to say. But they're more or less staying in position. Well, mine is. Twenties's target keeps walking to the edge of the compound room and looking over the side. I don't know if he's spitting or just admiring the bushes, but makes these periodic trips back and forth. He's at the edge right now.

"I'm gonna wait until my guy moves away from the lip of the building," Twenties says calmly. "Don't want him falling into the courtyard."

"Worried he'll knock on the front door on his way down?" says Exo.

Twenties doesn't reply.

I'm keyed in, listening for the sound of his suppressed N-18. My finger is ready to squeeze and end the zhee in my scope.

Crack-bdew!

I gently squeeze my trigger. My own rifle parrots the sound, and two zhee are dead on the rooftop. I don't feel bad. These zhee might not be in pitched warfare against the Republic, but they *are* militiamen working for our target. They've probably captured Republic citizens, held them for ransom. Possibly ate them. And if that wasn't on the menu, these are the types who fire rockets into the green zones of Ankalor. Just for laughs.

They say they do it because we're here. But we're here because they do it—plus a whole lot worse when left to their own devices.

Whatever.

Two less bad guys in the world.

"Two donks down," Twenties announces.

That's what we call them. Donks. Because the zhee look like donkey people, you see.

We wait to see if the sound of their bodies hitting the roof brings up any curious buddies. When it looks like no one's coming, Wraith orders our pilot to bring us over the roof.

This is when we're most vulnerable. A dumb rocket aimed from a window would take this bird down. A rocket that slipped into our open door would send us flying, and I doubt all of us would survive the blast.

But the featherheads in the cockpit are cool. They're pros. These guys are picked to fly Dark Ops around because they've got nerves of steel, showing unbelievable cool and calm in the face of furious conditions. Often escaping death by razor-thin margins and then going back to do it again.

With Twenties and Kags on the roof, the shuttle lowers into the drop zone. The compound consists of a single building inside a walled courtyard. We're hovering about as far from the house as we can, so close to one of the ten-foot walls that I could reach out and touch it. We're quiet, but even a system as sophisticated as a stealth shuttle can't prevent the dust and debris that gets kicked up by the repulsors.

We jump out, dropping five feet to the ground. When the last leej lands, the shuttle lifts off. It'll fly out of attack range, circling until we need it again.

So far, so good.

The building isn't huge. Flat-roofed and maybe eighteen hundred square feet. It does have two stories, so we'll rely on Twenties and Kags to clear the upper floor from the stairway leading down from the roof.

I run up to the compound's front door, Masters following to cover the swing side. My bucket's audio sensors pick up scurrying inside. A good indication that the zhee suspect someone may be outside. But just suspect. If they saw us for sure, they'd be shooting. Exo and Wraith disappear into the dark corners of the compound, taking an angle sufficient to catch any zhee looking to flank us from the rear entrance.

"I hear a lot of scurrying inside," I announce over L-comm.

"We're set to move downstairs on breach," Kags says in reply.

Wraith chimes in. "Chhun, blow the door. Don't bother with an ear-popper through the window. If they know we're here, the risk of them tossing it back out on us is too great. We go in hard."

I stick an explosive disk in place, then Masters and I run about eight meters to get clear of the blast. I press the thumb switch on the cylindrical detonator, and the compound goes boom. Dust and smoke swirl around the entrance of the building. The door is gone. My bucket can see through the smoke and into the darkened house. Zhee are scattered on the floor, attempting to push themselves up.

Exo is inside first, followed by Masters. Then me. Then Wraith. Two more donks hit the floor. Exo dusted one, Masters the other.

The front door lies on the floor at the far end of the room. The wall behind it sports a large dent where the door hit it, as well as a bloodstain from the zhee who was standing behind the door when it blew. That zhee's not dead, though. He's struggling to his feet and looking at me with those lifeless eyes. He moves a hoofed hand inside his cloak for something, and Wraith drops him with two quick blaster pistol shots to the head. A zhee knife drops onto the floor as the donk goes down.

A knife.

It was going to try and cut my bucket—and head—off. Given the situation, I'm hoping whatever zhee are left in the house try the same thing. I'd much rather run into bad guys with knives than bad guys with stolen Repub blaster rifles.

I move across the room—a spartanly furnished sitting room—to an uncleared doorway. I can see the stairs leading to the second level just inside this next room. I'll need to keep sharp, because that leaves a number of potential firing positions open.

"Target acquired," Kags reports over L-comm. "I've detained him in the second-story bedroom. Twenties is clearing the rest."

"Yeah, it's clear," Twenties chimes in. "I'm overlooking a banister at the top of the stairs. Second floor and stairs are clear, so don't shoot me if you come my way."

"I'm heading toward the stairway now," I say, glad that I only have to worry about what's on the ground floor.

The entryway by the staircase has a door, but it's open, giving me a clear view into a wide hallway branching off into bedrooms or bathrooms. Going through a doorway is the most dangerous part of clearing a house. There are two angles on either side where shooters like to sit, hoping to empty a blaster pack into you as you storm through.

It's a random cube shoot, because once I go through, I can glimpse left and then right to make sure no one's hiding in the corner, but I also have to watch to make sure hostiles don't pop out of one of the rooms to open fire down the hall. This is the place where a lot of leejes test their armor.

I move swiftly through the doorway, hoping my bucket's night vision in the darkened house will be enough to give me the edge over anyone looking to join the fight. I glance to my left and right, and see only empty corners. There could still be a zhee behind the door, though.

At that moment, one of the donks jumps out into the hallway, ready to unload.

My reflexes are faster. I double-tap my NK-4, hitting the zhee twice in the head.

But then my heart stops and a cold sweat builds on the back of my neck, in spite of the bucket's temperature maintenance systems. Because I hear a vengeful braying behind me, and the sound of the door being kicked open. I drop and spin.

A quick blaster bolt sizzles down the stairs, hitting the zhee center mass. It slumps dead in the corner.

"Yeah, you're good, Chhun," Twenties says over L-comm.

Exo enters the hall from one of the far rooms. We point our rifles at each other for a minute. "Oba, Chhun!" Exo calls out. "I almost shot you. One room left."

We take the final room, the one the zhee I dusted jumped from. It's a bedroom, and on the bed are three little zhee... I dunno, colts, I guess. They're unarmed, which isn't always a sure bet with zhee kids. I look down at the dead zhee and see that it's a woman. These kids just saw their mom get iced, right in front of them. No doubt her husband is dead somewhere else in the house, making these kids orphans.

"House is clear!" Exo announces.

I report the *exception* to Exo's report over L-comm. "Yeah, I got a room full of donk kids in here."

"We'll send in a translator bot to bring them to the nearest neighbor," Cap Owens says in response. "Is the courtyard clear of any leejes?"

"All clear," Wraith says.

"Shot-drop inbound."

Exo leans down to look at the kids. "Hey, donk kids, don't grow up to be like your parents. We're not the first legionnaires to lay the smackdown on some zhee, and there'll be plenty more of us in the future."

"Masters," I call over the L-comm, "swing over by the stairs and help Exo watch these baby donks until the bot shows up."

"On my way."

I hear the buzzing of the shot-drop grow in intensity, followed by a *whump* as the package embeds itself in the dirt of the courtyard out front. I'm looking outside, watching for a counterassault, but just by habit. We've got so many Legion eyes on us, we'll get the report of trouble coming long before it gets here. For now, it looks like the zhee are done for the night and don't feel like mixing it up with a crew that just took down the neighborhood badass.

"Translator bot's here," Kags says. "We bringing the target downstairs?"

"Hold him up there," Wraith says. "We'll exfil from the roof so the featherheads don't have to squeeze between the house and courtyard walls again."

I return to the sitting room and find Wraith checking the dead zhee for intel. "Anything?"

"Nah. But we should have some scanners along with that translator bot."

As if on cue, the bipedal translator bot steps awkwardly through the open door. Early on in robotics, someone got the idea that these bots should look like elegant servants. Most have polished metal casings, and higher-end models come encrusted with jewels that mimic various cultural or species-specific patterns. The Legion orders its translator bots in matte gray.

"Hello, sirs," the bot says. "What is your directive for this evening?"

Wraith points down the hall to the room where Masters and Exo are babysitting the donk kids. "There are some zhee children in the room down there. See if they have any family in the area. Escort them to the family if they're within a few blocks. If not, take them to the nearest neighbor's house and leave them there."

"Of course, sir."

The bot moves off stiffly. I can hear it conversing in the odd, braying language of the zhee. Soon it's returning with the zhee kids in tow.

"The zhee *deskha*—that's their term for young children—claim to have an uncle two houses down. I will lead them there. Will I be going alone, or under escort?"

"It's all you," Wraith says.

The bot takes a step back. "Oh. I see." It turns to face the children, saying something in their language that I assume means, "Come along."

They file out of the house just as two scanner bots float in, each about the size of a melon. These came in the shot-drop, too, and probably just finished up a surveillance of the exterior. As soon as they enter, they begin the process of scanning the room, recording everything and cataloging the dimensions and materials of all they see. When the report is done, we'll know how long the curtains were and what type of woods the rods were made from.

The bots flutter down and extract four legs from their spherical bodies. They crawl over to the dead zhee and take over for Wraith, rifling through the corpses for intel. They'll check the whole house for us. Kind of nice having a forward-operating Legion base in the green zone of Ankalor.

A boom sounds outside.

"What the hell was that?" Exo calls over the L-comm.

"Shotgun blast," Cap Owens announces. "Saw it on overwatch. Translator bot delivered the kids, and the uncle didn't take too kindly to it. Blew the bot's head off."

"Better it than us," Kags says.

"Copy that," replies Wraith. "Everyone upstairs for evac."

I wait for Masters and Exo to file up the staircase, then I climb the steps after them. Twenties and Kags each have an arm on the target. A sensory deprivation hood specially designed to fit a zhee covers its head.

What's this donk going to tell us?

21

"I'm afforded certain freedoms by the House of Reason!"

The reporter in front of us is saying it, but I can tell from the look in his eyes that he doesn't believe it. Not anymore. Not when a kill team pulled him off the street after a night of carousing in the green zone. No, he doesn't believe a word of that anymore. His red eyes still show the same fear they did when we pulled up in an unmarked speeder, kicked his date—I'm being generous using that term, because the guy we knocked over looked like he'd been paid to keep company with the reporter—into a fruit stand stocked with mullies and clot citrus, and then sped off after placing a sensory hood over his head.

We hauled him into an empty prep room inside an Ankalorian diner. A few credits convinced the kitchen crew to close down early and leave the place unlocked for us. We tied the reporter to the stool and pulled the hood off, flooding his senses with the hum of refrigeration units working against the Ankalor heat and the unnatural glow of cheap overhead lights, buzzing too-white and casting no solid shadows.

We're not wearing our armor. We're in our civvies, with only our shades, haircuts, and biceps hinting at our place in the Legion.

The first thing the reporter said, when he saw that we weren't zhee looking to chop him up in this kitchen, was about his rights as a reporter. He says it again.

"I'm afforded certain freedoms by the House of Reason!"

"You'll be afforded a kick to the junk if you don't shut up," Exo says.

We nominated Exo to do the talking for this part. Because he's good at it. Because he means it.

"No," Exo says, pacing like all he wants to do is pounce on the guy. "You know what? I don't want to hear this bleeding-heart journalist whine about his rights. Put the hood back on him. Guys like him are why I prefer jour-no-bots any day of the week."

"No!" the reporter screams in protest. "I'll... I'll calm down. I just... it was the shock of coming back into reality when the hood came off." He looks to each of the six of us, pleading. "I'm calm. I'm a professional reporter. I'm paid to be calm and factual. I'm calm. I'm calm."

"Okay," Exo says, bending over at the waist and putting his face within an inch of the reporter's. "Hood stays off. Man oughta be able to live out the last few minutes of his life seeing the world around him."

"You're going... to kill me?"

Exo shakes his head. "Nah. I'm not. My boss probably will, though. You screwed up, Steadron. You screwed up big and now we know about it."

Steadron, the reporter with the gray skin and red eyes, a ridge of pinched, leathery skin running along his jawline, Steadron of the Spiral News Network, gulps. He begins to sweat more than the Ankalor heat alone could claim responsibility for.

We don't actually know all that much. The zhee we caught isn't from Ankalor. His home world is Nidreem. But Ankalor has a larger Republic presence, so our zhee came to do double holy work: shoot rockets at the infidels and convert the Ankalor to the one truth—that the zhee gods created their people first on Nidreem. Which makes the Nidreem superior to all other zhee—the chosen ones. Any other zhee—and indeed, all other species—must be subservient.

Of course, if you're an Ankalorian or from one of the other two planets, you believe the exact same thing—except you insert your planet's name in place of Nidreem and fight any zhee who says otherwise.

But Steadron's not a zhee. He's just the guy our zhee pointed out. The guy who knew about the supply officer with the MAROs and tipped off the MCR. The guy who, for what I have no idea, got thousands of Republic soldiers killed.

The door to the restaurant's dining area is flung open, and Cap Owens strides through. He passes the shut-down line kitchen and into the prep kitchen. He's pulling a chair behind him, shades still on and looking like a hungry sand bear just woke up from hibernation. He practically tosses the chair in Steadron's direction, then sits on it backward, his arms resting atop the chair's back.

"I'm establishing three facts, right up front," he says. "First, you're Steadron Pawoe of the Spiral News Network. Second, you told someone something you shouldn't have.

Third..." Owens leans toward the reporter menacingly. "I'm the living embodiment of your worst nightmare."

Steadron stutters out an incoherent reply.

Owens holds up a hand. "We're waiting on one more."

Andien walks in. She's dressed in a core-world power blouse, looking like she just came from the Senate pavilion. I've never seen her like this before. Does she dress like this all the time? Whenever she's not in the field?

Why do you care, Chhun?

His thumb pointed at Andien, Owens says, "I'm not going to tell you her name, because you don't need to know it, and you're not *allowed* to know it. I'm going to ask you questions. I want you to look at her when you answer. She's the only one you're looking to please, because, us?" Owens looks around at his fellow Dark Ops leejes. "Our vote is a unanimous 'kill the traitor.' But her vote wins all."

"You're with the Republic," Steadron says, relief evident in his voice for the first time.

Exo leans in, apparently too caught up in things to remember the plan: shut up once Owens and Andien arrive. "We're the part of the Republic you don't want a visit from."

Owens nods. "A while back you told someone, Steadron, about a naval supply officer who had MAROs for sale. Two of them."

The color drains from Steadron's face.

"I... he..." Steadron begins. He's rattled and unable to control the tenor of his voice. "He was a naval officer. We'd been flirting. Talking. Just trading gossip."

Owens stares at Steadron expressionlessly, his dark shades reflecting Steadron's quivering lip like a black mirror.

The reporter looks to Andien. She's ice cold. No emotion. She just stands there, waiting. He clears his throat. Several times. Like there's just not enough moisture left in his mouth to do the job.

"Listen, I don't, I don't know what I did wrong. I spoke in a secured location in the green zone about rumors the zhee were selling for a pack of niks. If you want to know his name, or the name of the supply officer I—"

Owens stands up and hurls his chair across the room. He kicks the bottom rungs of the stool, sending it sliding backward, causing Steadron's spine to crash into a prep table several feet away. Cap then walks toward Steadron like a Wroemian bull cougar stalking its prey. "Don't *play* with me, reporter. You think we don't have that? All of that?"

He holds out a hand, and Andien places a datapad in Owens's big paw. Cap holds it up. Steadron recoils at the grisly holophoto. The dead eyes of a naval supply clerk, disemboweled with his throat slashed, stare from the screen.

"There's your supplier," Owens says. He brings up another image—an ugly, bug-eyed man with a snarling countenance. "And there's the guy who killed him. Ex-legionnaire named Grufua Cartyney. And I mean *ex*, not former. Kicked out when he should have been shot."

Steadron attempts to look away, but Exo is there to grab his head and hold it in place. "Don't make me pin your eyelids open with my vibroknife," he warns, adding a hissing epithet. "You helped *kill* our brothers."

Comprehension dawns on the reporter's face. The MAROs, the *Chiasm*, Camp Forge... It's the only story that's gotten any play since it happened. I see the moment when Steadron realizes that he's the guy who told the guy who met the guy... all the way to that damned day on Kublar.

"No!" Steadron manages, "I had no idea—no idea!—when I spoke to Tom that he would—"

"Show him the last picture," Andien says, her voice filled with malice. Maybe I'd forgotten that what happened on Kublar mattered to her, just like it matters to the entirety of this kill team. Just like it matters to the Legion.

Owens makes a gesture at the datapad, and it advances to the next holo. "There's your buddy Tom," he says. "Ex-navy with an axe to grind. Runs to the MCR, buys—thanks to you—ordnance he has no business having. He was there when the supply officer was killed. He's probably on his way back here to kill you next. But Dark Ops, we're smarter than the MCR. So you get to live... *if*." Owens lets the caveat sink in. "You get to live *if* you answer this next question to my friend's satisfaction."

Cap lets silence fill the room. It just hangs there until it's replaced by Steadron's ragged, excited breaths. He's going to talk.

"You're a lousy reporter," Owens says. "You make up half your stories, too busy chasing the bottom of bottles and the hot young men of Kublar to do anything important. You haven't told a real story since you spent six months embedded with the zhee of Nidreem. So it stands to reason, a guy like you, yeah, that guy isn't going to hear anything as big as two MAROs for sale from some zhee street junkie. But you *did* hear it from someone. And we think we know who. But you're either going to confirm it... or the *if* doesn't happen, and you don't live to see another Ankalor morning."

Exo slowly removes his service pistol. He's careful to stand conspicuously in Steadron's peripheral vision. The charge-pack primes, and the safety is clicked off.

Steadron looks around the room, searching for an ally. I get the sense he's about to remind us of the rights that have been afforded him by the House of Reason. But he doesn't. He slumps down in his seat, head bowed.

"Jarref Varuud," he says.

Owens turns around to look at Andien. She nods back at him.

"Congratulations," Cap says to the reporter. "You're one of the lucky few to meet a kill team and not end up killed." He looks to the others. "Men."

Masters and Exo grab Steadron by the arms and begin dragging him toward a walk-in refrigerator held open by Kags. The legs of the stool groan and pop as they're dragged along the kitchen floor.

"Wait!" protests Steadron as he's left sitting in the middle of the refrigerator. "You said... you said..."

"Said I wouldn't kill you," Owens says. He makes a wide gesture that encompasses all of us. "Said *we* wouldn't kill you. But I also told the zhee who worked here that we'd pay part cash and part meat. So they're gonna do the honors tomorrow morning. Sleep tight!"

Twenties slams the door, cutting off Steadron's screams and sealing him inside. I know that Andien said someone from the green zone would pick him up and remove him from Ankalor. I know that this is Cap's way of making the guy suffer—even a little—for what he helped accomplish. It doesn't matter if he didn't know, because he should have known better.

I know all this, but as I leave, I'm hoping that maybe the zhee day shift will show up a little early. That maybe Owens was telling Steadron the truth after all.

We're sitting in our squad room on board the *Intrepid*. It's a regular destroyer, a lot smaller than the *Mercutio*, but it's been designated as our base of operations in this sector of the galaxy. We're in the zhee cluster, the area of space between the four zhee home worlds. It's been about a week since we took a drop shuttle from Ankalor up to here.

Whatever kill team was on the *Intrepid* before us, they left us a pretty good pad. Enormous holodisplay, nice collection of games, adjacent weight room with cardio mills and oxygen controls. We're settling in, enjoying life on the ship. Appreciating how things have slowed down.

We've made the place our own and settled on calling our kill team Victory Squad. It feels right. We've gathered up what memorabilia we could from the company. Holopics of Rook, Quigs, Maldorn...all of our buddies lost. Kags was able to swing a deal through some old basic pals of his to have one of the blaster cannons from Pappy's combat sled recovered from Kublar—the Republic jumped in late to join the Kublaren side that seemed most likely to win—and shipped here. Its barrels are bent sharply in two opposite directions. We mounted it to the wall, with a holopic of Pappy below it. When we have visitors, we tell them how Pappy, probably with a tumbler bot still cutting through his body, hoisted himself out of our casualty collection point, climbed onto a sled to man the twins, and unleashed hell on the koobs until the flood pulled him under.

Ooah, what a leej.

I'm cleaning my NK-4 while Kags does pull-ups in a doorway. Exo and Twenties are going on hour number two of an argument about whether the preponderance of species in the galaxy should be produced as evidence for, or against, the existence of a deity. I have no idea where Wraith is, and Masters is watching something on the holo-display that his mom would definitely *not* approve of.

"So…" Kags says between grunts as he pulls his chin up to the bar, "why is the *Intrepid* sitting in zhee space? You hear anything?"

"I haven't heard anything," I reply. "You hear anything?"

"No."

"I haven't heard anything either," Twenties says, leaving his argument with Exo to chime in. "You, Exo?"

"Nah, I ain't heard quad stack."

Masters is too engrossed in his… entertainment choice to say anything. But I doubt he's got any idea why we're here.

A chime sounds as our squad room door swishes open. In steps Captain Owens with Wraith.

"Turn that garbage off, Masters," Owens orders. "My wife would drop a fragger down my shorts if she even *thought* I was viewing that kind of entertainment."

"Holoscreen off," Wraith says, not waiting for Masters to give the command. The screen goes black.

"Got something else for you to watch," Owens says, holding up a beat-up holodrive. "This doesn't leave this room, and it's courtesy our friend in Nether Ops. Who is single-handedly changing my impression of that organization. They want to catch the bad guys as much as we do. Or at least she does."

Owens syncs up the holodrive with the display, and we watch as an interrogation feed begins to play. A zhee, unrestrained, sits in a standard Republic navy interrogation room. He looks calm and unconcerned. A black bar in the lower right corner counts the seconds that go by.

Andien walks on screen. "Thank you, Jarref Kash Varuud, for agreeing to this meeting. It shows great trust in the Republic given our past history, and it's our hope that we can build on that trust for the mutual benefit of the galaxy."

The zhee gives its donkey-like equivalent of a smile. It speaks in heavily accented Standard. "The only benefit to the galaxy is to accept the four true gods and kneel before their first fruits, the Nidreem."

Andien smiles as if to say, "cute." She makes a show of scrolling through her datapad. "Be that as it may, we both know that's not the reason you're here."

"It is not," Varuud concurs.

"You have information about the MCR's illegal acquisition of Republic ordnance."

"A good day, was the destruction of the *Chiasm*."

"Man!" Exo shouts at the screen. "Screw this guy!"

We don't answer our brother's outburst, but I know we're all feeling the same thing.

In the holovid, Andien has said something I couldn't quite catch because Exo was shouting. I pick up her questioning at the tail end. "Is that true?" she finishes.

Varuud nods. "It is."

"And what's that contact's name?"

"Scarpia."

"Pause relay," Wraith says to the holoscreen. The image freezes at his command.

Scarpia. It's a name known to the Legion. He's an MCR arms dealer, a high-value target that no one has ever gotten close to catching, though more than a few Legion and Dark Ops missions have attempted. He's a ghost. And he's also the only reason the MCR even get close to making a dent in their planetary raids against local militias and police forces. They still can't stand up to the Legion and Republic military machine.

Or at least... they couldn't. Not until Kublar.

If Scarpia was behind what happened there, taking him down... it has to happen.

"From this point onward," Owens announces to the room, "bringing in Scarpia is the primary mission of this kill team."

Twenties is still staring at the holoscreen. "Do we have an idea where he is?"

"Yeah," Masters says. "Is that why we're not at Kublar?"

"Not exactly," Owens says, scratching his cheek through his thick beard. "But this is the place where we'll be in the best position to do it when the time comes. Ford, jump to the marked spot on the holovid."

Wraith commands the holoscreen to queue up a specified time stamp. Andien is seated, seemingly hanging on every word spoken by the zhee.

"But why here," she says, "if he's located somewhere farther in the edge?"

"The *Chiasm*—gods be blessed for its ruin—was, as you would say, the opening act. A greater destruction, a more glorious triumph, is being arranged by Scarpia. The fall of the Republic is destined to flow from the might of the zhee."

"And what is this 'more glorious triumph'?" Andien asks.

"This I do not know. But it will flow from the zhee."

"Then why stop it?" Andien asks, giving voice to the thoughts of my own mind.

Varuud splays his hand, as though his reasoning is self-evident. "The destruction of the Republic must not be accomplished by the planet Ankalor. When the Republic is toppled, it will be by the hands of the Nidreem, so that all may know to whom the gods have given preeminence."

22

You're Tom. Safe on Scarpia's ship. Safe.

Night on the *Smuggler's End* is a quiet time. Quiet and still. Nothing like being stuck in an escape pod with Frogg for three days' ship time. No, it's not like that at all.

So you lie awake in the night and tell yourself that no matter what the situation is, you're going to have a good night's rest. Because three days in the escape pod with Frogg and all his melancholy horror stories—along with the knife he constantly sharpened—well, honestly that got to you.

Six months' deep cover and your nerves are fried. It's to be expected, dear boy, is something X might have said. But never did.

And yet you think it would be wonderful, at this moment, if he *had* said that. That simple absolution could justify so much. Because internally you're coming apart at the seams after the rendezvous and the jump back to *Smuggler's End*.

It's to be expected, dear boy.

Blanket absolution would justify so many things.

Being Tom.

Disappearing.

Illuria.

Your heart stops cold when you think about her alone in bed. That's not true. It doesn't stop cold. It speeds and grows hot.

And so you get out of that bed in the wide cool stateroom that is the opposite of the cramped escape pod, and you pad quietly across the thick carpet to the balcony beyond. The night is cool, and the sea is covered in beaten silver. Some lonely island passes far off to port. There's not another ship out here on the sea tonight, and somehow that feels like the very picture you have of yourself at this dire, can't-sleep late hour. It is really you alone on the sea of the galaxy, and there is no known port on the map of your heart.

Is it midnight?

Isn't it always, lately?

You light a cigarette and push thoughts of Illuria away as you try to solve your two biggest problems.

"We're so glad you made it back, Tom," she said that afternoon on the landing pad. You could feel all four of her graceful green arms embracing you. You were awash in her pheromones. Drugged to the gills by the scent of her. The possibility of her. The trajectory of her.

And how bodies in motion exert some kind of gravity, that thing no one can really explain beyond one law describing it.

You once read a short story in university. Some ancient spacefaring tale.

Gravity is love in the swimming pool of the universe.

"Easy does it, my darling," Scarpia joked on the platform as the sea breeze tugged and pulled at your clothing and caught and tossed her hair.

Had he been joking?

"You'll kill our boy, Tom. He's been cooped up with Froggy. He's probably a half-crazed killer right now, what with that sort of influence."

Frogg smiled wanly at that comment as you were hustled below to the saunas near the pool deck. A place of privacy away from the crew. After all, things had to be discussed.

There were rubdowns. A medical checkup. Food, fruit, and cold liquor as your body was steamed and the grit washed off. The carnage on Ootani Station, and the escape pod afterward, slipping down the drains.

"How'd that go?" Frogg asked Scarpia, who made a face. Because of course we botched the job and didn't get away clean. In fact we left a ship and bot.

"Well... we got it half right, Froggy," Scarpia replied like a dissatisfied schoolmaster. As in, you tried your best, but clearly the material is beyond your ability.

Clearly.

The silence after this was enough for everyone to know that the botch was squarely placed on Frogg's shoulders even though you said nothing about what really happened. Of course, everybody—even Frogg—knew you'd saved the day. Knew that you made sure the two of you wouldn't be interrogated in some Dark Ops black site, spilling all the beans. Because when the Legion goes after you hammer and tongs, you confess.

Everybody confesses.

That hadn't happened.

"I'm so glad. Tom…" Illuria practically moaned as she watched you getting a rubdown. Everybody was there. Scarpia popping chilled pieces of gauki fruit in his mouth. Listening and talking. Illuria was going off planet for a shopping trip soon. She was very excited about the latest fashions. Scarpia smiled at her like an adoring father.

A rather informal debrief is what it really was. Down there in the sauna, once you looked past the pleasantries.

"I'm just so glad you weren't tortured, Tom," said Illuria again when the questions got a little tough.

At that moment, it was crystal clear to you that even if Frogg didn't gut you with that wicked little pigasaur sticker he kept on his fat little thigh, Scarpia was going to have you thrown from the top deck of *Smuggler's End* into shark-infested waters for seducing his girl by just being you. Tom, that is. Even if he had to import the sharks.

You smiled.

She smiled.

And you thought about…

Because you couldn't help yourself. Because that's what Tom would do, and you, after all, are Tom. Like it or not. For better, or worse.

Now you're standing here in the night on the *Smuggler's End*, a massive floating estate that resembles a high-tech version of some ancient pirate ship with a central tower that climbs up against the moon and the night, you're standing here and smoking while you're trying to solve all your problems and not think about Illuria.

You try to think of how to solve your—not Tom's—problems.

Problem number one: Find out where Scarpia intends to rendezvous with the stolen corvette.

Problem number two: Contact your handler and let him know that the kill teams have to come in now. Right now. They have to stop Scarpia before that rendezvous. Before the corvette jumps into the Republic's core system. Because something tells you that when that happens, all the planetary proximity jump protocols aboard that ship will be disabled. A screaming five-hundred-ton corvette will go in low and fast on the House of Reason.

And yeah... the death of the Republic a few minutes later.

There is absolutely no way.

You say that a lot. And it keeps being incorrect. But you don't see a way to get a message to anyone in the Carnivale.

And the day of the operation is getting close.

MCR officers, real live rebels, actually show up with their bankers at Scarpia's floating estate. And lawyers. Contracts are agreed on, and of course you're there, Tom, watching it all go down because Scarpia trusts you. Now more than ever.

Frogg's stock is falling after the botched job on Ootani Station.

You're the bright and shining new Tyrus Rechs. You never fail. You're Pericles. Or Agamemnon. Or Kurth of Dentaar.

The man of the hour as far as Scarpia is concerned.

So you're all there. Including Illuria, who's going on a shopping trip a couple of weeks before the jump to the rendezvous.

That night, to celebrate the contracts being signed and the transfer of half the credits up front, Scarpia throws a party for the MCR on a desert island.

Everyone is there.

The MCR buffoons all look so proud of themselves, and sick at the same time. Not that these guys ever do any real fighting for freedom. Still, they look sick because they're committed. Committed to taking the conflict to a whole new level. And aware that the wrath of the Republic, the Legion being the most common chosen method of that wrath, will come down hard on everyone it can find.

Few will survive.

But of course this too is for the greater good, the MCR cuckoos proclaim through toast upon toast.

And still there is no way for you to signal X. Because that needs to happen. Or... corvette into the House of Reason. And with that speed and payload, there's just no way of telling how large the fallout will be.

It will destroy the city. Of that you're sure.

Could it destroy the planet?

You tell yourself you're growing paranoid. Of course not. If it could, someone would have done it.

But you don't know. For sure.

You don't.

You need to tell X.

Pigasaurs are roasted over hot coals. Golden liquor flows, adding its own burn to revelers' throats as the smoke of the charred and salted meat rises into the evening. Dancers and drums are brought in from some foreign place to entertain. The beat is tribal and urgent. This party is life and all that is opposite of the impending mission of death.

The MCR officers guzzle and laugh, living as large as they can because they know there's not much more of it left to them... life, that is. They know they're finally poking the beast in a way that will no longer be tolerated. Something more than skirmishing with relatively unprotected planets. More than the *Chiasm* and Kublar.

Scarpia pours you a drink. "Look at them, Tommy. Fools." He's close to you, and drunk too. And the look in his eyes is pure neurotic coldness. No love. No empathy. No customer service from the galaxy's most affable and elusive arms dealer. Scarpia stares at his customers with disgust and contempt, and it's a good thing you are back, away from the firepit, among mephitic shadows that seem to dance across your faces in time to the drummer drumming for the lovely girls who undulate for the MCR officers.

"They've allied themselves with the zhee. The aliens will die for their cause on impact, and these rebels will die by the Legion in the fallout. What a joke." Scarpia spits this out with low disgust. "We'll be on our way to paradise, earning billions at a fixed rate, when they go to light speed."

And you're praying, hoping, *willing* him to tell you the rendezvous point right now, because the hour is late and now it's so desperate you might just hijack the ship's comm and try to get a message through, never mind the consequences.

So many dead. Those are the consequences.

But he doesn't tell you. And it seems, almost for a second, as his drunken eyes wander back to lucidity, he seems to know that maybe that's what you were waiting for.

The rendezvous coordinates.

Or maybe it's just a trick of the firelight and shadows. And the drink.

Maybe it's just your fear.

He smiles at you. Warm and genuine. Sorta.

"Fixed rate, Tommy boy. For the rest of our lives."

And then Scarpia wanders back to the fire and refills everybody's drink from a decanter of liquor so expensive a family on any of the best core worlds could live for a year off of the proceeds.

The MCR officers cheer and shout. Much of that liquor doesn't make it down their throats. Spilled onto the pure white sand of the island.

It'll all go down before the month ends.

You know that now. It all goes down that swiftly, and you have no idea where, or how to let X know to stop it.

The House of Reason and everything around it.

You head down to the beach, then back to the ship. "Tell Mr. Scarpia I wasn't feeling well," you tell the boatswain.

There's only one way to get a message through now.

Only one person.

23

It's Illuria who seduces *you*. Isn't it that way, Tom? Isn't it always that way? Haven't we seen this coming from far off? You go back to the ship because she didn't get to go to the party. It's business, dear, Scarpia had told her.

And she seemed genuinely hurt. Then.

Scarpia hadn't wanted some drunken MCR officer with nothing but fatalism and glory on his mind to take a shot, make a grab at her, and queer the whole deal. Toss away all that fixed-rate paradise.

"Bad form," was a thing Scarpia would've said in the party's foul aftermath.

So she'd stayed out of sight. Pheromones are dangerous. No use messing everything up over a girl.

So you go back, because she's going shopping the day after next on some pleasure world, while you, Scarpia, and Frogg take Scarpia's ship to begin the process of fitting the corvette with an untold payload, and then delivering it, formally, to the MCR. Care of the zhee.

Then everyone disappears to that fixed-rate paradise Scarpia has promised you all.

And if Illuria is going shopping for fine and lacy things suitable for Scarpia to display her in, then of course the operating and rendezvous timetable coincide with the end of her trip. Kill two birds with one stone. It's very Scarpia thinking.

All you have to do is find out where—once you seduce your messenger. Then get a message through.

So you return to the ship. Not because Illuria knows... but because she might deliver the message for you. But first... she has to want to.

Has to want to save the beings in that suicide corvette's path, and throw away all the fixed-rate fantasies of old pirates.

And also there is this... When Scarpia said she couldn't come to the party, why, yes, she had made that genuinely sad face. She loves parties. And music. And dancing. And food. And new friends.

But she gave you that look no one else caught.

The look that said... now. Tonight. Or never, Tom.

You're sure of it. It wasn't the pheromones. It was her. Wanting you.

And as you cross the waves out to the estate, Tom, or you, or whoever you've become on this night with everything on the line, you're desperately hoping Frogg didn't see her look too.

Because he's been watching you lately.

He's always watching.

And yes. There's always that knife.

The launch docks bob at the waterline of the massive float-ing estate. Most of the crew is either at station, or helping out with the party ashore. There *are* some on board, how-ever. And anything out of the ordinary will be noticed and reported. If it is seen.

But you've gotten good at being unseen. Who has seen through Tom?

And of course... this is as dangerous as it gets. This is where Scarpia has you thrown from the ship when you're far out at sea. In imported shark–infested waters with no place to swim and no Carnivale men in black to come and pull you out.

No kill teams to stop the impending loss of Republic life, or flip the board to start eliminating the lives of the Republic's enemies, either.

Or maybe...

No. That's why you have to do this. So they'll know.

And that's got to happen because someone—*two* someones from your other life; yours, not Tom's—why, they're *on* Utopion. Sub-luxury housing, courtesy Nether Ops. Very nice, just not Senate Council nice. They're wait-ing for you to come home from the wars.

Maybe it will be Frogg with the knife.

What?

Instead of the rented sharks out in deep waters.

Oh. No. Frogg's stock has fallen.

But this is how someone like Frogg gets back in tight with Scarpia, Tom.

Yes. It is. I'll be careful.

So it's vital that no one sees anything that shouldn't be seen right now, aboard the mostly quiet *Smuggler's End*. The perfect scenario is that somehow she's swimming in the pool. You imagine that. The water shimmering in blue and her in nothing beneath the water. You imagine that because she knows you're coming back for her. Has known it. Has really arranged it.

Because isn't she in charge, Tom?

Someone's got to be in charge in all of this, and it may as well be her. She's the only one who isn't a cutthroat and a killer. She only enjoys their company. And that's been the autobiography of your life these last six months.

In the company of cutthroats and killers.

Someone has to be in charge because you don't need to hear that it's all not going according to plan. You don't want to hear that the fate of the House of Reason, and the city on Utopion built around it, and perhaps the Republic itself, is actually dependent on your seducing a concubine. Because if the universe abhors a vacuum then we certainly can't imagine what it abhors about the fate of all those people.

It's hard not think of her body as you thread the through the ship, passing large maintenance rooms and dark storage bays kept in clean and neat order where all the toys wait.

And then another thought occurs.

Everyone is headed back here tonight.

Why not blow up the ship with Scarpia, Frogg, and all the MCR generals on board? Kinda solves the problem, doesn't it, Tom, or whoever you are?

Except it really doesn't, because no one knows what happens next. No one knows back at the Carnivale that the MCR has pitched so many of its resources—really to the point where this is their one shot—to buy enough dark market payloads, the stuff that makes MAROs look like fire-poppers, and stuff a stolen corvette full of it. Big enough to carry the load, still fast enough to get through if the jump takes you to the edge of the planet. Destroy the House of Reason and thereby destroy the surrounding city for the next atomic half-life hundred years.

No one knows about that plan anywhere in the Republic. But the MCR and their zhee buddies do. And they won't forget just because some of their officers and their arms dealers croak. In fact, they'll be stronger, won't they? Because then all they have to do is track down where Scarpia hid the thing amid the ruin of his financial empire, and the invoice is no longer due.

If the MCR was smart, you think, *they'd* blow this ship up with Scarpia inside it. But they're not.

And that's good, you tell yourself.

You enter the main deck. The "pleasure dome," as Frogg has called it in the past. Nothing is there waiting for you except the lonely deck chairs and the shimmering waters of the pool, gently undulating in the night as though someone has only recently swum and then left. You hear the quiet lap of the water against the sides of the beautiful pool. The light shifting beneath the water is somehow comforting. A perfect oblivion to drown yourself in.

For what you did.

For what you're about to do.

You weren't really going to seduce a woman not your wife in order to save the Republic, were you?

Tom?

Were you?

And you certainly weren't going to enjoy it.

Tom?

Tom has nothing to say. And that bothers you for so many reasons.

Illuria is nowhere to be seen. That's for the best, because your marriage is safe. It's just that all those people on Utopion are dead.

You light a cigarette and contemplate the technical difficulties of how to blow the *Smuggler's End*, with yourself on board. Because that's the last option. The only option.

You're thinking about the end of you when you notice the delicate, perfect wet footprints that lead away from the pool's edge.

Leading to the sauna.

As though she saw the launch leave the island and knew it was you coming for her. Finally.

She is in control.

You cast a furtive glance over your shoulder, Tom, at that island. No other launches. And even here, across the water, you can hear the drum and bass meltdown of the party to end all parties in full swing over there.

You have a little girl. A wife. You're a naval officer.

And a spy.

Those people *will* die.

So Tom walks into the sauna area where it's cool and dark and the echo of his footsteps on the tile is what walking into hell alone must sound like.

And you find her there. Waiting, as though this moment were seen coming from far off, from the very first moment when she said your name.

Tom.

"Are you worried?" you ask her. After. The two of you lying entwined on the rich fragrant planks of the heated sauna.

But regretful really seems to be the word you meant instead of "worried."

Because that's where you, not Tom, are at. Because even if you save the Republic and prevent that corvette from smashing into the House of Reason on Utopion... well, you will have to tell the mother of your daughter about this.

Will I? you ask yourself. Because it wasn't you. It was Tom. Tom committed adultery. Not you.

Tom can't commit adultery. Tom's not married.

This is all you. You did this. Not Tom.

You.

Own it.

So you'll tell her. Your wife. And she'll know the breaking point of your fidelity. All those people. But she'll wonder, if she takes you back in. She'll always wonder. What if it was half as many? What if it was just one life? What if it was because you wanted an excuse?

You take a drag off of your cigarette and hate yourself. If only for the idiotic notion that you could ever save what you had. It's really all gone now. Worse than what Utopion might be. Whatever you once were... it's gone.

And then there are things you'll never be able to tell her because details hurt. So you'll live with the pleasure, and the pain. And because Illuria, lost and happy Illuria, strokes your chest and you feel her tears on your skin. And she keeps whispering the name, that name that is not you, over and over as though it is a destination on a map she keep within her heart. Softly, in that velvety deep voice of hers.

You can't ever imagine forgetting her.

It's not as easy as it all looks, Tom. You.

"Illuria..." You speak softly. Softly because your voices echo in the deeps of the sauna complex.

This is as dangerous as it gets.

"Illuria..." you begin again.

She looks up at you with those dark doe eyes that you will never, ever forget. Not because of the pheromones you're drowning in. Not because of the six months of fear and terror, and the running down an alley being chased by mindless killers, monster donkeys known as the zhee. And all that time waiting for the math to work out in Frogg's head and for him to start cutting on you. And knowing you'll have no way to defend yourself from something that's more dangerous and vicious than it is human. And all the other late-night arms deals with killers and cutthroats who'd just as soon take your life as opposed to parting with their dirty, blood-covered credits. And pieces-of-junk freighters to forgotten end-of-nowheres so that you can, as X said, "Sink good and well, into the muck of the galactic underworld, my dear boy."

Not because of all that and so much more.

But because she sees you for whoever it is you are right now. Not Tom. Not you. Not the Nether Ops patsy.

She sees you as you when you found her in the sauna and she beckoned you to her, promising some other kind of oblivion. Promising to go all the way there with you.

And you surrendered and roared into her... as all that darkness disappeared.

"Yes," she says up at you in the quiet of the sauna. A pipe somewhere gently hisses.

"He's a monster," you say.

"Yes," she replies. "I know."

You sigh. You sigh because finally... after all this time out here beyond the perimeter, all alone, deep in a cover you've lost yourself in, finally you have an ally. One person you can tell the truth to.

"You've got to help me stop him," you whisper.

"I know, Tom."

Her voice is small, and frightened.

A chartered freighter takes Illuria away the next afternoon. You watch from your room. Staying well away from the window. Its thrusters fire as the repulsors lift the well-cut craft off the landing platform, and then it's speeding off toward the sun, and some jump to one of the core worlds for unlimited shopping. Nothing's too much for the great man's concubine.

Illuria will get your message through.

Now that you know where the rendezvous is going down.

You know now.

You've given her an actual handwritten message and a dead drop on the RepubNet to get it through to. Any hotel concierge will be able to accomplish that for such a pretty woman. Even without the pheromones.

"Is there anything else we can do to make your stay at the Epsilon Maximus more enjoyable, Miss...?"

Illuria in gorgeous silk, every eye in the lobby either coveting or outright lusting after her. The bodyguards Scarpia has hired to carry her packages keeping a respectful distance.

"Oh..." She leans in close. Smiling. The man's skin flushes. The guards know this is how she is. It's why people bend over backward for her. "Could you possibly send this message for me?"

Unseen, she presses it into the concierge's hands.

If the guards do see, they'll think it's a tip. Commerce. Business. To ensure proper service.

"Of course," the man says, his voice catching in his throat. "I'll take care of it personally."

And that's all you have to do, you've told her. Not Tom, because Tom would want the fixed rate. *You* told this to Illuria. Get the message through.

And so as the ship is well and gone from the deck of *Smuggler's End*, this is what you're hoping. Because that's all you've got now.

The MCR generals were gone in the morning.

The morning after, as you lay in bed. Exhausted and still smelling of her. Thinking of her.

You return to your room, take a shower, and try to remember the other people, the people in your real life.

But all you can think of is brave Illuria, beneath you and on her way to save the Republic.

And the message she carries.

Sign and countersign code words. *Hijacked corvette rendezvous with target in Makchuria. Stop at all costs. Will be used in terror incident on Utopion. Immediate use of kill teams recommended. Highest priority.*

The water in the shower cascades off you. But you're not even you anymore.

It's like you never were.

The mood is somber in Illuria's absence. And for a second, as you wander the quiet ship, you see Frogg in the gym working out. The look on his face determined. Far away. Murderous.

Vicious and dangerous.

And then he sees you and smiles back. Suddenly. But not sincerely. That's all gone now.

Maybe that's just your guilt.

Maybe.

You find Scarpia, or rather he finds you.

"Tom!" he cries almost too emphatically behind dark sunglasses. "Missed you last night. And this morning. Luria says goodbye."

Is he watching your face for a reaction?

She told you. Told you where the rendezvous was going down because she knew. Because he'd told her. And then she told you after you asked her to help you. During. One last time for the both of you with the lie that there would be another time on the other side of this.

"Tom... I know..." she whimpered.

But you didn't care at that moment because you were drowning in her and trying somehow to make it all right one more time. Or make it, that other life that you really are, go away.

"It'll be at Makchuria," she cried.

You tell Scarpia you weren't feeling well.

"Well, Tom..."

No "dear boy." Uh-oh.

"We'll be jumping out tonight. Got to prepare to make the rendezvous. Be ready. And frankly..." He pulls you aside on the pool deck. Within sight of the sauna.

Where she told you everything.

Where you promised more than you should.

Did she really believe you?

"You're the only one I trust, Tom. Froggy's getting a little weird lately. Just between you and me. I don't expect anything to go sideways, but you never can tell with these rebel types. They might want to keep as much money as they can. So bring any weapons from the locker you think you need, and a couple of holdouts. There's been a development..."

You raise your eyes.

You wonder if the water was hot enough to wash the scent of Illuria from you. And then there's that other part that never wants it to go away.

He, Scarpia, must be rife with her.

You don't treat me the way he does, she said. *To him I'm just a toy, Tom. With you... I am real.*

"The zhee are insisting that they not only crew the ship, but bring an entire battalion on board. Smelly, dangerous things'll be armed to the teeth in the best gear and tactical equipment I could sell them, and it'll all be a big old waste."

"Why?"

"Suicide battalion, Tommy. They consider this mission so great an honor, so important, that they'll be there until their last moment of existence. That way the Legion can't storm the ship before it hits, and they get to live vaingloriously in the next chapters of their holy books. Not that the Legion would have had the time to board the ship had *my* plan been followed to begin with. But... I'm in the business of pleasing my customers. And this is what they want."

So there's that.

And later that evening Scarpia's ship comes in and everyone boards. Gear and all. It feels like the end of all things. Or rather... the beginning of the end of all things.

Everyone, even you, Tom, is silent. Grim and determined.

Dangerous and vicious.

24

I'm crouched outside a blast door leading to the bridge of a Republic corvette, attaching two red bands of det propulsions. Blowing a door inside a starship is a tricky proposition. You're in a confined space, and the blast has to go somewhere. The hope is the force of it blows the door into the bridge. But these doors are tough, designed to withstand an incredible amount of force, because they're ours. You sort of don't figure to fight against your own tech. But maybe that's a chink in planning. We should have.

There are slice-boxes and override commands, but these security systems have redundancies and protections. Meaning that if the right person were to be on the bridge, they could stop any override command. An independent slice-box could take upwards of forty-five minutes, if not longer. And by my bucket's internal chrono, we've got exactly eight minutes, twenty-eight seconds left before mission failure.

So blowing the door is the only option. And while six det-bricks would do the trick, I can't guarantee the blast wouldn't wreck us as we hide behind bulkheads. Or worse still, tear open the hull so we get sucked out into the vacuum of space. Some good we'll do out there—six floating leejes in the darkness, waiting to die of oxygen deprivation.

That's what this det propulsion band is for. It works like a rocket booster. I attach it to the door, doubling up to make sure, and when triggered, it will shoot a constant propulsion. So much force that the door's internal mechanisms are forcibly reversed. As if a giant grabbed the thing and forced it open, locks and gear brakes be damned.

My hands are trembling. I should be cool, I remind myself. But we went through hell just to get to the bridge.

Masters was dusted almost immediately. Moments after we breached and landed on the deck. Too many zhee. We cleared the corridors and breached the engine room. That's what ate up most of our time. By the time the disabling charges shut the corvette's engines down, we had only twenty minutes to spare. And we lost Wraith to injury. So he's sitting back there with a pistol in each hand, popping any zhee that come looking.

It's a matter of survival now. How long can we make it? Can we get the job done in the time we have left?

Captain Owens made it clear: we do this or we die trying. No second chances. No Quick Reaction Force.

I get the det propulsion bands in place and signal for the operational members of the team to get back. I run behind the nearest bulkhead and activate the device. "Going hot!"

The corridor fills with the white-orange glow of the bands' localized thrust. Smoke billows, and our buckets change optics so we can see through it. Filters work. I smell no trace of what's going on outside. Within a second, the blast door's internal mechanisms groan. The groaning culminates in a snap, then the sound of gears being stripped out as the sheer power of the bands pushes the door open.

"That's an opening!" Exo calls out. He tosses a fragger through the open door just as I kill the propulsion bands.

Boom!

I follow Exo into the breach. The door is maybe half open, still plenty wide for a leej to move through. Exo fires once, and a cacophony of return fire sounds from within the bridge. A blaster bolt hits Exo square in the bucket, and he goes down hard. I want to stop and pick my buddy up, pull his body out of the line of fire, but that'll just get me killed, too. So I rush in past him, firing my NK-4 and dropping three zhee, all of them firing from the hip, in rapid succession.

These guys are barely aiming. They trust their gods to guide their bullets. Exo just wasn't lucky.

No time to dwell on him. I assess the room. There's hardly any crew, just a few humans in MCR uniforms. Where helmsmen, navigators, and sensor techs should be stationed, I see only armed zhee, their dead eyes lusting for my death.

The fragger Exo threw landed just to the right of the door. There's a ring of dead bad guys where it detonated. I dive in their direction, because the incoming fire is too hot for me to survive standing up and shooting it out. Kags and Twenties haven't come through the door yet, though they're still showing up in my HUD as in the fight. My only thought is that the zhee fire is so thick through the door, they just can't move.

I don't have a lot of room to maneuver myself. I duck behind a sensory relay station. It's being chewed up by blaster fire, but it's something. I pull out a fragger and toss it toward the zhee. I'm up the next second, firing my blaster rifle on full auto. That means I won't have much time before my charge pack goes black, but my hope is the firepower is enough to let Twenties and Kags join the fight.

One of the zhee stoops to pick up the fragger. A better choice would have been to kick it away, because it explodes and blows off his arm and donkey face. A few more of the aliens go down from the secondary fragmentation blast. Pieces of shrapnel pepper my armor, and the pain issuing from between my shoulder and chest boards tells me some of it got through.

Stupid. But at the same time, I'm not sure what else I could have done.

I keep firing as Kags and Twenties burst in. Twenties reaches my position, but Kags gets lit up, taking multiple blaster shots. My HUD shows him as dead before hitting the ground. Twenties and I are both hugging the relay station for whatever cover it can provide, but the donks are whittling it down with blaster fire.

"Changing packs," I announce, dropping my spent blaster pack and slapping home a fresh one.

Just the two of us left, with Cap Owens watching somewhere, unable to assemble anything that will help us. There are maybe six zhee out of what began as twenty donks, plus a few MCR. We're pinned down, but we can handle six zhee.

We have to. This is what the Republic pays us for.

"Let's pop 'em and drop 'em," I say to Twenties over the L-comm.

"Yeah," he answers, changing out his own charge pack. "On three?"

"Let's go on four," I say. I have no idea why. Just being a smartass in the last moments of my life.

Twenties counts down, quickly. The idea is to be synced, not dramatic. "Four-three-two-one."

We pop around our corners. As I drop a zhee with my NK-4, I feel searing blaster bolts rip through my armor and into my torso. The pain drops me like a sack of spun osmioid.

I'm dead. And as if the pain weren't enough, my HUD makes sure I'm aware.

LS-55, Lieutenant C. Chhun: KIA

About all I can do is watch Twenties finish the fight. He dusts the last of the zhee and makes his way to the corvette's helm. Just when he's about to enter an override code, the lights go bright and an alarm rings. Above us, in the catwalks, Legion instructors shout and scream. All of them providing feedback on our training evolution. At the same time.

"Way too much time spent in the engine room! That needs to be cut by a minimum of five minutes!"

"One of you pansies damn well better muscle up and carry an SAB next time! I don't care how much you love your tiny little guns!"

"Congratulations, gentlemen. The galaxy is screwed."

It's like being at Legion training all over again. But Captain Owens was right in bringing these guys, all of them squad leaders and seasoned leejes, in to observe. They're looking down at a roofless replica of a Republic corvette, doing everything they can to make this training evolution a success. And none of us are too proud to accept constructive criticism from a fellow leej.

I pull myself up from my "death" position on the corvette's deck. The dead zhee lying all around me turn back into target bots, their holographic projections ceasing with the conclusion of the exercise.

The failure. Again.

Exo pushes himself up from the deck. "That sucked. Shot in the face, are you kidding me? Donks couldn't shoot that good."

"Hey," Masters says over L-comm. "At least you made it that far. I got dusted like—what?—two steps outside the assault shuttle. I've been lying on this deck for the entire run. What's worse, this stupid shock technology didn't let me at least catch some sleep. Stupid Republic engineers and their combat optimizations."

"Group up on me," Wraith orders. "Let's run it again."

"Hold up," says Cap Owens. "I think we need to get you some chow first. Talk through it. Try once more after that, then we'll call it a day."

We're having chow in our squad room, buckets off and shoveling empanadas stuffed with some kind of bird-fish hybrid shuttled fresh to the ship's stores this morning. Or at least, that's what the guys in the galley told us. Generally, those guys know what's going on, though. And whether it's fresh or pulled out of a six-year-old stasis pack, it tastes good. I'm feeling ravenous, so I bite one of the meat pastries in half and chase the mouthful down with a big swig of black caff. I drink more caff than water since joining Dark Ops.

Cap Owens belches a benediction for his finished meal, then reaches for a bottle of water. He takes a swallow and summarizes the points of consensus reached over the table. "So priority alpha is shaving time off of the engine room, because that's non-negotiable. The exercise is an immediate failure if those engines aren't shut down."

"Most of the donks are in that room," notes Twenties. "Maybe we need to toss in some satchels of det-brick. Take them and the engines out at once."

I nod. "That would be easier, but the risk of causing a secondary reaction that would result in hull breach is too high. Fraggers, ear-poppers, and blaster fire are as much as we should bring. Even then… it's volatile."

"Agreed," Owens says. "If you leejes get sucked into the vacuum before taking the bridge, it's the same mission result as a total team kill in the corridors. All the steps have to be met."

"Access to the engine room is significantly better than to the bridge," Wraith says. "We all know what happens when we storm through the bridge's blast door. The engine room has far more entry points, and the donks can't defend them all en masse. We know we can take them down given enough time, we just have to fight our way to the reactors and then shut them down with a pulser charge."

We all nod. He's right. The engine room fight is one leejes will win fifty times out of ten.

"We can take the engine room without a full team. We saw that today. Masters got taken down in the corridors right away—"

"Thanks for reminding me, jerk," Masters says, eliciting chuckles from the rest of the group.

Wraith continues as if the interruption didn't happen. "And I went down in the first thirty seconds of the fight. But the rest of the team pretty much took care of business on their own."

"Yeah," agrees Exo, "but then by the time we fought through the corridors and onto the bridge, the clock was too wound down."

"So what I'm saying," Wraith leans forward and taps his fingers against our shared meal table, which is really just a coffee table cleared of all its crap, "what I'm saying is that we establish a foothold in the engine room and then split off. Three of us stay, and the rest of the team moves to clear the corridors and begin breach preparations for the bridge."

Owens listens intently. I think he's waiting to give his opinion until the rest of the squad has voiced their own.

"There's an assumption there that Masters doesn't keep getting shot in the face on exit from the assault shuttle," Exo barks.

"Dude!" Masters yells. "You're giving me a complex. I've only died like three times since we started this training cycle."

It's all in good fun. Or at least that's how it sounds. But we're not used to failing like this. Truth is, this evolution feels like it's meant to be impossible. Designed for failure. I don't doubt that there's some buried truth behind every joking comment. Exo really does think that some of us will die before reaching the engine room. And Masters really is getting skittish about the fact that he's been dusted three of the seven times we've run this scenario today.

"I think this plan can work," I say, deciding at that moment to lay it out on the table. "Here's the reality. We haven't been at top form during these training exercises. Masters, you're so psyched out about getting shot on these exercises that you're overly cautious, and it's getting you dusted. Exo, you're trying to carry the entire team and rushing the donks like a bullitar. I barely had time to shut off the breach thrusters before you ran through the door. You could have been cooked. All of us are feeling the fatigue of doing this exercise over and over. But let's suck it up and execute Wraith's plan.

"The corridor has been an easy fight once we clear the resistance around the assault shuttle. When we breach the bridge door, let's flood the room with fraggers and ear-poppers. Hull integrity can handle it, donks and MCR can't. So pack extras this time. One of the instructors said we need to ditch at least one CQC weapon for a big old squad automatic blaster. It's heavy and a pain to lug through the ship. But if I had that instead of my NK-4 in the bridge room, we would have completed the scenario successfully last time with minutes to spare. I'm sure of it."

"I can carry the SAB," Kags volunteers. There's a resolve in his face, and I see it in the other men as well. "I'm certified for that weapon from my time as a basic. I was part of a SAB crew before they grabbed me to work the twins on Kublar."

"Okay," Owens says. "More than okay. This is exactly what I expect from this team. One more go today. Let's kick this course's ass."

"Yeah, fine," Exo says dryly. "We'll kick its ass. Kick it right in the stones. But this op needs more than one kill team on it. We all see that, right? Two teams, minimum. One for engine, one for bridge. Or, if you've only got one team, you kill the engines, exit in your shuttle, and have a fighter squadron blow the whole damn ship up."

"True enough," Owens agrees. "But in Dark Ops, we don't train for easy mode."

"Cap," Twenties says, sounding like he's about to change the subject. "I know you haven't heard, but this all goes back to the *Chiasm*, doesn't it? The guys we're after, they'll be on a Republic shuttle?"

"No idea," Owens says. "But I've heard scuttlebutt from friends on other kill teams that this training module is happening all over. So if it's not precisely our personal vision quest, you can bet it's damn big all the same. Ooah?"

Ooah.

Legion Commander Keller paces alongside the massive port windows of the *Mercutio*, then stops to examine a panorama of Republic destroyers and frigates. He can't count them all, but he knows the number. Eighteen. An impressive display of Republic firepower, called out to this section of the galaxy because Nether Ops is sure, "primacy alpha," that the biggest threat to the stability of the Republic since the Savage Wars will show up here. Just outside of Makchuria.

The ships, all of them leaving their respective sectors of space thin should anything major flare up, were positioned by Admiral Ubesk so that any ship entering Makchurian space would be immediately engaged.

Kill teams throughout galaxy's edge have been training non-stop on a designed-to-fail evolution that involves breaching the ship, shutting down flight capabilities, and storming the bridge.

Marines and frontline legionnaires are waiting in assault shuttles, ready to take the fight to whatever resistance is aboard the target ship—supposedly a Republic corvette—while the kill teams secure their objectives.

There is the potential, Keller muses, for the corvette to have more Republic soldiers on board than MCR crew and defenders. God help any *actual* Republic corvettes unlucky enough to pop into Makchurian space today. Though none are expected.

"I don't like this."

Keller looks to his left and sees that the *Mercutio*'s captain, a man in the navy for life named Slooce Avery, had joined his portside vigil.

"There's more of the day behind us than in front of us," Avery notes. He sets a mug of cold caff on the port window's ledge. "My crew is growing fatigued, and the incoming shifts are as frazzled as the outgoing. Everyone is at high alert, and their nerves are getting shot."

Keller nods his agreement. "My legionnaires—not to mention the marines—have been squashed together in those assault shuttles all day long. They're eating from ration packs and using the same for waste collection. Getting the trash collected every three hours. And I can't authorize a chance to stretch out or get some air, because Nether Ops has this interdiction classified as Red Priority."

"Fate of the Republic," grunts Captain Avery.

"Damn well better be," says Keller. "Have you heard from Ubesk? Has he had any luck getting a status update from whoever Nether Ops squeezed this intel out of?"

"He's still in meetings. But if this all turns out to be nothing... this time Nether Ops doesn't get to shrug and walk away." Avery folds his arms and assumes the angry captain demeanor Keller has witnessed so many times in his career. When enough has become too much. "I'm telling you, Commander Keller," he vows, "this time the House of Reason will get an earful from all its admirals. And the

Legion, too, I hope. We've left the edge of the galaxy completely vulnerable by gathering here. And this *after* what happened to the *Chiasm*."

"Hell to pay," Keller agreed, staring once again into the vastness of space behind the bristling Republic destroyers.

The empty space.

With no corvette.

And time winding down.

You're Tom. Aboard the corvette, *Ankalor's Pride*.

Tom. Do something, Tom. Figure something out now and make it quick. Because this is... this is worst case. This is where hope is abandoned.

Do something!

You keep telling yourself that. You keep willing Tom to figure out a way out of this mess. Even as Scarpia lazily explains the change of plans to you and Frogg.

"The best-laid plans..." Scarpia says, as though this complete about-face is little more than a hiccup over dinner reservations. You thought seven, but they wrote down seven-thirty, and now you might be late to the show.

Do something. Tom. Do something.

It was all going so well. So well that you even let a sliver of hope enter into your life. Hope that got you through the conversion of the Republic corvette *Revive* into a massive bomb recomissioned into the service of the Mid-Core

Rebellion as *Ankalor's Pride*. The MCR generals wanted something more symbolic, like *Return of Liberty*, but concessions had to be made for the zhee crew who would actually fly the ship into the House of Reason. Killing all those people. Destabilizing the entire Republic.

Illuria's message got through. Of that you're sure. You're sure because, while you sat with Frogg and Scarpia in the lounge, while private contractors worked feverishly to convert every section of the ship into a hold to be stuffed with explosives, while that was happening, you watched Scarpia as he spoke with Illuria. You saw how relaxed she was. How she spoke about the beautiful things she'd bought, and hinted at the naughty things that were only for Scarpia. And, you thought, perhaps she could see you, sitting there behind Scarpia, visible to the holocam. Perhaps she saw you, and the promise of those things was for you. For a time imagined, when this would be over, with Scarpia dead or captured, and she was destined to be happy with you.

Because she believed that.

What?

That you were different. That you truly wanted her happy. That you were the one. The one who wasn't there only to use her like some plaything. The one who cared. Who loved.

But that was never the plan, was it, you sonofabitch? You used her. Used her to get the word out. Knew very well that if you survived, you'd never speak to her again.

That was Tom.

That was you.

But she's happy. Even Scarpia seems to notice. "Illuria, I haven't seen you this giddy in so long. I think more shopping trips are in order once this business is behind us, eh?"

She was happy, and that gave you hope. She was unburdened. She didn't have the weight of that message on her shoulders because it was delivered. And she hadn't changed her mind, because Frogg continued sulking. You know, instead of driving his knife into the soft underside of your head, just behind the chin. Pushing it upward until you could feel it pierce your tongue and pin it to the roof of your mouth while you gagged, slicing yourself farther and choking on your own blood.

That hadn't happened. So you were feeling pretty optimistic. Feeling good that the kill teams were ready. That Makchuria was where this would end.

That hope allowed you to formulate procedures for overriding the corvette's necessary safety protocols. The ones that prevent a ship in hyperspace from slamming into a planet. Because who would want to do that?

Hope let you look the other way when Scarpia had all the independent contractors—lured to this job with a pay rate that would set up their families for years—rounded up and placed in the airlock. Hope let you live with them being dumped into space to die painfully. No exceptions. No witnesses. No need for them to take up space and die with the rest of the zhee.

When the House of Reason falls.

But all that was okay, you told yourself. Because it ends at Makchuria.

But now that opportunity is gone, and you need to do something.

"You see," Scarpia continues, "I *told* the MCR that the plan I'd designed was their best chance at success. You both are aware of what can happen when a plan isn't followed neatly."

Frogg casts his eyes downward. These little backhanded jabs. These paper cuts from Scarpia. They'll drive him to greater devotion. He'll be more vicious. Ruthless. More fully realized. Scarpia knows this.

"The MCRs aren't willing to die on this mission. It's not in their makeup, which I understand. But the zhee are. So the rendezvous at Makchuria is off the table. We are to meet the zhee at Ankalor. A shuttle from the planet will meet us, full of their crew and warriors. And we'll depart on that same shuttle with the MCR and go our separate ways after a final jump."

"Ankalor has a minimum of three Republic destroyers," Frogg says, an edge of concern in his voice. Not fear. Concern. Over another failure. Something he can't afford to be tainted by, even if it's beyond his control.

"Indeed they do, Froggy." Scarpia flashes his devil-may-care smile. "But this corvette has all the proper registration and identification. The MCR have acquired naval uniforms and will claim to be stopping to pick up a VIP from the green zone. So if a destroyer does take an interest in us, we'll simply stall until the shuttle is aboard, make a pre-calculated jump to empty space, and then part with the zhee. All quite simple. A plan of my own making, though not as preferable as the first."

"Tom, what do you think of my plan?"

Do something.

"Tom?"

What do the legionnaires say? KTF?

That's what you'll do. You'll be the suicide warrior who beats the other suicide warriors to the punch.

"Hello…? Scarpia to Tom?"

You become keenly aware that both Scarpia and Frogg are looking at you. Scarpia with amusement, Frogg with suspicious scorn. You make a show, as if you were lost in thought. You were. You were lost in thought. It's not a show.

"I'm sorry," you say. "I was thinking about what you said. I know this wasn't your first plan, but this is genius. Really. You know that I'd say otherwise if it weren't so. I did when it came to the supply officer. Your second plan is every bit as good as the first, Mr. Scarpia." You add the mister, because you think that's what Scarpia needs to hear right now. "If anything, this plan is better."

Scarpia leans back in his seat and smiles. "It's settled, then. Froggy, tell the crew that we are now prepared to jump for Ankalor."

You focus on that smile. Scarpia's smug, self-confident grin. You start thinking of ways to detonate this horrific payload well before Utopion. You think of plans, contingencies, and potential obstacles. But mainly you think of Scarpia. And his smile. You wonder, will that smile remain plastered to his face, moments before he's atomized in the final moments of all your lives?

Will he smile then?

You will, Tom.

You will.

Captain Eliyah Deynolds sits in her chair overlooking the bridge of the *Intrepid*, reviewing the never-ending reports that always wait for her on her datapad. There was a time when she would have locked herself in her office, emerging to rejoin the bridge crew only when she felt that enough fires had been put out. But experience has taught her that simply being with her crew develops a bond that is essential to swift and decisive action when the need arises. Her officers and crew are professionals. Trained to operate in the best navy the galaxy—the universe—has ever known. But even that can be improved upon.

Captain Deynolds is present. She is accessible. Respected. One to watch.

That she will be given command of a destroyer, perhaps even a super-destroyer, in the mid-core is considered all but certain. And that will be fine.

But serving at galaxy's edge is also fine. If the core is where sailors learn to become politicians, galaxy's edge is where they become warriors. And with the *Intrepid* alone to watch over the volatile zhee planet cluster; with word of the *Chiasm* still fresh on everyone's minds, though it was months ago; with all of that... a warrior is needed on the bridge.

Her number one, a Senate appointee, Commander Wulf Mercall, is not a warrior. Captain Deynolds knows this. Has observed this in how differently he's treated by the legionnaires on board. She has never been the subject of such scorn. And she knows it had nothing to do with rank.

The commander is an aspiring politician. So she rarely gives him the bridge. Even if that means sitting idly in her chair, denying what seems like the hundredth request to remove the massive corvette training ground the Legion has installed—not that the supply crew making the requests knows that's what's taking up so much of their precious cargo space.

She denies the request without comment and takes a sip of steaming spice-leaf tea. With just a few drops of cream. Enough to cloud the drink and give it a velvety smoothness.

"Captain Deynolds!"

The voice belongs to an ensign newly assigned to one of *Intrepid*'s bridge sensor stations. Ensign Pollet, the captain reminds herself. The ensign sounds stressed, worried, excited.

"Go ahead, Ensign Pollet," Deynolds says calmly.

"A Republic corvette has just jumped into the system. It's holding just above Ankalor."

Oba, Captain Deynolds screams to herself. This is it. It's happening. She calms herself. Controls the spikes of adrenaline. "Hail them. Commander Mercall."

"Yes, Captain?" The point seems surprised to be called upon.

"Communicate with the corvette. See what they have to say. We have no reports indicating that any Republic vessels are scheduled to arrive over Ankalor."

"Captain," the weapons officer calls out. "Shall I ready batteries for assault?"

He must sense the tension on the bridge, Deynolds thinks. Tension that she must be exhibiting. "No, Lieutenant Rasham. Give no indication of combat readiness whatsoever."

She looks over to the commander, sees him engaging with a Republic uniformed human in what appears to be a friendly conversation. She hears hints of the subject. VIPs. Special pickups. Unscheduled.

"Captain," Ensign Pollet says from the sensor array, his voice low, as if whoever the commander is communicating with on the corvette might hear him, "I'm detecting a shuttle of non-Republic make leaving Ankalor on a projected course for the corvette. Confirmed by planetside observations."

This is a decision point. The captain knows it. She contemplates waiting on the commander's report. He seems engaged in idle conversation. Deynolds's first thought is that he's being stalled. That, or the person in the corvette is an old friend from Academy.

Wait, or act?

The captain is a warrior commanding a destroyer on galaxy's edge.

The choice is clear.

She stands up from her chair. Her teacup spills onto the luxurious carpet, splashing onto her mirror-shined shoes. "Connect me to the all-ship comm."

The communications officer's hands fly across her console. "The comm is yours, Captain."

"Keep weapons offline," Deynolds reminds Lieutenant Rasham before keying open her comm. "This is Captain Deynolds," she announces. "All combat personnel, scramble for immediate assault. Deliver-Actual."

26

I'm in our squad room, bucket off and beginning to peel away the synthprene to examine the massive bruise on my shoulder. I slammed it hard into a bulkhead while diving for cover in our final training evolution of the day. The way I hit that solid impervisteel, I would have shattered my arm were it not for the armor. As it stands, my squad logo is blurred and scraped up from the impact.

My hair is drenched with sweat. I flick my tongue across my upper lip. My stubble pricks against my tongue as I taste salt. I need to shave. After a shower.

That's all I really want, and I suspect that's all the rest of the guys want after getting our asses handed to us on the corvette course one final time. But we were really close. Literally thirty seconds short. The instructors actually let us finish the scenario, only to tell us after the fact that we all, in fact, died.

That was a kick in the stones.

A shower will fix it. Maybe slap on a heated tissue reconstructor to take care of the bruise. Though sometimes I like to let the hurt linger. A little reminder of my own mortality and the need to stay focused.

I've just begun to tug at my forearm armor when the all-ship chime sounds. Captain Deynolds isn't the sort to give those cheesy all-ship bulletins like some skippers

I've spaced under. If she's going to all-comms, it's because she's got something important to say.

"This is Captain Deynolds. All combat personnel, scramble for immediate assault. Deliver-Actual."

I knew from the way she said her name that something serious was going on. By the time she says the word "combat," I've switched from armor-removal mode to armor-up mode. So has everyone else.

"Sket!" Owens says. He runs to his gear locker and begins to strip. He's been wearing the T-shirt and athletic shorts most of the instructors wear during training evolutions. "Get to the launch-one assault shuttle. First bird off the destroyer. I'll catch up, but *leave without me* if you have to. I'll hitch a ride with the marines."

The all-comm message repeats, and we've got our buckets on before the captain finishes.

Everybody rushes to their lockers to grab a mission bag. We have several of these made up, each for a different environment or situation. I grab my CQC—Close Quarters Combat—shooter bag, the one I use for rescues, captures, stuff like that. It's optimized for ship-to-ship or building CQC ops. Very light on survival gear, extra fraggers and blaster packs, more tech solutions for getting around sophisticated tech locks without blowing doors down. Yeah, I won't need all this for the corvette, but it's better to take the bag and leave what I don't need in the assault shuttle than it is to waste time digging things out now. Plus, I'll probably forget something crucial and get us all killed if I don't take the whole bag.

"I don't have enough blaster packs for this SAB," Exo says, hauling his own shooter bag onto his shoulder. This is a problem because the squad automatic blaster came in real handy on our last run through the course.

"Grab some packs from some marines on the flight deck," Wraith orders.

Even though he's trying to sell it like he's fine, Wraith is moving with a slight limp. He turned his ankle pretty bad while we were ducking blaster fire on the bridge. I'm not the only one who notices.

"You okay to go, Captain Ford?" Kags has his bag over his shoulder, his NK-4 strapped to his chest. He reaches out to help Wraith hoist up his own bag. "I can carry that for you, keep the weight off your ankle, sir."

Wraith shoulders the load and shakes his head. "I'm fine, Kags."

If anyone could carry two bags and still be primed for the fight, it's Kags. I remember back to when he climbed up to Outpost Zulu on Kublar. I was sucking air like a fat kid sucks milkshake, and he was barely breathing heavy. But Wraith is carrying his own bag.

Leaving Cap Owens to change, the six of us sprint down *Intrepid*'s corridors en route to the hangar bay. Sailors, enlisted and officer alike, give us a wide berth. When the captain calls for all combat units to scramble, and you see a black-clad kill team squad running your way, you *move*.

Thankfully the hangar is placed strategically close to our squad room. Or maybe our squad room is placed close to the hangar. Semantics. We're there in almost no time, our boots pounding the flight deck as we rush toward the assault shuttle positioned at the front of the launch queue. Fire teams of marines are running to and fro, as are deck crew and launch techs. It's glorious, organized chaos.

I live for these moments.

I get paid for what comes after launch.

We're fifty meters from the assault shuttle's open load doors when I see a marine. He's doing a slow spin, looking lost. Like he got separated from his buddies. Not a hard thing to do with all the comings and goings inside the hangar. I see that the guy is part of a SAB crew. He's loaded down with the specialized charge packs. "Exo," I call, pointing the marine out to my squadmate. "Found your ammo!"

Exo separates from the pack and grabs the marine by his flak jacket. "Hey, hullbuster! You're comin' with us."

The marine says something to protest, but Exo isn't having it. He practically drags the kid to the assault shuttle. "Don't worry. We get to go in first. That means you won't have to wait as long to die!"

I see Captain Owens coming in fast like the squirts after eating at a prueher food buffet, his surge shotgun in one hand and a haversack tucked under the opposite arm. I stow my gear bag under my jump seat and strap in.

"Okay, kill team," the pilot says almost as soon as our squad gets on the shuttle. "Mission is hot and we're cleared right now. Strap in."

"Hold up," Wraith calls. "We got one more coming. Fifteen seconds."

"Fifteen seconds," the pilot repeats, "and then the doors close."

Captain Owens hurls himself on board the shuttle with five seconds to spare. "Hey kids, miss me?"

"We're good," Wraith tells the pilot.

"Closing doors. Prepare for immediate launch."

The engines of the assault shuttle hum with intensity. We're the lead bird, so the gauss accelerators are already lined up with our shuttle. We should slingshot through the hangar's shielding in a few short seconds. I can't tell if our guys are tense, but the marine looks like he's going to be sick.

"Hey, hullbuster," I say. "Remember to tuck your chin and stay with us when we get on board the 'vette. You'll be fine."

The assault shuttle blasts out of the hangar and we're feeling the gees rearrange our insides. If this really is a Republic corvette, there are probably better ways to drop in and pay a visit. But if it's not…

Our pilot confirms that this is the real deal. "Corvette is positioning for a jump. Impact in twenty seconds."

"Don't jump," I hear Owens repeating in whispers over the L-comm. "Don't jump."

"Five seconds," the pilot calls.

I count down in my mind. We hit at what feels like three.

The corvette's hull is nowhere near as thick as the hull of a destroyer or the Ohio-class cruiser. We should have a good breach without any extra work on the shuttle's part.

"Okay, kill team," the pilot says over the comm. "We've got good penetration. Right above the primary north-south corridor. Seal integrity looks… outstanding. We're one with the ship. Hey, uh… but before you lower the ramp, I'm picking up a concentrated number of hostiles moving from the shuttle bay."

"Marines looking to repel boarders," Twenties suggests. "Yeah, this is MCR for sure."

"I've got visual on the external holocam," the pilot reports calmly. "Looks like… zhee."

Okay. So that's no surprise. The zhee have been part of our training evolutions. Whatever the Legion wanted Dark Ops to train for, we're about to do it.

Pings and clangs pepper the hull.

"Zhee are unloading on the ramp," Masters says. He's sitting closest to the door, so he's no doubt hearing the hornet-like buzzing loudest of all. Couple that with the fact that he's gone down more than once during training, and I'm worried he's going to get twisted.

"We can't drop the door like this, man," he says. "They'll chew us up."

He's right. Nerves or not, he's right. We drop that door and the blaster fire will come in so thick, there's just no way we'll avoid casualties. "Hullbuster!" I call. "You got a cutting torch?"

"Yes, sir!" The marine passes down the torch.

I hand it to Masters. "I want you to cut a fragger-sized hole in the ramp."

"Yeah," Masters says, taking the torch and thumbing it live. "I see where you're going."

Blue-white flashes light up the interior of the cabin as a glowing circle takes shape in the ramp door. When the circle is almost completely cut, I tap Exo on the shoulder. "Get ready to send a grenade outside as soon as the hole opens."

"Fragger or ear-popper?" Exo asks, digging into his hip pouch.

"Why not both?" Wraith suggests.

"Ooah," Exo says. "Time to KTF these donks."

Masters knocks out the cut-circle with a sharp jab of his armored elbow. Exo leans over and sends the grenades through the opening. First the ear-popper, then the fragger. A red blaster bolt sizzles and impacts the lip of the opening, sending sparks inside.

Exo pulls his hand back and wiggles his gloved fingers in front of his helmet. "Bastards almost blew my digits off!"

Boom!

The ear-popper is loud enough that I feel the vibration on the deck of our shuttle, bright enough that the flash fills our cabin with white light.

Boom! Boom!

The fragger goes next, two successive blasts sending shrapnel in every direction. Thankfully, the blast radius doesn't extend to our little peephole.

"Drop the ramp!" Owens shouts.

The shuttle doors go down and we fill the opening with blaster fire. We unstrap and jump to the deck. The zhee around us are crawling, and blood is everywhere. A few of the donkey-like creatures are struggling to raise bleeding limbs perforated by the fragger's shrapnel. Trusting that their gods will guide their blaster bolts.

We dust them before their gods have a chance to hear their prayers.

"Kill every last one of these donks," Owens orders, sending a shotgun blast into a zhee who's belly crawling toward his feet, a blood trail snaking behind.

We leave no survivors as we head to the engine room.

"Damn," the marine says as we turn the corridors, muscle memory guiding us to our target and destination. "You guys need to think about what just happened. I don't mean to jinx it, but that was over a dozen zhee who managed to get guns trained on a deboarding assault shuttle. I've never heard of that happening without serious casualties. You guys didn't even take a scratch! You're untouchable. And you just rewrote assault shuttle doctrine. That's history, man. That's indelible."

"Looks like this hullbuster's been reading textbooks in his spare time," Twenties jokes. "Using a big word like 'indelible.'"

"That's us," Masters chimes in. "The Indelible Six. Captain Owens calls us that all the time. Right, Cap?"

"Oh, yeah," Owens deadpans. "I even write the name in my journal. Dot the i's with a heart."

We grow quiet as we move through the empty corridor, weapons at the ready. In the training evolutions, we didn't encounter hostiles until breaching the engine room. Here, I don't know what to expect. But so far, it's been remarkably similar. I feel the sensation of the deck vibrating beneath my feet.

"You guys feel that?" I ask.

"Feel what?"

"Yeah," Wraith says, "I felt it."

"Felt what?"

Owens sighs into his comm. "Corvette just made the jump to hyperspace. We're doing this op on hard mode."

27

You're Tom, on the bridge of the corvette, *Ankalor's Pride*.

Think, Tom. Just... just calm down and think. You tell yourself that there's still time. Still time to blow this boat up. Still time to rid the galaxy of Scarpia. Time to tell your wife that what you did with Illuria... *to* Illuria... was for her. For her and your daughter. For the galaxy. Hell, even for the Republic.

But that's if you can actually have a bridge console to yourself. Without Frogg or someone else—one of the MCR crew—looking over your shoulder. Because they'll see. Warnings will need to be disregarded. Alarms muted. Overrides provided.

They'll see that, Tom, won't they?

Oh, yes, they will.

Frogg will see it, and his froggy eyes will widen and he'll send that knife right between your ribs. Deflate your lungs, pierce your heart. And he'll smile, satisfied. And Scarpia will call him old boy.

And you'll be dead.

Which is the worst thing that can happen to you right now.

The jump to Ankalor will be finished in moments, and then, as far as Scarpia is concerned, your job is done. This is a waiting game. On the bridge. With the MCR in their stolen Republic uniforms.

"What could you possibly want with a console, Tom?" Scarpia would ask.

And Frogg would lick his lips. Because what *would* you want with a console when the job is done and you're just waiting for a shuttle full of zhee to come aboard so you can take said shuttle and enjoy the good life? Fixed rates, and all that.

"We are in Ankalor space, just above orbit," the MCR navigator announces.

The head zhee, not a sailor but still the captain, says nothing.

"Shall we hold here and await the shuttle's arrival?" another MCR officer suggests, showing deference to a clueless captain.

The whole bridge feels like grown adults playing a kids' game of war. But... the payload. The House of Reason. They're playing for keeps.

"Do not burden me with your formalities," the zhee says, dismissing the MCR lackeys with a wave of his hoof-hand.

Nobody knows what they're doing on this bridge. Unreal.

You don't know what you're doing.

I do.

You do?

I know what I'm doing. I just don't know what to do.

Ah. Tom knows what to do. Take the money and run, Tom. Fixed rates. You've gone so far. Murdered thousands.

Bedded Illuria. Why not just call it the start of a new life? As Tom.

We're Tom.

You shake the thoughts from your mind. This is the part of you that's trying to hold on. Trying not to die in a fiery, self-made explosion. But you have to die, if others are to live.

"Sir," a sensor tech shouts from his display. "There's a Republic destroyer within range. The *Intrepid*."

Scarpia raises an eyebrow at this wrinkle.

You hear Frogg hiss, "Exactly what I thought might have gone wrong. Scarpia, we need to jump now. Zhee honor guard be damned."

Scarpia turns to you, inviting your thoughts. Your heart is racing, because a Republic destroyer means at least one kill team. Which could mean...

No. You have to focus. Answer Scarpia. As Tom. Tell him what Tom would say.

"Frogg's right. We're not supposed to be here. If they launch assault shuttles quickly, we may not have the opportunity to jump."

Scarpia considers for a moment longer. He raises a hand and steps toward the MCR officer who most ought to be the captain, and the zhee captain who should not be a captain. "May I have a word?"

The zhee, the rebel, and the arms dealer form a triangle without lines. They speak in hushed tones, but it's clear to you what's happening. Scarpia is suggesting a retreat, the zhee will have none of it, and the MCR officer is doing his best to find a compromise.

"We're being hailed," calls the MCR comm tech.

The man who perhaps should be captain straightens himself. "If you'll excuse me, I should answer this. I'm certain that I can stall the Republic until our shuttle has boarded. I know how to talk to these types. I served in the Republic navy for almost two years."

Two years. This is the sort of experience the MCR has to offer?

You wait, and listen to the conversation. The subterfuge about unscheduled arrivals and picking up VIPs. You don't think about Illuria. Or your family. You think about the captain of the *Intrepid*, though you don't know their name. You find yourself willing—praying?—for them to launch assault shuttles.

See through this paper-thin excuse of an officer.

The conversation between the two ships continues. You begin to worry that the MCR officer may be able to stall the captain of the *Intrepid* long enough. Whoever he's talking to, it's as if they're old friends.

Salvation comes in the panicked voice of the MCR sensor tech. "They've launched assault shuttles!"

Assault shuttles!

With kill teams. And marines.

A dumb silence falls over the bridge. You see the MCR who would be captain looking at the now-blank holodisplay. Frozen in his place.

It dawns on you that no one is going to do anything. They don't know how. All you have to do is wait and then… what? Raise your hands? Lie on the floor and hope the kill team takes you alive? X never walked you through this final part of Operation Ghost Hunter.

How do you prove you're not a traitor?

"Tom!" Scarpia shouts, his voice high and edgy. "Take command! These fools are worthless."

You stand there, unsure what to do.

Tom would assume command of the ship.

"Tom!" Scarpia screams again. "Get us out of here! *Do* something!"

And so you do. Because to do nothing would mean a knife from Frogg, who could probably figure out how to jump the corvette without you.

You rush to a command console and instruct the ship to re-angle to make the jump to hyperspace.

"If we're going to get out, we need to get out now, before the shuttle docks in our hangar bay," you announce to the bridge.

You hear a clack, a blaster rifle being primed, just behind your left ear.

"No." It's the zhee. "They will board. Or you all will die."

This is immediately contested. The MCR-who-would-be-captain storms toward the zhee. "Now see here, the agreement was—"

A sudden burst of blaster fire rips into the MCR man's stomach. He clutches his wound and drops to the floor.

Frogg takes a step, but the zhee has a distance advantage. It swings the blaster rifle and stops Frogg cold in his tracks. The ex-legionnaire backs up and stands beside Scarpia. You can't make out your erstwhile employer's face from your vantage point.

You imagine him looking sick.

"I can wait," you say, keeping your calm. "But that likely means an assault shuttle will breach the ship."

The zhee gives a reverential bray. "The chosen warriors of our four gods will repel them."

"The shuttle from Ankalor should dock in one minute," the sensor tech reports.

You nod. "I'll prepare the jump coordinates. Utopion is pre-selected. We can dump out en route and formally transfer command to the zhee."

The zhee in front of you says nothing. He stands unaware of the little things you've done to buy extra time. Closing the hangar doors so the shuttle will be forced to wait as they ponderously reopen.

Frogg would have noticed something like that. But the zhee has removed Frogg from your presence, like a sultan would one who displeases him. So no Frogg on hand, no one to notice you delaying the jump timer by three hundred seconds.

The lead assault shuttle is closing, and the Ankalor shuttle carrying the zhee has docked. The zhee are no doubt pouring out like space rats from an infected hold right about now.

"They are on board," the zhee captain shouts. "Make the jump!"

"Not that easy," you say. "The MCR you blasted must have tinkered with the hyperdrive's jump delay. It's counting down but I don't have the override codes."

That's a lie. You do. The secret ones hardwired into the system so that you'd always have a backdoor key.

"I could try to guess at it, but that might force a reset and we'll wait even longer to make the jump."

"Bring it up on screen," Scarpia orders. "I, for one, wish to see how close we're shaving things."

You curse to yourself. You had hoped to reset the counter one more time. But this will close off that option. Your only hope is for assault shuttles to arrive before you make the jump.

The bridge doors swoosh open, and armed zhee rush inside. They form a perimeter and point their blaster rifles at every non-zhee in the room.

You feel the corvette shake, and a blaring klaxon fills the bridge.

"What's happening?" the zhee cries out.

You suppress a smile. "Republic assault shuttle just penetrated all the way through to the main corridor."

The zhee captain brays orders in his native tongue, and several of his species run off, gathering others as they go to lead a glorious assault on whoever's inside that shuttle. You watch the countdown to jump.

"When we jump, we *all* go to the House of Reason," the zhee captain informs the bridge. "No second chance for the Republic to meddle in the will of the gods. You will die for the glory of Ankalor, and the sacred texts will remember your names."

You look at the sensor array. No other shuttles will arrive on time. Their ETA is too far out. The clock will strike midnight and this corvette will disappear before their eyes.

It's up to this kill team—it has to be a kill team, first in war, first in ops like this, always—to stop this ship from reaching its target.

And you, Tom.

It's up to you to help them.

28

"Save the fraggers if you can—we'll need them for the bridge!"

Kags lays down a steady stream of blaster fire from his SAB. "Yeah," he grunts, "if we make it to the bridge. These zhee are making it so we gotta stop and fight for three minutes just to take a couple steps closer to the engine room."

We're in a protracted blaster battle. The corridor we're attempting to push through forks into a 'Y' and then loops around the entire engine room. The zhee have set themselves up in in that fork, right in front of the main door to the engine room, and are putting up a good fight.

I line up a zhee who's been jumping around a corner to empty a charge pack with full automatic blaster fire. He's done this three times, jumping out, unloading, braying about his gods, and then jumping back in. The firefight has been thick, affording him this opportunity. But after the third time it just pissed me off. So I'm looking for him. And when he pops out, I double-tap, splitting his head open at the mane.

But for every donk we kill, it seems like there's another taking its place. Far more than we experienced in the simulation. It's practically a miracle that we made it out of the assault shuttle with these kinds of numbers on the ship.

The real problem are the two zhee in the middle of the floor, taking cover behind a pair of cargo containers that must have been dragged to their location in anticipation of an assault on the engine rooms. These donks are laying down rapid-fire blaster bolts with such intensity that we aren't able to get off a clear shot.

Reality is that we're pinned down, but only by these two zhee. When one of their zhee buddies tries to corner-peek to get in a few shots of his own, we drop the kelhorn. But we've gotta do something about the blaster MGs raining holy hell on us.

Fraggers were the first go, but with how low the ceilings are in the corridor, we had to chuck the grenades like we were throwing fast balls. That made for too much exposure. Not to mention the first couple we threw detonated well shy of our targets.

"Hey, hullbuster," Kags calls to the marine. The kid is on the opposite of the corridor, about ten meters south of Kags. "I need one of those extra charge packs you've got. I'm running low."

The marine nods. Unlike a conventional charge pack, the one required to keep an SAB going is a heavy piece of work. In the Legion, they're usually strapped into the webbing of the legionnaire equipped with the weapon. It's not the sort of thing you can just toss to whoever needs it. Which means the marine is going to have to run the resupply to Kags, or Kags is going to have to run to the marine.

Since Kags is using the SAB, we don't want him out of the fight.

We lay down covering fire for the marine, but it's not enough to get the two zhee to duck down behind the cargo containers. They're feeling real safe and snug. I see us take our first casualty. A fusillade of blaster fire slams into the deck around the marine's feet as he runs. The zhee adjusts upward, and the blaster bolts tear into the kid's leg, up to the thigh. He goes down hard, a few steps from Exo.

Exo pulls him to cover, but the kid is screaming. I can hear him as our fire slacks.

"Ah! Ah! Oba! It hurts! It hurts!"

The zhee behind the container begin to laugh. Then they mock the kid. "Ah! Eet hurts! Eet hurts!"

More donkey laughs.

This *seriously* pisses me off. "Why don't you two take your knives and let's settle this?" I shout. "You women. You *cowards*."

The zhee laugh again. They're having a grand time. "Why you don't sleep with your sister?"

I doubt the zhee have a firm enough understanding of the grammar of Standard to realize they more or less insulted themselves. It doesn't matter. Had they taken the bait, I would have dusted them with my NK-4. You'd be surprised by how often enemy combatants fall for the "come out and fight like a man" lure.

"All right, Victory Squad," Captain Owens says from behind the cover of a bulkhead. "Time is seriously draining. If the real-time window is anything like the exercise window, we're in some deep dung."

The marine cries out again. We don't have a medic, and other than Exo, no one's in a good position to reach him.

Once again, the zhee mock his pain, saying in broken Standard, "Oh! Oh! Please, help me!"

I'm beginning to hate them as much as the koobs.

"Dude," Kags says over L-comm, "I got this."

Before any of us has a moment to answer, Kags steps out with his SAB, holding down the trigger and firing full auto. No burst fire. No aim, really. He's shooting from the hip and sending an overwhelming stream of blaster fire down the corridor. The zhee are caught off guard. They both disappear behind their containers.

Kags begins walking down the hall, still firing. The cargo containers and the corridor wall behind it are riddled with black scorches from the innumerable blaster bolts. A zhee attempts to run out and stop the onslaught. Kags swings his SAB in the alien's direction and just about cuts it in half. Another comes from the other side, only to be dropped by Wraith.

We're following behind Kags, moving up by the power of what is now relentless firepower. Kags is in the middle of the corridor, maybe a meter away from the cargo containers.

When we reach the 'Y' where the two zhee are camped out, Masters turns corner port, Twenties turns corner starboard. Leejes back them up, opening fire on the shocked zhee in the forking corridors—who did not expect to see a kill team advancing on them so quickly.

Kags doesn't stop firing. His weapon's barrel is glowing, but it functions. He just holds down the trigger until he's right on top of the two zhee. They make attempts to point their own weapons at Kags and fire, but he simply sways his arms and the two zhee are torn apart beneath an avalanche of blaster fire.

The corridor falls silent. We've wiped out the resistance. All that's left is to breach the door to the engine room.

I crouch next to the door while the rest of my team stacks up. We had good success with a slice-box, so I reach in my kit to retrieve one. But without warning, the door simply slides open. I'm looking inside, slice-box in hand, at two dozen zhee. Each of them seems just as surprised to see me, like they weren't expecting the door to open either.

Before either side has a chance to make a move, the engine room fills with vented steam. It blasts directly onto some of the zhee, and they begin wailing in pain. The rest of them open fire at the door. I fall on my butt and begin to scurry backward like a crab to escape. I reach a bulkhead, but I'm cut off from my team still stacked against the door.

"What happened?" Wraith asks over L-comm.

"I don't know," I answer. "The door just opened."

"Okay," Wraith says, and I can tell he's not really satisfied with that answer, but it's what we've got. "We saved a lot of time with that trick out of the assault shuttle. Let's not split up. Toss an ear-popper through the vapor and let's go in hard."

I'm looking for an opening to move back up with my squad. Blaster bolts sizzle past me down the corridor. Too many. My guys are pinned in there and I'm pinned out here.

Great.

I'm waiting for an opening that won't get me shot in the face when I hear a private-channel chime over my bucket.

"Chhun," I hear Captain Owens say. "You need to take the bridge. Right now."

"What?" I'm having trouble believing what I just heard.

"Do what he says, Chhun." The voice belongs to Andien. Somehow she's communicating through my L-comm in spite of the fact that I'm on a ship traveling through hyperspace. Nether Ops has some legit gear.

"I don't..." I begin, genuinely unsure what I'm supposed to do. Follow orders, I guess. But this was not part of the training evolution.

"The ship is little more than a hollowed-out bomb," Andien says. "And it's heading directly for the House of Reason. Based on the jump time recorded by the *Intrepid*, we'll have impact in fifteen minutes unless either the hyperdrive is cut—which gives us twenty minutes—or you take that bridge and change course."

I started running at the word bomb.

You're Tom. And you're not sure how long this will go unnoticed.

"Twenty zhee dead!" the zhee captain bellows. "Killed in one swoop at the mouth of the assault shuttle. And where were their brothers?" He slams his hoof-hands onto a nearby console.

The MCR sensor tech answers. "Holocams indicate that the other zhee seem to have gotten turned around.

They entered a restricted area—a payload hold—got themselves stuck via a door malfunction, and ended up looping around to the airlocks. Cams went offline shortly after that. Most likely due to the kill team."

The zhee captain stares with disdain at the MCR sensor tech. This report was not at all welcome.

"If these legionnaires cannot be stopped," the zhee captain rails, furious as he brays, "then how can I honor your request, Scarpia?"

Scarpia worked out a deal with the Ankalor zhee that made keeping him alive—keeping *us* alive—well worth their time. But this conditional agreement hinged on the elimination of the kill team. A team that was now advancing rapidly on the engine room.

"I'm sure I don't know," Scarpia says. "Your warriors were brought aboard precisely to assure that no such event would happen. And yet here we are." The arms dealer smiles that self-assured, smug grin. The one he uses when he's sure that he has the ultimate upper hand. Which he always does. "Had my *original* plan been carried out, you would already be celebrating the destruction of the House of Reason in the afterlife."

The zhee captain snorts in response to this.

"I will still yet reach the zenith of our gods." The zhee stares at Scarpia with its dead eyes. "The question is, will you be there too, groveling before the gilded throne I will be given?"

"I certainly hope not," Scarpia says dryly. "Froggy?"

Frogg steps forward. "Yes, Mr. Scarpia?"

"Do you think *you* could do something about this kill team?"

A wicked smile curves across Frogg's face. Is there anything he'd love to do more? And can you stop him from your place at the console? Ostensibly you're maintaining the ship's travels in hyperspeed, preventing the nav computer from dumping once it realizes you're on a collision course with Utopion. Ostensibly, and at the moment, actually. Because if not you, it'll just be someone else. The number of blaster rifles pointed at you tells you that much. The mission will continue, with or without you. You're expendable.

You always were.

Frogg clears his throat and flips his knife once up into the air. "Oh yes, Mr. Scarpia. I fancy I can do something about this kill team. Something very nasty indeed."

I've slowed my run into a cautious patrol as I move past the assault shuttle and back toward the main bridge. My bucket's audio sensors strain for a hint of any zhee who lie ahead, but all my ears are met with is the real-time L-comm transmissions from the rest of my team.

"One more pocket to clear out," Masters says.

I hear Owens's shotgun boom repeatedly, at what I don't know.

Kags screams out in pain, and my stomach sinks. Is he hit? Dead? I listen to the scene like it was a scripted drama.

Wraith: Kags, you okay?
Twenties: Kags!
Exo: He ain't movin', man!
Masters: Sket! No wait, I just saw his arm move.

More blaster fire.

But my focus needs to be on what remains ahead of me. I have five fraggers and three ear-poppers. Plus my breaching gear and NK-4. I don't know if that'll be enough to clear the bridge, but what other choice do I have?

I continue down the main corridor, my blaster rifle tucked into my shoulder, at the ready. I stop. Ahead I can hear two zhee sentries speaking in their odd language. Praising their gods, I imagine.

Okay. So how do I dust them?

I'm not skilled enough with a vibroknife to pull off a double blade kill. I settle on creeping as close as I can and going hot with my blaster pistol. It's suppressed, and hopefully won't draw attention.

I prepare myself to creep forward when a side door, one of the barracks doors that was always sealed in training, quietly slides open. In a panic, I point my suppressed blaster pistol at the open door, expecting to dust a zhee walking through at any second. But... nothing comes.

Something tells me to walk toward it. I look inside. The room is stuffed from deck to ceiling with explosives, but there's a narrow path. I follow it. At the end of the path, another door opens before I get there. As if I'm being led down some enchanted pathway.

Each corridor is empty. Each room is safe. I realize from my walk and the lay of the ship that I'm being guided past the sentries. I'd already be on top of them if I had moved this far up the main corridor.

Someone—a friend—is walking me safely through. Andien?

I'm weaving through doors and rooms. Corridors and holds. Sometimes I wait, and I can hear zhee talking just on the other side of the door I'm on. I lower my L-comm to little more than a faint background noise to better hear what's outside. The zhees' frenetic voices fade and disappear. And I move on.

The bridge is close. I can feel it. I know it instinctively from the number of times I've been on this ship when it was a mere training construct aboard the *Intrepid*.

And then I reach the door that I know opens onto a waiting room that in turns opens onto the bridge. I've been brought to a side entrance—on a ship where the entirety of the bridge crew will expect the attack to come from the main corridor.

But the door doesn't open.

I wait. Wondering if my friend has left me.

My bucket's sensors pick up motion on the other side of the door. I hear yelling. Wild, furious screams in Standard.

"Tom!" the voice on the other side shouts. "Damn you to hell, Tom!"

The voice pauses between every outburst, as if waiting for Tom to reply from somewhere.

"I know it was you, Tom!"

"I can see it now!"

"I'll gut you for this, Tom!

"Tom!"

I'm not sure what to do. This guy isn't going anywhere, and I can't keep waiting. I kneel down and retrieve a det-brick. If I have to blow this penultimate door, so be it.

The lights in my room flash. Whoever is guiding me doesn't like this idea.

Is it you, Andien?

Or is it Tom?

Or is it the man on the other side of the door?

I stow the det-brick and stand up. I raise my NK-4 to my shoulder and point it at the door. Finally, the door slides open with a whoosh. I don't see anyone in the room.

I've taken one step forward when a man—short, powerfully built, and ugly, with bug eyes—rolls from around the corner and leaps at me. I fire my NK-4. He absorbs the shot; he must be wearing armor. He crashes into me and my rifle goes flying. We're tangled together on the floor.

The man straddles me. He raises a knife, and I see the viciousness in his eyes.

29

My attacker attempts to plunge his knife into the unprotected spot between my bucket and chest guard. I get my arms up and grab him by the wrists. I let his momentum rock me backward, and I kick him off me. He does a flip and lands on his back.

We're on our feet at the same time.

"So you're what's left of the kill team, eh, mate?"

He tosses the knife back and forth from palm to palm. My NK-4 is on the ground. I reach for my sidearm, hoping my draw is quicker than his knife hand. But the little guy's reflexes are something else. As I reach for the pistol he lunges, forcing me to jump back to avoid several expertly aimed slices and jabs. As I'm dancing around the room, it's instantly obvious to me that I'm going to bump into a wall or he's going to get lucky before I manage to draw and fire.

I decide that talking to this odd little man, compactly built and full of muscles, is my new strategy. "Yeah. I guess I've made a habit of surviving."

The man takes another swipe at me, but it seems almost playful. Like he wasn't actually trying to cut me. Like he's enjoying this now.

And why shouldn't he? Time is on this suicide bomber's side.

"See what you are? That should have been me," the man says. "I was Legion. And I know that you know I was, because this is how the Legion teaches you to fight with knives. Of course, experience has led to some modifications on my part."

He thrusts for my head. I dodge, and the blade glances across my bucket.

No harm.

"I was Legion, and I was good. Damn good. Best killer the Legion ever had, don't you ever forget it. And what does a killer do but kill? So I killed who deserved it. Who I felt needed it. And a lot of buggers needed it."

"You sound charming," I reply, hoping to get him off his game.

"Thank you kindly. The legionnaires, they didn't like the killing. Or maybe they did and it was the House and Senate who lost the stomach for it. They hate us, you know? They hate legionnaires because we remind them that they need men with guns to bring about the change they call 'natural' to the galaxy."

Another swipe, another near miss.

"So they drummed me out. When they should have put me on a kill team. Put my talents to use."

"They made the wrong call," I say.

The man gives a half smile and inclines his head, as if to hear more. "Oh yeah?"

"Yeah," I say, maneuvering myself behind a det-brick that fell out of my pouches while dodging. "They should have killed you."

I kick the det-brick at the man's face. It hits him square on the chin. He takes a step back, and I deliver a shoulder tackle, driving him into the deck.

The man howls with rage. He slices along my chest, but my armor absorbs most of it. The very tip of the blade finds home through my synthprene, enough to draw blood, but it's nothing too deep. I grimace behind my helmet.

I don't know if you remember, but I'm something of an amateur GFC fighter. And the ground game is where I tend to excel.

I rub my armored forearm across the bridge of the guy's nose until he sends his non-knife hand to pull my arm away. I've got his knife hand gripped by the wrist. I let him pull my arm away because this opens up his face. Unlike him, I'm wearing my bucket.

I slam my helmet down with a head-butt that I don't even feel. It hits him on the mouth, though I was aiming for his forehead. I see blood right away, and he spits out two teeth onto the carpet. I lift my head back to bring down another head-butt. He sees the opening he's given me and lets go of my forearm, placing his palm over my bucket to hold me off.

I'm still in a good spot. I take a few jabs at his head, but they're glancing blows. All the while, our legs are jockeying for position. He's trying to roll me off him and I'm riding the wave, trying to stay on top. We're both panting and groaning, putting all the strength we have into this fight. I know only one of us is getting up from the deck alive.

He must know it too.

I grope for his neck with my free hand, hoping for a choke. He tucks his chin, and my hand moves up and onto his face, even while his hand finds the opening beneath my bucket and begins to squeeze my throat.

This guy is a powerhouse. I feel my air supply dwindling, which makes the arm I'm using to keep the knife at bay grow weaker by the second. He's starting to turn this around.

My hand rubs against his face until I reach his eyes. I gouge my thumb into his eye socket, pushing hard with everything I've got. In case you're wondering, a human eye when crushed by a thumb feels more like a bag of jelly than a hard ball.

My opponent wails in pain and moves his head, causing my thumb to pop out of his eye socket. It lands by his mouth. He bites down hard, and I can feel the pain through my gloves. I scream inside my bucket. "You sonofabitch! Just die!"

He's pushing the knife toward me and I'm hanging on for everything I've got. I get my hand free from his mouth and wrap it around his neck. We're literally choking the life out of each other. I can see the color change in his face. I've got an advantage because my bucket is increasing the amount of pure oxygen I'm breathing as my breaths grow shallower. He'll have to cut my air supply out entirely, and I don't think the little guy has the stamina left.

I feel a knee attempting to ram home into my crotch. But that's an armored area. I squeeze with every ounce of strength in my hand. I think I feel his grip loosening.

"Surrender," I manage to rasp. My throat feels like it's on fire.

He doesn't answer. I squeeze tighter.

"Surrender!"

Still no reply, but now I can feel the strength in his knife arm ebbing. I'm getting more air. I begin to steer the blade toward his face. His lone intact eye looks at the weapon with fear.

"Surrender," I say one more time.

My would-be killer is silent. He's watching his own blade in his own hand move toward him. I stick the point of the blade into him, just below his mandible. He screams, but his voice is weak. I use the opportunity to tighten my grip around his throat. I slide the knife farther in and down, flicking it back and forth until, at last, I sever his jugular vein.

There's a slick, wet sound. His strength fades rapidly now as the blood gushes from the wound. His hand drops from around my neck. His breathing grows faint. He pulls his hand off the knife and lifts it up. For a moment I'm expecting a final, desperate strike to my head. Instead the hand seems to caress my bucket, the helmet of a legionnaire like he once was, before drifting down to the floor.

He's dead.

I roll onto my back and take deep breaths. I feel as though I have no strength left. A trickle runs down my arm. For a moment I fear that the blood I see on the deck is from the cut he made on me. That it's my blood pouring forth as much as his. I'm afraid to look at my arm. But my sense returns. My bucket would notify me of such a wound.

I'm okay.

I'm okay.

There's still a job to do. It felt as though we struggled for hours, but I know only a few minutes passed. I bring myself to my feet and retrieve my NK-4. "Okay," I say to the ether. "Any more like that, or do I get to use my rifle on the bridge?"

I'm ready to go in hot. Just waiting for the bridge door to open. But it doesn't.

I sense that I'm not alone. I turn and see Wraith step through the door. He's still limping a bit, but it looks like the adrenaline has kicked in. Twenties, Masters, and Owens trail him.

"Where's Kags?" I ask.

I don't get a response. And then I remember that I lowered my L-comm volume to almost nothing. I turn it back up and repeat the question.

"Bro," Owens said, "didn't you hear on the comm? Kags is dead, man."

"So's the marine," Twenties adds.

I feel so numb from the fight that the words barely even register. I move to the door. "Did you shut down the hyperdrive?"

Owens nods. "Remote detonation. That way we can control it at the last second. We breach, throw in fraggers and ear-poppers. Brace ourselves, kill the hyperdrive, let them fly around the room. KTF."

It sounds as good as any other plan to me. "Let's stack up."

"Don't you gotta blow that thing first?" Exo asks. He's carrying Kags's SAB. We'll need it.

"Stack up," I say, aiming my rifle and ready to blitz. "It'll open once we're set."

My kill team sets up, but Owens steps back. He grabs two men by the shoulders. "Hold up."

I can tell he's getting something over his comm. Having a discussion on a private channel.

He looks up at the ceiling in exasperation. "Okay, Victory Squad, this kill team is not allowed to go in with fraggers."

"Are you shittin' me?" Masters asks. "That's the only reason we even sniffed passing this in training."

"Wish I was. There's more. Under no circumstances are you to EKIA any humans. Uniformed MCR or otherwise."

"Why the hell not, dude?" Exo says. "I'm gonna kill every scumsack in that room."

"So what's the plan?" Wraith asks. "Because we gotta go now."

Owens pumps his shotgun. "Same plan minus the fraggers. Door opens, I kill the hyperdrive, and we go in."

We stack up in anticipation. I wonder what Andien, or whoever is watching me, is thinking about our little pow-wow. Doesn't matter.

The door opens and Owens blasts the hyperdrive. I can hear the rumble. The corvette is ripped from hyperspace, and the sudden change causes everyone who wasn't holding on to something—like we were—to go tumbling while inertial dampers struggle to minimize the change in momentum.

Our kill team pours onto the bridge. Exo is first. He goes blind corner right and sees nothing but some zhee to shoot.

Twenties is next. He goes straight down the middle. I'm behind him, going blind corner left.

I see a zhee crouching in Twenties's blind spot, carrying a shotgun. He pops up his weapon. I swing mine over.

Not soon enough.

Twenties doesn't see the blast. Probably doesn't hear it, either. It hits in in the back of his head and... his head... it... he dies.

I pump four shots into the zhee, sending him straight to hell for what he just did. "Leej down," I call over L-comm.

We roll over the bridge, shooting every zhee we see. The humans, for their part, are on their knees with their hands up. But at least one in a Republic uniform goes for a blaster rifle. Masters makes him pay.

The bridge is secured within thirty seconds. Owens goes immediately to the helm. We can see Utopion in the viewport, coming up quickly. He keys in an emergency course adjustment and the corvette begins to nose up, narrowly missing the planet and skimming off into orbit.

We've left six humans—four in Republic uniforms, two wearing finely tailored civilian clothes. There's also one zhee who stood with them. I'd guess he's the big boss.

My boys are like rabid animals.

"Get on your knees!" Masters and Exo scream. They force everyone down, and I'm pretty sure they're going to dust the entire crew.

I'm pretty sure I'll let them.

But then one of the humans, a handsome guy—familiar. He drops to his knees, hands laced behind his head. He looks... sad. Relieved and sad. Like a living nightmare just ended. Then it hits me. This is the guy we saw in the holovids. The guy who helped knock off the dirty supply officer. The guy I tussled with was the ex-legionnaire. I'm looking at Tom. The same Tom the guy I killed was raving about. The same Tom who must have...

"Stand down!" I shout to Masters and Exo. "We have our orders and they're there for a reason. Do not harm the humans."

The zhee just looks at his dead crew, his eyes every bit as lifeless as his friends. Wraith walks up to him, removes his pistol, and shoots him once in his donkey head. The zhee drops hard. We're all looking at Wraith.

"Orders were not to shoot the humans," Wraith says.

"Looks like that zhee tried to pull a knife," Owens replies.

We slow the ship. Men-at-arms come in and begin taking the prisoners away by shuttle. A crew of explosive-ordnance techs is trying to make the corvette something less than a super-bomb.

I notice that the two humans not dressed in Republic uniforms—Tom and the other guy—they get special treatment. Instead of a man-at-arms taking the other guy away, I see an admiral's aide show up and remove his ener-chains. The man rubs his wrists, smiles a smug little satisfied grin, and follows the admiral's aide to who-knows-where.

Tom stays cuffed, but his escort just screams Nether Ops. I think I picked up the look from Andien. As Tom walks by us, he says, "Hey. This all should have never happened. I'm sorry. I need you to know, I'm sorry."

The shuttle jump back to the *Intrepid* is devoid of any joy or goodness. My face is a mask. Whatever Owens is thinking, it's hidden behind his beard and shades. Wraith, as always, is wearing his bucket.

Masters shows it, though. His eyes have been perpetually wet and his jaw has been jutted out. The sign of a man trying not to lose it. I wonder how long he'll be able to keep it in.

Exo is dealing with his rage by pacing up and down the shuttle deck, slamming his fists against armored thighs and growling curses to himself.

Twenties and Kags lay single file on the deck. Sealed in casualty bags.

I turn Kags's bucket over in my hands and think about the day I first met him, when he asked what KTF meant. I told him, "You survive our trip to market, Basic, I'll let you know."

Kid ended being a good leej. He'll be missed.

And Twenties. I don't think about Twenties. I *can't* think about him. Not now.

Captain Owens draws in a big breath of air. "Listen," he says to the surviving members of our kill team. "I've been thinking. What happened here... I don't even know what to say. Our friend Andien from Nether Ops filled me in some things. Stuff she shouldn't have said."

Exo stops his prowling. "Like what kind of stuff?"

Owens lets out a heavy sigh. "More bad times, man. Bad times like this. Like the *Chiasm*. Something's coming. The whispers are there. Out in the shadows beyond the edge. And they're coming worse than we can imagine."

"Where you going with this, Cap?" I ask.

"It's time Dark Ops acts a bit more like Nether Ops," Owens says, rolling his neck and popping his vertebrae. "What you accomplished on that corvette was outstanding. But a kill team can only do so much, and our work comes *after* the bad times have already arrived. We need someone—*I* need someone—to get ahead of things. Or try, anyway. To drift out to the edge. Watch. Blend in. Become part of the fringe. Because when the bad times come... we've gotta know first."

Nods begin to swell like a rising storm in the shuttle.

Masters sniffs. "If it means making sure our guys didn't die for nothing—I mean, you all saw the same thing I did. Those two pricks on the bridge... they're not gonna be dusted."

"This is how we save lives," Owens concludes. "But one of us has gotta disappear, and it can't be me. So what I'm asking is: which one of you is our volunteer? Who's starting a new life for the Legion?"

Wraith looks at the group. "I'll go."

EPILOGUE

X did not know the end of his puppet. Of Tom and who he returned back to being. The real end. The only end that should have ever concerned a human being, a being, a citizen of this Republic on the constant verge of collapse...

Who knew? Who really knew, he thought to himself, as he closed out the file. Beyond his tiny window the sky had turned dark with the coming of early night.

Not all things are known to those paid to know all things, thought X, and this thought comforted him. There are, he thought to himself anew, as he held a cup of warm tea and watched the darkness... there are some things that must remain private.

He had attended the ceremony after the recovery of Tom. After the rescue by the boys in the Legion. The killing boys. Shakespeare was right. The dogs of war was what they were... and when they were loosed... havoc.

X had attended to the debriefings of Tom. The *endless* debriefings, and then the hushed remonstrations in which everybody was reminded under pain of death, that to talk was to open oneself up to that particular option.

"After all, we can't have people knowing the MCR almost got this close to slamming a starship straight into our House of Reason, can we?" That particular bureaucrat had cried aloud during one particularly horrific set of quiet afternoon meetings in the deep caverns of nowhere, located well beneath the most innocuous of government admin buildings.

And what was left unsaid by everyone, because X felt all their staring stares, was: *And we can't let them know it was our man who destroyed a starship and bombed a forward legionnaire base in a particularly contentious war zone.* Can we?

Our man being... Tom.

We can't.

And of course it was all X's fault.

But X knew where some of the bodies were buried, so everything was neatly annotated and then erased. Bureaucracy even in deception. Even in grand deception.

And what of Scarpia?

What of him? Someone had pulled enough strings to get him out of hot water. "Need to know, and you don't, dear boy," some Mandarin had warned when X went asking.

X was sure Scarpia would turn up again and be about as useful as he could be until one day when he wasn't. And then X could have him like some devil waiting patiently for a particularity unrepentant sinner.

That was understood.

Until then... Scarpia was free to move about the galaxy and make his particular brand of mischief.

X made a note to revisit.

And of course there were awards and promotions. Not for X. But for everyone who wasn't really involved. They got those things. It helped them in their constant upward quest to make all the right moves. All the House of Reason moves.

But the pimps...

Hookers...

Murderers...

And everyone else who served the Carnivale, except for one, got nothing. They got the privilege of a thorough dressing-down, and the chance to try again. Even though the Mandarins dressing them down knew that their continued failure was inevitable. In fact they looked forward to it, so that they might profit from it.

Yes... X had his enemies. Just like everyone else.

No one thanked him for saving the House of Reason. Instead, the way the narrative had played out, he was—and this was unspoken—he was the responsible party. It was as if he had planned and almost destroyed the House of Reason himself. Never mind Scarpia, the zhee, and the MCR.

X had played his little espionage games and counter-terrorism tricks, and "this mess" was all his fault.

X smiled to himself, sitting in his squeaky, old, yet comfortable chair in his tiny office. He smiled and sipped a cup of tea. Watching the loose leaves at the bottom swirl as he thought...

It was always that way with the House of Reason. Blame the victims and apologize for the perpetrators.

He'd stopped asking "why" a long time ago.

Why try to understand insanity?

Instead he was trying, in his own unspoken way, in some part of his own consciousness he was barely aware of... he was trying to save everyone from them. He was trying to save the galaxy from the House of Reason and all its toadying toadies. All its cronying cronies.

He was, if you thought about it, trying to save them from themselves.

And when they fire you...

He finished the tea and turned out the light at his desk.

Then it will all be someone else's job.

He imagined fishing... if they let him live.

And what of Tom?

His assignment is over. He can go back to being that other person he once was.

But even X knows this is a lie. A comforting and polite lie. But a lie nonetheless.

And still...

X walks through the quiet offices of the Carnivale. Everyone is gone. They'll be back tomorrow to play their little games. But for tonight, on this early evening, they have all gone home to their loved ones. They will hold them tight and lie awake, knowing they must protect them from the darkness.

And Tom?

X steps out onto the street. It is empty and silent and only the shop down the way casts any light beyond the orange streetlights battling the light night mist.

And Tom?

The House of Reason wanted to give him a medal.

X smirked bitterly, knowing what they had in mind and seeing it for all its awful crassness and craven manipulation.

They wanted to award him the Order of the Centurion, in fact.

And of course all the Legion generals went nuts.

But as ever, the House of Reason had its way, playing its dirty laundry games to ever get what it wanted.

Why, X asked his man inside.

Why give the man who was partly responsible for so many Republic deaths their highest honor? The Order of the Centurion.

Because, he told you—your man inside, your savvy operator—because it makes everyone dirty. And dirt ensures everyone will remain nice and silent.

And so you went, Tom. You went to the award ceremony and looked as sick about it as I felt. And you stood there with Legion brass not even bothering to show and some low-level functionary presenting the award you can never admit to.

And you smiled in your navy uniform, because after all it's a pretty big deal for anyone outside the Legion to ever get an award for "disregarding one's life in service to the mission of the Legion and its brotherhood."

That's what your medal commendation read, Tom.

I don't think you even looked at it all that rainy afternoon as I did your last debrief and walked you to a speeder that took you back to your old life. To that other name.

You felt phony, Tom.

And they wanted it that way.

Shame abounds. No one ever wins but the House of Reason.

I watched you go. Back to where you came from. Back to where we summoned you from. Back to them, your wife and child and your other life.

I did want to tell you something, Tom. I wanted to tell you that long before I was X, ringmaster of the Carnivale, I was a kid in a bucket. A legionnaire. And I can tell you, Tom, you did legionnaire's work out there in the dark.

They'll never know it.

They'd tell you that's a lie.

But I know what it cost you.

I know what you bought.

You disregarded your life for the mission.

You earned the Order of the Centurion.

And no one will ever know it.

So I'll let you go now, thinks X as he watches the train depart. The train carrying "Tom."

You'll ride that train for the rest of the day, and by late afternoon you'll reach the private estates of your grandfather. The famous admiral. The one whose shadow you were raised in. The one you've always been measured against, even by yourself.

I know you, even though your name is no longer Tom. I know you'll walk the last miles from the station to your ancestral home. And I don't want to think about what you'll think about. I only hope you'll find some pleasant memory that's enough to hold on to... knowing what you'll have to do next.

Knowing that you're a sinner seeking absolution. Knowing that she's your priest. Wondering if she'll forgive you for saving everyone.

I hope you're not thinking you have to tell her about the dead, the lies, the murders, and all that other "Tom" life. But I do suspect you'll confess to Illuria... because you're that kind of man. You will have to tell her the truth. Because someone must know. Someone must have the opportunity to forgive you, Tom.

Someone.

In time you'll reach the door.

And they will have seen you coming from afar, like some fabled hero from our shared ancient history. Some warrior who sailed the seas and bested monsters and came home changed.

She'll be watching you from a window high in the nursery. She's been doing that since you left. Waiting for you. Because she loves you.

The whole house will erupt at her sudden cry. Knowing you've come back. Knowing you're alive. Just knowing.

Because where you've been... there's no knowing.

And because she loves you, she'll take up your child from her bed and rush down the stairs, racing ahead of the bots and your father who can't believe this wonderful thing that has happened. She's racing ahead of them all to claim ownership of you.

And when the door opens and she's openly weeping, you'll smile, and she'll briefly sense something and ignore it because...

Because...

Because... you're back. And that is enough.

She won't see the look of too many done things. Or all the dead and shame of such things.

Or Illuria.

She will see only you.

And because she is a mother, she will hold the hand of your greatest prize, presenting her to you. The young girl you were saving the galaxy for. As though she too is a soldier giving a report of duty maintained and service faithfully rendered.

And in that moment when you embrace the little girl, so much bigger than when you'd last seen her, close to you and dare the galaxy to come between you…

Will it all have been worth it?

Will it?

I know, thinks X. *I know you will be thinking about that Tom-not-Tom. I know you will hold her and whisper your daughter's name…*

"Prisma."

Yes. Because someone must.

The shuttle that hauled them out to the edge, the very edge of the galaxy, was crewed by Repub Navy types, wearing civilian clothes.

Anonymity was the order. Scarpia guessed they were about to be quietly disappeared.

Frogg would have known the type who did this kind of work. Known they were killers. Takes one to know one, he would have thought to himself with a grim sense of satisfaction. And during the jump he and Scarpia would have kept to themselves in their bunks.

They would've made a plan. A plan to bargain, kill, deal, manipulate their way out of this. But honestly, there was no way out of this one. This was... the end.

"Close one, that," Scarpia would have murmured as they lay in their bunks. Frogg would have been above and thinking his silent, ever murderous thoughts.

Scarpia wondered if he would ever see Illuria again. Only briefly wondered. Wondered what she was doing and if she was happy. At this final end-of-things moment that seemed of some import to him.

He closed his eyes and listened to the nothingness of hyperspace. To him it was like a howling void that could never be satisfied.

A day later they landed on a dry desert world. Way out beyond any kind of life. Barren sands, burning heat, and the flinty ranges of distant jagged-cut mountains promised nothing remotely resembling life.

It was then, as the Repub Navy types ushered them out onto the hard-packed dirt of a long-dead lakebed that Frogg would have murmured, "I think they're going to cut us loose here, chief."

Frogg was dead. But Scarpia heard him. Scarpia only had Froggy left. And he was just a ghost.

Scarpia swallowed hard. His baleful eyes took them all in and glanced down at Frogg. Yes. For all intents and purposes, it did look like they were about to be abandoned to their fate.

A fate that most likely promised starvation, heat stroke, and extreme dehydration.

They wouldn't last two days out here. Wherever here was. And it's nice to know the name of the place where you're going to die. Not required. But nice all the same.

The end wouldn't be pretty. That was for sure.

Once they'd been backed far enough away from the shuttle, it raised its boarding ramp, spooled up its engines, and lifted off on the hum of its repulsors. Gears folding inward, pilot pivoting for course track.

And then...

Silence.

The silence of the desert.

The silence of their minds dealing with their impending mortality.

The silence of arriving at the end of all your bad decisions.

Scarpia was sure Frogg would snap and murder him right there on the dry clay of an ancient lake. Get one last one in before...

They began to walk toward the low mountains.

They walked for the better part of a day. At night they lay down behind a rock and watched the few stars come out. Their mouths were dry and thirsty for moisture. In fact, they were already dying of thirst.

The next day they crossed over the low jagged mountains with fantasies of some small outpost on the other side. A place of water, and cold beer, and smoked meats.

Each of them not daring to make their final confessions for all the evils they'd done. But close to...

That would be a kind of heaven, a paradise to them.

But what they saw on the other side of the mountains was even more stunning.

On the plain below, the mammoth keels of what must be three massive battleships lay alongside one another. Construction crews moved about the distant and massive ships like tiny ants. And beyond this was some kind of sprawling military compound comprised of wire, high towers, and wide, watched kill zones. Within it lay tents and barracks and concrete bunkers. But it was all empty, for the most part anyway, a place waiting to be filled. Expectant for the promise of a future.

Yet it was the incredible and gargantuan ships that lay out there below them, like the skeletons of prehistoric monsters out there in the waste, that captured Scarpia's imagination. Froggy's, too. They would be nothing like anything the galaxy had ever seen. The ships were immense, and they were identical.

They heard the Repub Navy shuttle in the skies above. A different one this time. One with an admiral's flag stenciled near the cockpit. A moment later it set down near them on the ridge, blasting them with boiling dust and flung grit.

Scarpia raised his long hands to his eyes to shield them. Frogg merely watched like some murderous little animal determined to kill and live for as long as the time remaining to it.

The boarding ramp lowered, and out came a navy captain. He walked briskly toward them.

He was smiling.

"Mr. Scarpia…"

Scarpia and Frogg stared dumbly back.

"Commander Devers sends his welcome, sir."

The officer turned to the massive ships. He gazed at them with adoration and pride. Then he turned back to the two desert wanderers.

To Scarpia the arms dealer and Frogg the deceased murderer.

"Do we have your attention now, Mr. Scarpia?" the officer asked. "Because we're going to need a lot of weapons."

The ghost of Frogg licked his dry and cracked lips.

Scarpia looked down at Froggy. Then up at the officer.

A lot of weapons.

Scarpia gave a thin smile of satisfaction.

Read on for a special note from the authors.

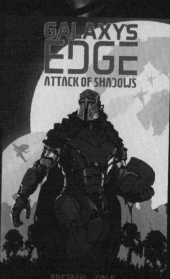

AUTHORS' NOTE

Hey there! It's us, Jason and Nick, back to thank you again for reading another installment of *Galaxy's Edge, Season One*. This is either the third book (if you're reading in order of release—in which case we hope by now you've gotten a sense of why we wrote this story in the order we did), or it's the second book (if you're reading in chronological order—in which case we hope you enjoy *Galactic Outlaws* next!).

Either way, you thought enough of this world to dive back in for more, and we greatly appreciate that.

So what to say about *Kill Team*? You noticed as soon as Tom showed up that this book was unique, didn't you? Of course you did. Because you're Tom. And Tom doesn't miss things like that. No, my dear boy. But perhaps the single most common email we get about this book is excitement about Ford's decision to go out into the cold to become Captain Keel and the revelation that Tom is a Maydoon. We just love those "aha!" moments when things start to come together. There will be a lot more moments like that as we continue through the series.

There will also be a lot more layers to peel back—more machinations, organizations, and puppeteers like X and Dark Ops and Nether Ops. You'll find in this series that, just like in the real world, there are forces behind the scenes pulling strings and making decisions that end up putting soldiers—or in our case, legionnaires—on the front lines. And the results aren't always pretty.

Up next, in *Attack of Shadows*, we'll finish up what we call our "on-ramp." By the end of book four we'll have all the pieces in place for an epic conflict that will shake the galaxy for the rest of the series.

If you haven't yet read *Galactic Outlaws*, spoilers follow in 3... 2... 1...

So at the end of *Outlaws* we meet Goth Sullus, who orders an ominous attack once he has been handed over the fleet commanded by Devers. *Attack of Shadows* is that attack. The entire book is one relentless battle localized on the planet Tarrago and its moon. When the dust settles, the galaxy will be irrevocably altered, and in book five, we'll see Wraith and Victory Company reunited and fighting for what they believe in. And then... hold on, because the intensity only goes up through the end of the series!

We really hope you're enjoying yourself as much as we enjoy writing these stories. If you haven't already, head over to our Facebook group and share your thoughts. We'd love to hear from you.

KTF!

— Jason Anspach & Nick Cole

PS. Amazon won't tell you when future books come out, but there are several ways you can stay informed.

1. Enlist in our fan-run Facebook group, the Galaxy's Edge Fan Club, and say hello. It's a great place to hang out with other KTF-lovin' legionnaires who like to talk about sci-fi and are up for a good laugh.
2. Follow us directly on Amazon. This one is easy. Just go to the store page for this book on Amazon and click the "follow" button beneath our pictures. That will prompt Amazon to email you automatically whenever we release a new title.
3. Join the Galaxy's Edge Newsletter. You'll get emails directly from us—along with the short story "Tin Man," available only to newsletter subscribers.

Doing just one of these (**although doing all three is your best bet!**) will ensure you find out when the next *Galaxy's Edge* book releases. Please take a moment to do one of these so you can find yourself on patrol with Chhun, Wraith, and Exo for their next gritty firefight!

THE GALAXY
IS A DUMPSTER
FIRE...

OTHER GALAXY'S EDGE BOOKS

Galaxy's Edge Season One:
- Legionnaire
- Galactic Outlaws
- Kill Team
- Attack of Shadows
- Sword of the Legion
- Prisoners of Darkness
- Turning Point
- Message for the Dead
- Retribution

Tyrus Rechs: Contracts & Terminations:
- Requiem for Medusa
- Chasing the Dragon

Stand-Alone Books:
- Imperator
- Order of the Centurion

ABOUT THE AUTHORS

Jason Anspach and Nick Cole are a pair of west coast authors teaming up to write their science fiction dream series, Galaxy's Edge.

Jason Anspach is a best-selling author living in Puyallup, Washington with his wife and their own legionnaire squad of seven (not a typo) children. Raised in a military family (Go Army!), he spent his formative years around Joint Base Lewis-McChord and is active in several pro-veteran charities. Jason enjoys hiking and camping throughout the beautiful Pacific Northwest. He remains undefeated at arm wrestling against his entire family.

Nick Cole is a Dragon Award winning author best known for *The Old Man and the Wasteland, CTRL ALT Revolt!,*and the Wyrd Saga. After serving in the United States Army, Nick moved to Hollywood to pursue a career in acting and writing. He resides with his wife, a professional opera singer, south of Los Angeles, California.

Honor Roll

We would like to give our most sincere thanks and recognition to those who helped make Galaxy's Edge: Kill Team possible by subscribing to GalacticOutlaws.com.

Marlena Anspach

Robert Anspach

Steve Beaulieu

Steve Bergh

Wilfred Blood

Christopher Boore

Brent Brown

Rhett Bruno

Marion Buehring

Mary Ann Bulpitt

Peter Davies

Nathan Davis

Richard Fox

Peter Francis

Chris Fried

Hank Garner

Michael Greenhill

Phillip Hall

Josh Hayes

Angela Hughes

Wendy Jacobson

Chris Kagawa

Mathijs Kooij

William Kravetz

Grant Lambert

Danyelle Leafty

Preston Leigh

Pawel Martin

Tao Mason

Simon Mayeski

Jim Mern

Alex Morstadt

Nate Osburn

Chris Pourteau

Maggie Reed

Karen Reese

Glenn Shotton

Maggie Stewart-Grant

Kevin Summers

Beverly Tierney

Scott Tucker

John Tuttle

Christopher Valin

Scot Washam

Justin Werth

Justyna Zawiejska

N. Zoss

Made in the USA
Middletown, DE
07 February 2020